WHO WILL WATCH
THE WATCHERS

WHO WILL WATCH THE WATCHERS

by Edwin Fadiman Jr.

Little, Brown and Company
Boston - Toronto

LIBRARY OF CONGRESS CATALOG CARD NO. 71–103949

FIRST EDITION

*Published simultaneously in Canada
by Little, Brown & Company (Canada) Limited*

PRINTED IN THE UNITED STATES OF AMERICA

This one is for my three —
Susan, Mark, Kenneth.
Surely, a good and sufficient
reason for everything.

Sed quis custodiet ipsos custodes?
—DECIMUS JUNIUS JUVENAL
A.D. c.50–c.130

Author's Notes

This book is a work of fiction. Except for some historical characters and incidents, any resemblance to persons living or dead is purely coincidental.

1 ❧

THE bedroom of the small apartment was warm. There was a not unpleasant smell in the air, the scent of a young, healthy girl's body, which hung close to the stripped Hollywood bed and thickened about the open closet door. Some ten summer dresses were neatly hung in the closet, almost concealing the disarray of shoes on a shoe rack beneath. There was a small wooden dressing table and a plain mirror above it. The bathroom was unexpectedly spacious, with a stall shower, a tub, and a white table loaded with cosmetics. Incongruous, and therefore noticeable, were a tube of shaving cream, a man's razor, and some men's bedroom slippers neatly lined up next to a pair of pompommed mules.

Hung on the inside of the bathroom door was a woman's dressing gown in pink — very feminine, very frilly — and, clasping it in inanimate ardor, a man's terry-cloth robe.

From the bedroom, a telephone shrilled four times and stopped.

It was five-thirty of a hot July afternoon in Washington, D.C. The building was coming alive. Doors opened and closed. The smell of cooking began to permeate the apartment, drowning the subtler odors. The air conditioner in the living room coughed once and changed its pitch as the compressor clicked on.

A key rattled in the lock.

The girl who swung the door shut behind her did not switch on the lights. She transferred a paper bag from her hip to both arms, and walked to the kitchenette. She banged the bag down on a small utility shelf and rushed for the bathroom. She swung the door half closed behind her.

The phone rang.

"All right," she muttered. "Give a girl a chance, will you?" The phone rang again. She sprang out of the bathroom, just ahead of the roar of the flushing toilet. She picked up the phone and said, "Hello."

". . . I was shopping."

"Please come as soon as you can. It's a special dinner, darling . . . You know, you always call when I'm in the bathroom. It's a conspiracy." She laughed and switched on the small light that stood by the phone on the night table. "I'll see you in an hour. Don't forget the wine." She listened, laughed again, made a kissing sound and hung up. She swung her legs onto the bed and lay back, her head on the pillow. Then she put her hands under her head and was still.

At twenty-four, Deborah Bernstein's beauty was Semitic, a darkly blooming flower. Her eyes were large. The irises gleamed a golden black in the shadowed light of the lamp. Half-closed, the fine long lashes seemed artificially perfect. Her ears were small and neat. Her face, with its high cheekbones, glistened slightly with the heat of the afternoon. Her nose was thin, slightly hooked, with flaring nostrils, brooding now over her wide-lipped mouth. The chin was strongly modeled. Even in repose there was no relaxation in her throat or her fine, taut underchin.

Her breasts pushed at the thin summer material of her blouse. She reached down one lazy hand and partly unbuttoned herself. Some sweat glistened in the hollow between her breasts. Debbie looked at herself through half-closed eyes. She thought about Jeff: he liked to push his nose in there, burrowing like a small boy. Her insides began to dissolve, and she spread her legs. Her wide lips smiled vaguely, and her minidress, caught up around her hips, revealed her thighs. Her legs were long, lean, and smooth.

4

When they made love, their heads were almost at the same height. She was a big girl. She thought of herself twenty years from now, and realized that her young firm promise would by then have turned into lushness. But that was all right, she thought. Every age had its own beauty. If she were careful, she would simply grow more voluptuous, more exciting. The sight of her own nakedness was pleasantly stimulating. The heat enfolded her with a warmth that reminded her of Jeff's.

With a sigh, she swung her legs over the side of the bed, smoothed down her skirt, and stood. She yawned once, stretched, smiled again into the silvering dusk, and hurried to the kitchen.

She peeled shrimp. Both she and Jeff were fond of shellfish, and one of Debbie's enthusiasms was shrimp cacciatore. "For a girl who takes her Jewishness so seriously," Jeff had once said to her ironically, "how come you eat seafood? And make ham sandwiches for picnics?" She'd laughed with him. Later, after he'd gone — it was a night in which they were not together; they'd decided it was best to ration sex until they were married — she'd thought about it for a moment and then dismissed it from her mind, as she had in fact long ago dismissed her Semitism.

She peeled shrimp. Occasionally she glanced up at the sign she had hand-lettered and pasted onto a cupboard door. The letters were carefully curlicued. DON'T FORGET THE MOST IMPORTANT INGREDIENT: LOVE. She thought about how she loved Jeff as she popped tomatoes into boiling water, blanched them, peeled them. She thought about him as she sliced and quartered them, expressed their seeds, and put them with a spoonful of olive oil into a heavy aluminum pan. She doused the frying tomatoes with a little tomato puree and stirred it all with a wooden spoon. She thought about Jeff while she salted a pot of water, into which she tossed the shrimp. She thought about herself then, and how lucky she was, how lucky indeed, to be a woman, to be alive at all, as she fished out shrimp now pink and smelling of their own perfume. She thought, with detachment, of her last orgasm. It had seemed to come from the roots of her being, shaking her body in concentric waves, leaving her breathless, holding on to Jeff with both hands and, as she noticed later, while she was putting Merthiolate on the scratches that ridged his back, all nails. She had believed she was pregnant. Pills or no pills, nothing that deep, nothing that violent, could have resulted in — nothing. She had *known* that something had been made, and she had gasped, "We did it. Darling, we just made one."

Her period began a week later. She had cried then, in the office, tranquil tears that coursed slowly down her cheeks and caused no pain. At one point Simon had stopped by and asked, "Something wrong, Debbie?"

"Why no," she'd answered cheerfully. She was unaware she was crying.

The tears stopped as mysteriously as they had begun.

Now she added transparent slices of onion, two cloves of garlic, and covered the steaming mixture. She punched the heat button to low. Then the doorbell rang.

Hurrying toward the front door, she thought fleetingly, "I should give him a key." It wasn't a new thought. Jeff mentioned it every so often, lightly, casually, so lightly that it was obviously important to him. But it seemed, for some reason, an ultimate surrender. She could not force herself to it. Her desire for privacy was almost as strong as her desire for Jeff. She knew somehow that she could never give anyone the key to her door — until they were married. Then, of course, it would be *their* key, and a new apartment. She supposed so, she hoped so.

From the moment she opened the door and Jeff kissed her, she could feel his tension.

"I brought some white wine," he said. "Almadén. A half gallon." He put down the paper bag and kissed her again. Her mouth opened under his.

"Hungry?"

"Yes."

"But we'd better eat first," Debbie said. "Everything's almost ready. There's French bread left." She hefted the bag. "I'll put this in the fridge. It'll stay cool. You too," she said, avoiding his arms.

"I've got some interesting news," Jeff said.

"With you in a minute. Sit down and do nothing. Or make us a drink."

Debbie went into the kitchen, leaving the door half open. Jeff dropped onto the couch, on the left-hand side where she could see him, framed by the half-open door. He lit a rare cigarette, and Debbie knew he had really important news. He smoked only when he was excited.

She turned on the tap in the kitchen sink and then just stood and watched him. Jeffrey Whitson. Twenty-three. Harvard, cum laude. His hair was blond, but coarse, a brush cut. Jeffrey had a General Service rank of 8. Seventy-two hundred dollars a year. Jeff insisted that you had to reach a civil service rank of at least a GS 10 before you could let your hair grow. But the short hair suited his face, gave it character. In profile his nose looked positively snub. His skin was fair and unlined, his chin narrow. His eyes were blue. My little blond, blue-eyed Aryan, Debbie thought fondly to herself.

She wanted him badly. She was ready, more than ready, and they hadn't even eaten yet.

Actually, looking at the upper half of her fiancé as he leaned his head back on the sofa, it was simple. She loved him so much she sometimes resented him.

He was built well, with the smooth, long, well-bred muscles of a swimmer and a tennis player. Nothing corded or ridged. His head sat easily on his neck. She thought of the flat muscles of his back, the excellence of his shoulder blades (they were still young, winged, somehow pathetic) and his flat stomach. It's not so much that he's built like a

Greek god, she thought, it's that he's built to my taste. A warm glow of possession enveloped her. There were freckles on his cheekbones, a powdering of freckles on the back of his neck, and his eyebrows were thick yet transparent. His stubble was as blond as his hair.

His hands were set upon his wrists with a perfection that could make her dizzy. She remembered how they looked as they stroked her body. Often, she would lean forward and kiss his hands; they were as exciting to her as his sex.

Debbie took a quick look at the shrimp. They too were ready. She opened the bottle of wine and poured two large glasses. She liked to drink wine, as did Jeff, in greedy gulps. No connoisseurs we, she thought, as she filled two water glasses and backed her way out of the kitchen, opening the door with her hip.

"Here," she said. "You want this now, or with dinner?"

"Both."

"No martini?"

"I'm too bushed," Jeff said. He smiled at her, and his blue eyes under his fair eyebrows glinted in the light. He had switched on one lamp. The living room was alive with the sensuality of dusk. A swimming-under-water time, Debbie called it. She had once tried to define for them both why they loved this time of day, especially in summer, but it had remained a mystery — until the morning that found them at the Metropolitan Museum.

They'd gone on a gay, swinging weekend to New York. After a while, the montage of bars and restaurants seemed suddenly not enough. Debbie had dragged Jeff to the Metropolitan and had stopped in front of a Monet canvas on temporary loan, entitled *Impression*. She had stood before the oil painting — a round bright sun and the sea and the shadows of fishing smacks — and something inside her stretched, an inner eye opened. She exclaimed, "That's why!" She was full of her discovery. "The air is alive.

8

It's not nothing. It's real. It affects things, especially at dusk. See?"

Jeff had patiently indulged her excitement. It was a tight moment of ecstasy he had not been able to share.

The living room was drowned in dusk, singing with it. She sat down next to Jeff. The wine was cold and semisweet. She took a large swallow.

"So tell."

"I'm going out-country," Jeff said.

"An assignment?" Debbie was wide-eyed.

"Yes. Simon phoned me. I'm to stop by his office tomorrow. He'll explain everything then."

"He will?"

There was a pause. "Well," Jeff said, "perhaps not everything."

"Just enough to get on with the job." They both laughed. Working for the Central Intelligence Agency was probably, certainly at Jeff's level, one of the least glamorous jobs in the entire federal structure. Jeff had been with the CIA one year. He had spent that time in a semidetached cubicle, working at a battered steel desk. He reviewed interdepartmental memoranda. Paper work and more paper work. On his desk was a long listing of mysterious combinations of letters and numbers. Against these Jeff checked correspondence references. The papers were, to anyone who didn't have the proper code key, meaningless gobbledygook. Jeff didn't have that key, nor would he for some years. Not until his clearance — he was cleared only for sensitive and secret — expanded to include top-secret. But you had to have a GS 12 rating and above for that to happen. And make thirteen thousand a year. Jeff was four years away from anything like that. Meanwhile, he would continue to check references he didn't understand against a senseless listing.

Simon, who was Jeff's boss and whose secretary Debbie was, had come up the hard way. Though he knew how intolerably frustrating Jeff's job could be, he would have done the usual about it — nothing — if Debbie hadn't spoken to him a week ago.

For some months, she'd noticed Jeff's growing disgust and boredom. She remembered the Friday afternoon it came to a head. She'd made an excuse to stop by Jeff's office, just to say hello. He'd had his door closed (you *could* close your door, but there was an unwritten law that employees of Jeff's status didn't require such privacy), and she'd knocked hesitantly. When there was no answer, she'd stepped in and closed the door behind her.

Jeff was staring into a glass of water which he held cupped in both hands. He looked up unsmiling. Debbie decided not to be subtle.

"What's the matter?"

"Nothing."

"You had your door closed."

"Yes."

"I just wanted to stop by to say hello. Are we having dinner?"

"Yes," Jeff said softly. "Sure." He looked up. "On you. You make more money than I do, you've got more responsibility, you've been here longer, why the hell should I pay?"

"I'm prettier too," Debbie said lightly. "And sexier." She left immediately and made her preoccupied way back to her office. Jeff was usually cheerful, if for no other reason than that he was in good health and felt well, truly well, most of the time. But there had been an undercurrent of real bitterness to his rudeness. Debbie knew he resented the fact that as Simon's confidential secretary, she outranked him by two ratings. How could he help it? She knew too that he resented the fact that she couldn't tell him about eighty percent of her day.

Her relationship with Simon Lee was unusual. It was close — it would have had to be, for they shared many secrets together, and, being human, the sharing had created a bond between them — but they had managed to keep their intimacy depersonalized. As she turned into her own small office, she made up her mind. She knocked on his door after checking her watch. It was four forty-five. Simon Lee was a man of routine. He took coffee at a quarter to five every day, and he enjoyed it. He made it on a small electric burner in the back of his office, an outfit hidden by the curtains the rest of the time. The burner was strictly nonregulation, and he was not supposed to own one. When he had brewed his coffee, and sugared it and poured into it just the right amount of synthetic powdered milk, he would sip it with the same concentration with which he did everything else: totally absorbed in the flavor, in his relaxation. If he was ever approachable, it was now. Debbie had this on good authority from Simon's wife. "If you ever want to ask my husband anything," she had said once, quite seriously, "wait until his coffee break. That's the time."

Debbie tapped on Simon's door.

She entered immediately. He was staring out his office window, his back to her. She could see the small coffee cup in his hand, and the room was filled with the sharp smell of Italian espresso.

"I always feel like saying, My, how you've grown," Simon said. He didn't turn around. Debbie knew how he felt. Headquarters covered nine acres in the bucolic township of Langley. The CIA owned one hundred and forty acres of land. There were over a million square feet of working space utilized by over ten thousand employees.

Simon had been with the department since the days of General Smith. He had worked for years in the battered old United States Public Health Service complex, in the gashouse section of Washington known as Foggy Bottom. He would still refer to "the Hill" with affectionate nostalgia.

"What can I do?" Simon asked. "For you, I mean."

Debbie wondered, not for the first or last time, how a man

who had spent his life as an underpaid career civil servant could still remain so sensitive, so prescient.

"A personal favor, Simon," Debbie said. He turned and faced her. Simon Lee was a man of fifty-five, with only the suggestion of a pot belly. His shoulders were still broad under his gray suit. His face was deeply tanned. His hair was long, wavy, and shining white. He wore a small beard. His eyes were bright blue. His fingers were lean and delicate, with well-trimmed nails. With luck, Debbie thought, Jeff might look like this in thirty years.

"It's about Jeff," Debbie said. "He's bored and discouraged."

"Oh?"

"I mean, he needs a change. Something to take him out of his rut."

"If you would speak more plainly, Debbie," Simon said. "And perhaps a little less in clichés."

"He's been with the department a year. All he's done is sit at his desk and check code on interdepartmental memos." She sounded whining, unpleasant to herself. Abruptly, surprisingly, she foresaw the bitterness of future years, during which she would have to do this many times: brace Jeff's softness with the rigidity of her determination. She would never tell him, at least not until he grew up enough to understand that this too was part of love.

Yet there seemed no way of putting what she wanted into words without destroying a little of Jeff — and of herself.

Simon walked to his desk. He looked at a brown-leather-framed picture of his family for a second. "But he's white," he said at last, almost helplessly. "My whole department is white."

Debbie said nothing. Central Intelligence was divided into "white" and "black" employees. If you were "black," you automatically knew, and knew *well*, anything up to twenty-one languages. You had lived through the CIA conditioning course which, by comparison, made marine basic seem like a stroll in the country. The edges of your brain had been as toughened as the edges of your hands in karate. You were a killing machine as well as a thinking, fact-gathering machine. You would then be stationed as an operative anywhere in the world.

For every operational employee, there were twenty like Jeff and Simon, who sat behind desks.

"I'll think about it," Simon said gently. "Your young man seems to have a good deal going for him all in all. You're certainly not the least of it," he added, dismissing her. She saw his hand punch the inconspicuous button beside his yellow phone, the button that lit a red light above his office door. Whatever he was about to do now, she would never know. At best, she would be given fragments of work to do. Bits and pieces carefully farmed out to other typists too, so that the total jigsaw puzzle would remain indecipherable. At times, since she was alert and intelligent, Debbie had guessed a rhythm, conjectured a pattern, and because she *was* alert and intelligent, she had immediately stopped thinking. It was one of the ways of keeping her job.

As it was, she knew too much. Keeping secrets, she had discovered, was a bore. They were not the sort of secrets she enjoyed. They had nothing to do with growth or love or emotion. Debbie had decided long ago that she was apolitical.

Now, sitting in her apartment by Jeff's side, holding her half-empty wineglass, she thought again of his jealousy. Not that he had ever admitted his feelings in so many words. But lately his dissatisfaction with himself, and especially with himself in relationship to her, had been growing.

God bless Simon, she thought, knowing that whatever this assignment was, it was make-work.

"How long will you be gone?" she asked, finishing her wine.

"Don't you know?"

"Nope."

"You're usually in on all these things," Jeff said, smiling. But his eyes were humorless.

"Simon doesn't tell me anything if he can possibly avoid it. You know that."

"I'm picking up a briefcase," Jeff said. "Combination lock. I don't know where I'm going yet. I'll be away two or three days. That's all I know."

"I'll be typing up your travel orders in the morning," Debbie said. "I'll let you know where you're going."

Jeff moved uneasily, then rose. "Are we going to eat?" he asked. The mood had changed. Dusk had deepened into night. The skin-prickling atmosphere of desire had vanished. Debbie looked almost coldly at the tall, spare young man whom she was going to marry within three months, who had been her lover for almost a year. Then, as she snapped back into emotional focus, she blew him an apologetic half kiss which he didn't see, and went to the kitchen.

The air conditioner murmured. They ate together, their chairs almost touching, making the dining-room table intimate. Debbie lit two candles and the clear gold and blue flames wavered in the air-conditioned breeze. They ate with the recklessness of the young. They finished the shrimp, and a quart of white wine, and a loaf of French bread, and a half of a large sacher torte that Debbie had picked up at the only authentic Viennese pastry shop in town. Jeff made coffee while Debbie did the dishes, and they took the coffee back to the living room. They sat in a darkness mellowed by the one dim lamp they had switched on earlier, and sipped their coffee, dulling but never quite drowning the edge of intoxication that came not so much from the wine and the brandy (Almadén brandy; Debbie sometimes thought they supported the damn company), but from their own pleasure in being close to one another.

Over the year of their intimacy, they had discovered the value and the power of silence. Quiet could shape a mood, create an excitement more intense than talk or action. They held the chalice of their happiness between them, a cup of silence filled with anticipation.

Jeff put on the *Trout* Quintet. His tastes in classical music, Debbie thought, were undeveloped. But she had to admit that nothing suited this evening more than the sugary Schubertian strains. After a while she felt Jeff's hand upon her knee, and she moved sideways fractionally, to make it easier for him. He stroked her thigh almost absent-mindedly and then buried his face in her neck.

She held his head with both hands, and as the pressure of his insistence increased, as she could feel the tension mounting, she crisped her fingers in his hair, and they rocked to and fro together. Debbie began to purr, a low vibrant sound in the back of her throat. It was a sound that Jeff could never hear without its trebling his own excitement. It was one of the private things between them.

"You're purring," he said softly.

"Yes."

"For me?"

"Yes. For you, only for you." He kissed her, and she said, "For me too."

"I'd like to do something too — like that."

"Go ahead."

"I don't know what to do."

"You're doing fine," Debbie murmured. He began the long slow stroking of her thighs and legs that she loved. Debbie leaned back on the sofa and closed her eyes. Under her bra, she could feel her nipples stiffen. Her breasts and belly felt gigantic, her thighs and legs seemed Corinthian pillars of marble. Then her body softened and flowered. She was deep in the center of her own whirlpool. It is amazing, she thought with the part of her mind she kept hidden and inviolate from sensation, it is astonishing how selfish I can be.

Jeff's hands reached for her panties, and she arched her

15

back, purring again. She felt his mouth pinch the inside of her thighs, and then his hands were forcing her apart, and he was kissing her . . . And the act of divorcement began. Debbie concentrated now on her physical sensations; she wanted to flow, to begin the long, greedy coming that would culminate in release. But before that, she had to exorcise her lover. Jeff was to become a tool, a faceless man, still Jeff, yet all men. This was what Debbie could never tell him: that when she thought of him, of Jeff the person, though it was always sweet, she could never be released. Jeff held her in bondage; man liberated her.

His mouth explored the petals of her genitals.

She put her arms behind her head, and her closed eyes saw circles of pink and yellow and purple, circles widening then dwindling again, to the rhythm of her blood.

"Oh. Yes," she said.

His mouth was becoming imperative. She could feel the excitement in him. Regretfully, she postponed the moment of her orgasm.

"Let's go to bed," she said.

They undressed swiftly, and their bodies came together on the bed in a minor explosion. Within a moment, Debbie found herself there again.

"In me," she said. "Hurry."

The man took her. She could feel the smooth hardness of him and then the rhythmic push, and she wrapped her legs around him and buried her face in his anonymous chest. The man was working now, straining, his breath labored. Debbie approved. A long path opened, blue and red under her closed eyelids, and she began a golden ascent, knowing now that nothing could stop her, nothing could inhibit her flow and her release.

"Now?"

"Wait."

"I can't."

"Wait. Wait."

It was time.

"Come," Debbie whispered to the faceless one above her. "Come now."

Their orgasm was almost simultaneous. Through the ripped silk and velvet of her dream, she heard his groan. Her body arched, her fingers clawed the sides of the broad back, and her fulfilment was a triumphant singing in herself. Her head snapped forward on the pillow, then back. She held Jeff in her.

"Don't go," she said. "Stay with me." As always, full of her secret, she was now apologetic.

"I use you," she said to him. He smiled.

"Anytime."

"It's not fair." She stretched, contracted her stomach muscles, and they were separate again. Jeff rolled over on his back.

Debbie put her hand on his stomach. She could feel the ridges of his ribs. She poked her finger gently into his navel.

"Could it be something important?"

"What?" Jeff was half asleep.

"In the briefcase."

"Who knows?" He stretched. "I like your toes." He slid down the bed and took her big toe in his mouth. Debbie giggled.

"You look funny," she said.

Jeff slid back up. "It's my thing," he said, "like your purring. Now I've got a thing too." Debbie looked at her toes. They were long and slim, more she thought, like fingers than most toes. If Jeff were to develop a toe fetish, she would have to take good care of them.

Debbie rolled over and kissed him. Her hand explored his groin; she took his penis in her fingers. "I don't know . . . I think I like you better small."

"It won't last," Jeff said.

Debbie began to excite him, slowly, almost absentmindedly.

"There's nothing on that I know of," she said. "Nothing out-country except 'black' work."

"I'm going to be an international spy."

"James Bond."

"Double-oh seven. I'm one up on the average spy," Jeff said.

"How? You're growing."

"Told you it wouldn't last." He teased her breast with his fingers, and watched the nipple swell. "I've got the sex already."

"Everything's growing," Debbie said. He had come to full erection again. She felt, as she always did, the thrill of power. She found herself wanting to kiss him there, a desire that was rare with her. She slid down.

"Copycat."

It took some time for Jeff's second orgasm. When he finally came, Debbie put her head on his thigh and closed her eyes. She felt peaceful, replete with victory, with tenderness.

Jeff pulled her up to him and kissed her. Then he relaxed, one arm across her breasts, and within five minutes he was asleep.

After sex, Debbie could not sleep. It was a time when, her mind free of her body's demands, she could think. She was utterly relaxed. She felt the pleasant warmth of a perfect circulation. She turned her attention inward upon herself. . . . and nibbled at her happiness.

Always, when she was this much at ease, she would fight against recalling her childhood, but sooner or later she would lose. She remembered in the same pattern, as though her mind had provided tracks along which there rolled with an even speed the same memories, like a long freight train, each memory hooked to the one behind. She remembered her mother's face and the terrible stories she would tell, sitting in the kitchen of their small Manhattan apartment on West 113th Street. Debbie recalled 801 West 113th as an apartment house with a canopy, a steel-framed entrance, and a gnarled gnome of an elevator man who was always stretched out on the shabby lobby couch, sleeping.

The Bernsteins had moved there in 1949, when Debbie was only three. Her memories began about 1950. By that time Debbie's father was himself a memory. Debbie's room had been small and pink, and full of her mother. She could recall with photographic sharpness Leah Bernstein's dark face, with the bent nose and hollow cheeks. Her father was only the ghost of a smell — a compound of cologne and tobacco, a brown masculine scent, mysterious and comforting.

But she remembered her mother's high, sweet voice best of all. After her father's death (she later learned that, in delayed obedience to the SS guards who had ruled his death-in-life for five years in a concentration camp, he had killed himself one night, carefully capping the jar of sleeping pills and putting it back in its proper place in the tin medicine cabinet) the stories had begun. It was as though Leah Bernstein had to exorcise a ghost and exercise her hatred in a constant oral reliving of five years branded on her soul, less visible but certainly more painful than the numbers tattooed on her arm.

She talked more to herself than to Debbie. A little girl, serious-faced, listening with large eyes to the greatest horror story ever told: the story of the Final Solution, a fragment of that story recounted by a thin woman with a high, sweet voice and work-roughened hands as she cleaned up the dishes or peeled vegetables or just sat with a cup of cold tea in front of her. Leah thought the child was too young to understand. She was wrong. Debbie understood, and what she did not understand she imagined. Her imaginings were more awful, if that were possible, than the reality. The horror kept her silent, her face immobile, her eyes devouring her mother's face. She would swing her legs against the rungs of the chair, while a Caliban named Adolf

Hitler, who had been almost a decade dead, rose, fanged and clawed, to tear at her insides.

Debbie was a practical, tough-minded little girl, and it took almost a year for the effects of Leah's monstrous self-indulgence to become visible. The child began to lose weight, and night after night she would wake screaming from nightmares of which she could not be made to speak. When Debbie's gaunt white face and deeply circled eyes finally frightened Leah into a doctor's visit, it was almost too late. To the gentle white-haired Austrian doctor Debbie finally confessed her dreams; he sent her immediately to a psychiatrist. Three sessions later, the psychiatrist sent for Leah.

Debbie never knew what happened during the hour and a half that Otto Zweig and Leah Bernstein talked. Her mother was white and shaking when she returned home. She would not mention what Dr. Zweig had said, repeating only, "How dare he . . . how dare he!"

But the stories stopped.

"No," Leah would say when, with a peculiar semisweet terror in the pit of her stomach, Debbie asked her to tell again about Papa and the camp. "No, the doctor said it was bad for you. I will never forget," she would add, her eyes staring at the kitchen wall with a certain comprehension of the shadows moving, unseen to anyone but her, upon its surface. "No one will make me forget that time. It is all I have left of Papa," she would add, never realizing how cruel a blow those words were to her husband's memory. "I will never forget," she would repeat, her voice now sad and musical, an actress's voice, plangent and self-conscious.

Debbie's nightmares stopped.

As she grew older, she discovered that there were books, many books about the Final Solution and the concentration camps where it was carried out. She read Reitlinger and Shirer. She re-created for herself, from her mother's stories and from the books she read, a picture of the camp of Leah

Seehligson, of the intense dark-faced Jew, Ludwig Bernstein, who was a camp Prominent.

He had taught architecture in a great Viennese school before he became an *untermensch* marked for extinction. Ludwig was not a particularly devout Jew — he was too urbane for that. A gentle scholarly man with visions of buttresses and pilasters in his head, he tried to teach the principles of his art to a class of young men while buildings like flames danced in his mind's eye.

Most of the young men had liked him; some had respected him; a few had genuinely loved him. He was a fragile, tight-jointed man with a delicate precision about his body, his talk, and his walk. He was affable and courtly to his young men and to the young women whom he occasionally met. He lived totally alone, with not even a cat or a potted plant, in a small apartment near the school. The living room was good-sized, the ceiling gold; there were plaster cupids at the four corners of the room and a faded Turkish carpet on the floor. The kitchen, reached through a long narrow corridor, was bare. A porcelain stove made it possible to warm the professor's pajamas on a cold winter's night. There was a bathroom done in faded green velvet, with an ornate tub, and a small bare room with a narrow bed where Doctor Bernstein slept. He took care of himself quite economically, living the circumscribed life of a bachelor who desires little beyond his work, his books, and his sleep.

There were books everywhere, overflowing from the walnut shelves that lined the living room, heaped on the kitchen table, surrounding the narrow bed. Many referred to his specialty. The professor's only extraneous love was wine, which he imported at some expense from the Pyrenees. It was foul wine, pale and rank, but he loved it and bought it by the case, and drank it slowly, enjoyably, every night, over his work or as he read his books.

His salary, which was more than adequate, went into a nearby bank. His life was simple, almost Spartan. His cleaning woman went shopping once a week. Frau Lichler was a motherly person who profoundly disapproved of the Herr Doktor's way of life. Her weekly purchases of fresh vegetables and her thick peasant soups — almost indestructible they were, able to stand in the cool larder for days — kept him alive and well. He ate what there was with absolutely no gourmandise, no interest. If the cheese came to hand first, then it was eaten, and the soup became dessert. But it was often the other way around. He ate little, and he stayed slender.

The night of the Anschluss, along with most of intellectual Vienna, Ludwig Bernstein kept to his home. He changed his routine not one iota. Days later, when Hitler appeared on the balcony and the great hoarse shouting of the crowd vibrated through the walls of his apartment, he did lift his head, blinking his eyes rapidly. But then he went back to his book. The sound of his world ending did not interrupt his quiet evening.

Ludwig was not a political animal. He refused to be drawn into the Hitlerian atmosphere of intrigue and yeasty hatred that made of Vienna a city fragmented into tight little knots of men standing and talking under streetlamps, a city of booted, black-shirted SS, and the constant two-tone alarm of the police cars and fire trucks as they raced to more violence, to more arrests.

It took almost eight months for Hitler to come to Professor Bernstein. One morning the head of his department, Herr Apfel, took him to a coffeehouse and through a mouthful of strudel told him: "Professor Bernstein, my good friend." The older man, all untidy mustache and bushy eyebrows, paused and sipped his coffee with a discreet noise. "You know what is going on here, *nicht?*"

Ludwig made a gesture with his shoulders which said nothing.

"You realize," and to his immense surprise Ludwig saw Herr Apfel's eyes water, the veined white turned slightly red, "you must understand, dear colleague, I have nothing to say in the matter." He paused and sipped more coffee. The pause invited a statement on Ludwig's part. Beginning to understand what was coming, Ludwig felt the stir of dismay and anger inside him. He said nothing, deliberately.

"I receive orders. I do not know who gives them. That is apparently none of my business." The older man patted his lips delicately with his napkin. "You are therefore dismissed, Professor Bernstein . . . My dear Ludwig . . ." and to Ludwig's horror, Herr Apfel's voice broke, and he began to cry, snuffling like a sixty-six-year-old child, sitting at a corner table in one of Vienna's better coffeehouses, blowing his noise with a large lavender silk handkerchief. "My dear colleague, you are not the first. I have been forced to say this to five other members of the academy, all" — and here Herr Apfel's voice broke in a high, indignant note — "responsible educators. The reason you know. It is . . ." his voice lowered to a half whisper, "absurd, insane . . . But there you are." He paused and lit a fat oval Turkish cigarette, puffing noisily, as though to hide his emotion behind a thick cloud of smoke.

"I suppose I must leave at the end of the term?"

"Oh, no. No, no! Ludwig, my dear man, you must leave *now,* this moment. I will have your things sent to you . . . yes, I will. It may cause trouble, but I will have your desk cleaned out and the contents sent to your home. Where, Herr Professor, I hope, I sincerely hope, you will *not* be to receive them."

Herr Apfel blinked a horrible conspiratorial wink through his tears and rose. His portly belly shone under its casement of English vest, the material originally excellent, now threadbare and shiny. "You must now excuse me." He opened his cigarette case and took out three of his gold crested Turkish specials. "Smoke, my dear colleague. Think. A word to the wise . . ." Leaving Ludwig Bernstein staring incredulously after him, the administrator walked away with small, almost mincing steps. He waved once, without turning his broad fat back.

Ludwig Bernstein looked for a long moment at the three cigarettes lying on the café table. With a swift movement of his hands, he swept them to the floor. His anger frightened him. When he rose to leave, the waiter pointed out the four-schilling bill. Ludwig paid, realizing that in his confusion and pain, Herr Apfel had forgotten about it. There was nothing to do now except to go home, in the middle of the day, at two-thirty in the afternoon. What of his four o'clock class?

During the time that followed, the memory of all those waiting classes was a cruel spur roweling Ludwig to despair. Again and again as he sat in his apartment, listening to the strange sounds of the city beyond him — the sounds of Vienna had changed; they were no longer familiar, no longer pleasant, but obscurely disturbing, dissonant — he could picture the faces of his students and the battered lectern, empty.

It never occurred to him that anyone else had taken his place.

He tried, pathetically, to return once or twice to his academy, but there was a guard at the gate through which the young men had used to walk freely, and you had to have a pass to get in. Ludwig was reduced to standing some five feet from the ornamental iron fence that enclosed the campus, watching his young men walk back and forth, unchanged, with round throats and smiling faces, unlined and confident. It seemed to him a paradise from which he had been banished.

When they finally came for him, they knocked twice, at ten-thirty in the morning.

Ludwig Bernstein opened the door and found himself facing three men. One was in uniform, with the zigzag lightning of the SS on his collar. The others were plainclothesmen, both cut to a pattern: shiny healthy faces with strong chins, a weakness about the eyes. All three were in such beautiful physical shape that the first thing Ludwig thought of was his rather slender body and frail musculature. In comparison to the young men's blooming health, he felt awkward and weak.

"Ludwig Bernstein?"

Ludwig nodded.

"You have fifteen minutes to gather your things. Then you must come with us."

The plainclothesmen took up watchful attitudes on each side of the door. One of them reached into his greatcoat pocket and took out a greasily wrapped sausage sandwich which he proceeded to eat. Crumbs and bits of sausage dropped to the carpet. Ludwig went into his room to pack his suitcase. There he was paralyzed with terror and indecision. What books should he take? How to choose at the most four books, to accompany him and sustain him during the unknown times ahead? He turned in despair, and the SS lieutenant was behind him.

"Might I make a suggestion, Herr Professor?"

The young man's tone was crisp and incisive. Ludwig nodded his head.

"Take warm clothes — and food. Bread and water. Never mind anything else. Just a suggestion, of course."

Ludwig nodded again and did as he was told.

They rode away in a Citroën, a shabby car with smelly leatherette upholstery. The motor was not in good condition.

"I have been promised better transportation," the SS lieutenant said, as though reading his mind. He laughed. "The army does not always keep its promises — unlike the Fuehrer," he added hastily, aware of the plainclothesmen sitting in the back seat.

"We have no car at all," one of them said. It was the first time he had spoken.

"We walk everywhere or take buses. It is not dignified," the other said. They fell silent.

"Where am I going?" Ludwig asked, clutching his suitcase. His palms were damp. The slow, amiable ride through the city was indescribably threatening.

The Citroën stopped obediently as a white-gloved policeman halted the traffic flow.

"You are being repatriated," the lieutenant said. "You will have an opportunity, Herr Professor, to practice your profession. You will be building a city. A small city to house you and your kind." He paused. It occurred to Ludwig to ask, what kind? But he said nothing. "You have friends," the lieutenant said. "It is due to them that you are being treated with respect. I am myself interested in architecture. So, I understand, is the Fuehrer."

"I see."

"Well, we are almost there. You pass from my jurisdiction when you leave the car. Do not be afraid. It may not be too pleasant a trip, but if you are careful, you will survive it." The small car stopped outside the railway station. It was ringed with huge searchlights looking superfluous in the bright light of day. The station was incredibly busy. The square outside was filled with people, mostly family groups. Young and old, rich and poor, the people milled about the station and the open space in front of it, surrounded by bored German guards with submachine guns. This final expression of a fascist state was ludicrously democratic. Bankers and scholars rubbed elbows with butchers and bakers and candlestick makers. They had only their Jewishness in common, a fact that both ennobled and degraded them. Professor Bernstein felt, for a moment, the weight of a vast tragedy upon his heart. The car stopped, and its doors opened into hell.

During that hot summer day, Ludwig sat on his suitcase watching the people around him, speaking to no one. There was a constant weeping all about him, a subvocal wailing. The people slowly settled to their wait, forming ghastly little picnics here and there, eating, borrowing water and food from each other. Professor Bernstein ate his bread and cheese, and sipped from the battered half-gallon canteen which he had filled earlier at home. Toward late afternoon Ludwig felt a need to urinate. He rose from his suitcase and, carrying it, went to the nearest German guard. The sun shone on a pleasant face, shaved, with clear eyes and cropped hair that caught sparkles from the dying light. The boy stood with his submachine gun at ease on his hip, his eyes remote.

Professor Bernstein cleared his throat.

"*Grüss Gott*," he said. "Could you tell me where —"

The young guard turned and looked directly and with great distaste at Ludwig. Economically and neatly, with a gesture that spoke of long practice, he swung the barrel of his weapon, hitting Ludwig on the side of the head with enough force to knock him off his feet.

Ludwig sat sprawled on the dusty asphalt, his head ringing, his stomach churning. Had he had much to eat, he would have vomited. He retched a number of times, and felt something wet trickling down his cheek. His fingers reached, and he dabbled in his own blood.

"*Heil Hitler*, Jew," the young guard said. "You must learn to speak only when you are spoken to. Wipe your face." He turned his gaze away and resumed his reverie. After a moment, Ludwig clambered painfully upright. His problem had, incidentally, been solved — in quite a shameful way. But the heat of the sun would dry him soon.

It was the first lesson.

At eleven-thirty that night, the train finally puffed into the station. It seemed endless. It consisted of two shabby coaches, one at the head of the train and one at the far-distant tail. Here the guards of the convoy would sleep in shifts. Between these two antediluvian relics of World War One splendor, with their faded and broken velvet hangings and their overstuffed chairs oozing cotton intestines upon the floors of the cars, there were one hundred cattle wagons.

Most were roofed; some were not. Their sides were still stained with dung; they had been only cursorily hosed down. The doors were secured with massive iron bars.

The people were herded together in quasi-military formation, and the doors were opened. Then the second lesson began. The German guards were now no longer detached. They seemed to want the thousands of human beings instantaneously boarded, and they began to use their rifles as clubs. This caused some confusion, especially among the women, some of whose children's heads were split open. On the whole, however, the people boarded the trains with great energy, hurling themselves into the recesses of the cars with superhuman vigor, dropping their possessions in their frantic efforts to protect themselves from the incessant hail of blows.

As each car was filled to capacity, and beyond capacity, the younger children were hurled by the guards onto the heads of the packed people. Then the doors were slammed shut and bolted, and all up and down the track, there was the metallic clang of doors.

Overseeing all this activity, a young SS officer stood slightly removed from the tumult, with his stopwatch in his hand. It took twenty-two minutes and twenty seconds to herd over twenty-five hundred people into ten cattle cars, two hundred and fifty people per car.

The SS officer admitted to himself that it could be done faster. In fact, it had been done faster, in Poland and Hungary. But these were German Jews for the most part, and they did not respond quite as satisfactorily to firm treatment. There was another factor: his men could not quite understand that the people they were penning up were not human beings. Until a few hours before, they had all been considered part of the Reich. Subhuman they now were, but the SS officer noted for future reference that there were gradations of subhumanity.

Ludwig was lucky. He was chosen by accident to remain

part of the clean-up squad. Some fifty men and women were set to work to wipe the blood and the vomit from the street and station floor. The few corpses — mostly those of young children who had stopped too hard a blow — were piled onto a baggage cart and spirited away. On his hands and knees Ludwig mopped at the agony of his fellows.

That was his third lesson in humility.

After the floor was spotless again, the doors to one of the cars were reopened — it was a car with a roof on it — and he and his fellow workers were jammed in. The doors were bolted behind them.

Ludwig found himself facing the side of the car. He could move his head and his arms, but he was held motionless by the pressure of bodies next to him. The sounds the people made were indescribable. He had held onto his suitcase, battered and torn as it was, and he managed to balance it on his head like an acrobatic porter, and waited for the train to start.

An hour went by. People somehow began to make more room for themselves. A few lapsed into unconsciousness. The more vigorous of the men began to plan and talk, not of escape but only how to make their present situation less ghastly. The unconscious were rolled into a corner. Some elderly people began the chant of the dead, and the minor strains filled the cattle car.

At last, deep in the night, the train gave a great shudder and began to move. For a while, the people were lulled by the movement of the train. Something, however, had to be done about primary necessities such as food, water, urination, and defecation. Those who needed to relieve themselves banged on the side of the car, until the guard who sat on top of the car yelled down. It was not an inspiriting dialogue.

"Keep quiet, you bastards!" the guard yelled.

"But we have to go. We must relieve ourselves." An elderly man close to Ludwig, in a suit of impeccable cut, wearing gold spectacles, began to cry.

"I've got to go ah-ah and peepee," he said in the voice of a small child.

"Shit where you're standing," the guard said.

"There's no room."

"I'll make room," said the guard, "but you won't like it." The threat was unmistakable. The people quieted.

Some took the guard at his word. The stench of human feces filled the cattle car.

"We've got to get this organized," a hoarse male voice said authoritatively from behind Ludwig. "We won't last five hours this way."

"I agree," Ludwig found himself saying. "If we organize ourselves . . ."

"I have matches," another voice said from the evil-smelling dark.

"I have a candle stub."

Many had provided themselves with candles. They did not so much light up the car as soften and humanize the dark. But there was just enough light to see by. The young and strong wedged their way until they were together. They began to move people about. The children were lifted up from the floor, where they inexorably slipped. The train had been under way now for some three hours. There were some dead and a few insane. The sick, the mad, and the corpses were shoved together in one corner of their rectangular world. Somehow, a little space was made.

"What have you got in that suitcase?"

Ludwig looked. The speaker was a girl about twenty-two. A tremendous bruise discolored her neck and part of her breast. Her blouse was torn.

"Nothing. Just clothes." Ludwig found himself lying.

"It's something good, I'll bet."

"Not at all."

She edged closer to him.

"I haven't eaten for twenty hours. I'm thirsty."

"So are we all," Ludwig said.

"Please help me." Her hand went about his shoulders. "I'm afraid," she whispered.

"What?"

"I'm dizzy, weak. I'll slip and fall into *that*." By now, the floor of the car was a malodorous, terrible mixture. "Hold onto me," Ludwig said. He was glad she no longer spoke of food. "Try to sleep."

The girl giggled. It was a sound so inappropriate to the hell in which they were slowly dying that Ludwig felt a flash of anger. "It's possible if you're tired enough," he said. "You sleep for a while. I'll hold you up. When you wake up, I'll sleep, and you wake me when I begin to fall . . ." Hell was already beginning to subdivide itself, Dantesque fashion, and the innermost ring was on the floor, where people would suffocate and die. Some children had already done so.

The girl slept, her head nestled against Ludwig's shoulder. He held her up for what seemed an eternity, and then shook her awake. He slept himself. When he woke, at her insistent call, she was hanging onto him for dear life.

"Another minute and you'd have been gone," she said.

Dizzy, numb, he stood swaying to the long roll of the train. A number of the younger men had formed a human pyramid, reaching to the tiny, iron-barred window that let in the only air. After much slipping and swearing, a light-haired boy of eighteen, looking more Aryan than the Aryans, climbed to the top of the pyramid.

"It's getting light," he called down. "Soon there will be light again." It was as though he had said, "Soon there will be life again." Everyone relaxed a little in the promised luxury of light.

"What do you see?"

"I don't know." His voice was strained. Something snapped within him. He screamed, a terrifying inhuman sound. "I see fire!" he screamed. "A mountain of fire in the distance! Death and fire!"

When they got him down, he was mad. He gibbered about a mountain of fire and smoke for a while, until the people had had enough. Someone knocked him down and rolled him over onto the growing pile of corpses. Other lookouts took his place. All that could be seen in the gray light of early dawn was a long marshy plain. An occasional peasant stood and stared as the train rumbled by.

The girl said, "I must have something to eat or I'll die." It was a statement of fact.

Ludwig whispered, "Quiet."

They were bound together now. He reached into his pocket and took out a tiny morsel of bread and cheese. He slipped it into the girl's hand. She ate the way some alcoholics drink, making sure she was not noticed. He gave her a swallow of water. She said, "I feel better."

Ludwig ate too. Outside, the gray had begun to turn to gold. It would be another beautiful day in the dim, far-distant world of men and women. They passed through this world at a painful lumbering gait, but they never stopped. Their divorce from humanity had begun. It was real, it was painful, it was terrifying.

"I must pee," the girl said. "Help me."

He managed to help her get her pants down, and she urinated, her legs apart. He became aware that she was looking at him.

"We're all going to die," she said flatly.

"No."

"I know it. No one would treat us so if we were supposed to live." Ludwig said nothing. He could not deny it. The girl looked at him again and pressed herself to him. Ludwig had tried throughout the long night to close his ears and eyes to the sexuality in the car. But couples, convinced that this was their last night to live, made love openly, and no one cared. It was difficult to find space; it had to be done standing up. The people would move as best they could to one side, to let a couple alone, and the man would hoist the woman upon him. The night had been ripped open with shrill cries. It was difficult to know which were the sounds of pain and terror and which of pleasure, for pleasure and pain, despair and life, had narrowed to an almost invisible line.

"Do it to me," the girl said simply. Ludwig was aware of a tremendous erection. He coughed. "I don't . . ."

"I'll show you." There was an edge of hysteria to the girl's voice. "If you don't do it to me, I'll ask someone else."

She undid his pants and took out his erect penis with a small triumphant gasp. "Do it to me now," she said, and she half climbed upon him and wrapped her legs around his body. He held her, wondering that she weighed so little, and she moved and reached down a hand, and he was in her. He came almost immediately, with little pleasure, and as he did so, she screamed aloud her triumph, her pain, her horror.

"What's your name?" he asked her a moment later.

"Leah."

He would have asked her more, but the train abruptly stopped. They had been riding thirty-four hours.

Ten loaves of hard, sour rye bread were tossed into the cattle car by the guards. A gallon jug of water was given them.

A section of the roof was opened, and the guard's face, gun at the ready, peered in. His nostrils twitched at the indescribable stench.

"Throw up your dead," he said.

Of the two hundred and fifty people, some seventy-five had died. Almost all the children were dead now. They formed the majority of the corpses. It was difficult for the exhausted people to hand up even the light bodies of the children. But when they had finally cleared the car, there was more room to move about, and the people were able to take stock of one another in the semidark that spelled full sunlight outside.

"How much longer?" someone yelled to the guard.

He poked the snout of his submachine gun down in answer. There was a mad scramble for the ends of the car, out of the range of the gun, and some people were hurt.

The train started again.

During the next two days and one night, Ludwig had Leah many times. He didn't want her, but the brief minutes of forgetfulness that tumescence and orgasm brought were an indescribable relief. She seemed insatiable. Having no frame of reference, he could not know, as they coupled like the beasts they had been turned into, that this was not love, not even lust, but a dead thing that served a pathetic purpose. Outside, feet dangling from the car's roof, their keeper smoked and watched the flat plain roll slowly by.

Somehow, rationing out Ludwig's food, the two managed to stay alive. When they reached their destination, the car was comparatively uncrowded. They were standing ankle-deep in their own ordure. They had — it seemed impossible, unbelievable — grown used to the stench.

When the train finally stopped, they did not know it. They waited for three hours in the dark, and then, with no warning, the doors were thrown open. A line of some two hundred guards, machine guns at the ready, were lined up in military formation outside.

"*Alle Juden raus! Raus! Raus!*" A huge voice bellowed. The people clambered out of the car. Most were dizzy, and some fell while dropping to the ground from the car. These were immediately shot and their bodies dragged to the side. Dizzy as she was, Leah would have lost her balance and fallen, ensuring her immediate destruction, if Ludwig had not held her steady.

A dais covered with green velvet stood at one end of the platform. The entire platform was ringed with armed guards. A clean handsome man, his hair brush-cut, stood on the velvet soapbox. He waited impassively, his eyes seeing nothing and everything, while the people were herded together in a ragged formation. This took about fifteen minutes. When the survivors of the train were lined up before him, the Kommandant spoke.

"Jews! This is Judenstadt. You will learn it is not a rest home. Here, you work. If you do not work, you die." He paused. "Here, you are respectful. If you are not respectful, you die." He paused again. "Here, you are obedient. If you are not obedient, you die. But — if you are all good children, if you work hard and obey your superiors — you will find fair treatment here." He glanced at his watch. "It has been a strenuous trip. You are tired. You will be temporarily barracked now. You will get soup, and you may rest. Roll call is at three forty-five. When you are assembled, you will be organized." He turned on his heel and stepped down.

"Move!" the guards began to shout, "Move, pigs! Move, you sons of bitches, you mother-fuckers, you scum!"

Already the blows and curses had become a part of life, no more to be resented than the weather or bad luck. Holding onto Leah's hand, Ludwig ran toward his future. He kept his eyes on the path. For a while he was lucky. Then he felt the jolt of a truncheon as it descended on his back. He let go Leah's hand and covered the back of his neck with his fingers. He kept running. A gate appeared. Carved in pseudo Black Mountain style over the archway, he read WORK BRINGS FREEDOM. Running under the shouting and the whipping, he entered Judenstadt. Leah was no longer with him.

Later, after he had somewhat recovered from the horror of his first hours as a Judenstadt greeny, he deduced that she must have been taken to the women's compound. He remembered little of what had happened to him during what the guards called "indoctrination time." He had run full speed, spurred on by lines of prisoners and guards who shouted at him continually and hit him constantly, so that the blows merged into one another, a dull background to the stripping, the kicks, the ice-cold shower, the barbering and haircutting. The barber, a prisoner with the green circle of a criminal sewn onto his sleeve, had taken his hair in one huge horny hand and passed the clippers over his head, shearing him like a sheep. All these cruelties propelled him into a schizoid state. He felt that nothing was truly happening to him; that his ego, that discrete powerful kernel of himself that allowed him to function all his life, had hidden somewhere deep within him, cowering like a child who has been too much punished; and this visceral abnegation of self had both saved his life and destroyed his soul. His numbness was mental, spiritual, physical. He moved in a haze.

This was a dangerous time. Everywhere about him, lying on the wooden boards that served as beds in the Judenstadt barracks which were originally a stable, men, shattered by tremendous spiritual and physical shock, went insane and died. There was a time when Ludwig Bernstein could feel his body deciding whether to continue or give up. His cuts and bruises made it impossible to sleep. It was a time for decision, a life-or-death decision in which the most important part of Professor Bernstein had no say, for his true self crouched in a corner of his brain, inoperative, sleeping, traumatized. The decision for life was made by his body, communicated to his brain without his volition. He lived. He endured. He would continue to endure.

He listened throughout that incredible first night. He heard a hoarse whisper: *"Shalom,* friends. I want to die."

A mutter.

"Friends. I am on a packing case. You cannot see me. Push the packing case away. Someone will help you in your turn."

A singsong voice, with a cantor's intonation.

"It is a sin to take one's life."

"Shit. You call this life?"

"We are tired. We know nothing. Let us sleep and see what the day will bring. Surely they cannot mean to kill us all."

Surely they cannot mean to kill us all. With the words echoing in the canyons of his skull, Ludwig Bernstein fell into unconsciousness.

Ludwig survived his first week in Judenstadt by remaining in his detached state. Blows did not reach him. They only numbed his body further.

He attended his first selection the second morning of his camp life.

They were routed out by kapos at a quarter to four in the morning. The flimsy striped convict garments did nothing to ward off the crisp coolness of the summer night — it was still pitch-dark outside. The huge searchlights that surrounded the assembly area were on, bathing that torn and tired patch of ground with merciless clarity. No green grew here; the earth was gray and tortured, trampled down by countless feet. The only moisture it had known, outside of rain, was the blood of the slaves who assembled there, many to die as they waited for their masters. Once in formation, Ludwig and five thousand others were introduced to the cap drill by the head kapo. The Germans chose prison overseers from among the prisoners themselves, and they chose with their own peculiar sense of fitness. All kapos were from the criminal class, men sent here for crimes such as murder or miscegenation or robbery. The most brutal of these men were made to oversee their fellow inmates, and over Jews especially they had the power of life and death.

The head kapo was a huge bearded man named Schmidt, whose original civilian offense was lost in the mists of time. He was a professional concentration-camp inmate. His leathery skin was scarred with countless blows. He bore these stigmata as proudly as he displayed his vices: sadist, glutton, homosexual, murderer so many times over that any application of these terms to him was meaningless. Schmidt liked *pipels* — little boys. He kept changing them with fickle frequency, renewing his harem from the new convoys which arrived in Judenstadt on a weekly basis. The children he discarded were usually killed. Some, if they were especially fat or looked appetizing enough, were carried behind the latrines, where they were murdered, quartered, and their flesh sold for food.

Schmidt, naturally, had all he wanted to eat. His forearms were brawnier and fatter than the waists of most of the Jews in his care. There was only one way of appealing to his good nature, and that was with a bottle of *schnapps* (any kind of liquor at all was called *schnapps* in Judenstadt). The little boys whose bodies he used were his personal servants, and the clothes he wore — a strange uniform, with gorgeous epaulettes and crimson-striped trousers tucked into polished boots — were kept immaculate by his small servants. Every night, in his eight-by-eight cubicle, Schmidt was served a formal dinner on his card table. The table was laid with a patched, threadbare cloth, pressed and cleaned by his latest *pipel*. The glow of the room was the glow of hell, for there was crepe paper hung on the electric light bulb, and in this strange crimson demigloom, Schmidt would dine, and then, calling the little boy who served him, would close the door. The prisoners in the common barracks room beyond would hear the groans and screams of his pathic degenerating into high childish sobbing as Schmidt achieved his pleasure.

Schmidt's gorgeous uniform was a sample of his masters' humor. So were his privileges. The Germans would often enter the barracks to watch the kapo at his meals, doubled over with laughter to see this enormous ape counterfeiting an officer's manners, dining like a monkey in a circus. They thought him comic as well as useful, and they let him live and gave him his perquisites. Later, they married him in mock ceremony to an inmate from the women's compound, and as Schmidt distastefully went through the required sexual duties of a bridegroom — the marriage had been none of *his* idea — the German guards watched, drinking and laughing and banging on their helmets when Schmidt performed manfully. The young girl lay, her face white and closed, a patient anesthetized upon an operating table. The next morning she killed herself, but that went unnoticed. Schmidt's wedding night was a typical Judenstadt joke, less grim than most.

This was the man who led Ludwig and his fellow inmates through the cap drill. The caps were shapeless convict headgear, and the idea was to remove them on word command and slap them sharply against the thighs, in perfect unison.

This perfection seemed impossible to achieve.

"Caps — *on!*" would come Schmidt's parade-ground roar.

"Caps — *off!*" Five thousand caps hit five thousand thighs with an enormous cracking sound. Perhaps there were not quite that many, for there were always twenty to thirty corpses lying at "attention" in their proper places in the ranks. These were the men who had died during the night. They were not allowed to disappear into the camp furnace until they had been properly counted the next morning.

Schmidt's ears were keen, and he always noted a slight imperfection. "We do it again, whoresons!" he would bellow. They did it again. They did it from a quarter to four in the morning until nine-thirty, when their masters appeared, rubbing the traces of a sound night's sleep from their immaculate faces.

Schmidt ceremoniously turned over the command to his superiors.

"Five thousand *figuren* ready and accounted for. Thirty-two dead."

Somewhere, the camp inmates had lost not only their names — the numbers had been tattooed on their arms that unforgettable first day — but also their very humanity. The Germans referred to them as figures — *figuren* — cardboard cutouts, performing their two-dimensional dance of death and pain in a two-dimensional hell. Numb as he was, the horror of the term penetrated through Ludwig's numbness, to be felt as a faint stab of unimaginable spiritual cold somewhere at the roots of his being.

"Jews of Judenstadt," the SS lieutenant said. His face was quite dark; his eyes black, the eyeballs white and rolling. "Today we find out what you're good for. If that's possible. We need clerks. Will all Jews who polluted the colleges of the Reich step forward."

"*No. Don't move.*" The hiss came from behind Ludwig's right shoulder. He knew who it was: an "old bird," three months in the camp and still alive. He stood steady. Some two hundred men stepped forward.

"Good," the SS lieutenant said. "Gather on the right."

He paused and looked at a list in his hands.

"Carpenters?"

"Yes," the voice hissed from behind him. Ludwig stepped out. The group was quite small; the greenies figured that carpentering would involve hard manual labor.

"Return to barracks," the SS officer said. "We will deal with you later. All others, form work details. Schmidt!"

"Yes, Herr Oberlieutenant?"

"Form work details. Move them out."

"Yes, sir."

The "clerks" were shot and burned that very day. The masters did not wish the intelligentsia to live.

The camp day had begun. In the barracks, Ludwig waited. They were empty and somehow more horrible than during the night, when the inmates were packed on their wooden pallets, looking like the corpses most of them would soon become. This "selektion" was already worth something to him. Until called, he could indulge in the luxury of doing nothing. He was not allowed to sit on his bunk during the day, of course, but he could stand, and for one precious half hour no one would hit him or tell him what to do.

He did not think much. When he did, his mind moved

uneasily over scenes of pain that had somehow penetrated past his defenses, into the small part of him that was still alive and human. He remembered the clepsydras, the "water clocks"; men marked by a blow on the face, counting their life in hours, who were taken away the next morning to be shot and thrown onto the huge pyres of roasting flesh that polluted the air of Judenstadt night and day. Their sullen red could be seen at dusk, indirectly, lighting up the sky.

These men reacted in strange ways. There were no mirrors in the camp, and many of them could not tell if they had been marked by blows. They fell for the most part into a rigid state of pure terror, feeling their faces with their fingers, counting the hours. Ludwig, like all of the others, had grown to hate his face, could he have seen it, since it could so easily prove to be his death warrant. What one could not get used to was the randomness of life and death here; men lived or died by insane whim, a whim without pattern or rhythm. There was no way of making sense of this world. The best thing was to go mad, or become a *mussulman,* a walking dead man, long past caring, not even for food. But Ludwig had discovered in himself an insensate desire to live, to endure at any cost. This will fought against the numbness of his being, and it was slowly winning. He was coming back to life, not as Ludwig Bernstein, of course — he had died long before — but as a Judenstadt "old bird," cunning in the ways of the camp, concerned for himself alone, expedient, somehow adjusted to an environment which was deliberately created so that one could not adjust.

When Schmidt came for them, he looked less menacing than usual.

"You bastards," he said. "You've got luck. Unbelievable luck. You know where you're going, you filthy fuckers?"

The eight men in the barracks stood stiffly at attention.

"You're going to help build an addition to the Kommandant's house. You're getting clothes. How the fuck did

41

you know when to step forward?'' Schmidt sprang with his wooden truncheon, and it descended upon the back of a small man who had never planed a piece of wood in his life; he'd just stepped forward automatically.

But even in his rage, Schmidt was careful, unusually careful, not to injure permanently the Kommandant's newly formed work force.

"Speak up, you whoreson, you circumcised filth of a Jewish bitch."

"Yes, sir," the man mumbled. He wanted to rub the spot where Schmidt had struck him, but his arm hung at his waist. He did not dare. "Yes, sir. You're right, sir."

"Outside, you bastards. I'll take care of you tonight. Double time — march!"

Into a truck waiting for them (what luxury!) and up to the truly handsome little house in "SS country," where the Kommandant lived with his plain wife, his handsome daughter, six cats, and three dogs. The Kommandant loved gardens and animals of all kinds. He had made many plans in his life but until now, he had never had the chance to make them come true. Now he luxuriated in absolute power — power over an inexhaustible, free labor market, extensions of his own hands that could, and would, build him anything he wished. His adoration of the Fuehrer had been lifted to empyrean heights. The Kommandant needed no money. All he had to do was say, "Let it be done," and it was done. Had he thought of it, he might have built himself a pyramid.

The Kommandant's thoughts did not dwell on death — except professionally — but on how good life was. Yesterday he had eaten a hen, South German style, with white wine. Tonight he would have a cold platter, and his cook had been told to prepare *kaiserschmarren* for dessert.

The Kommandant's wife liked to ride. He would build her a riding ring, like Goering's — better than the Reichsfuerer's, in fact. He would use walnut throughout.

42

The Kommandant's wife liked flowers, not only during the brief and torrid Judenstadt summer but the year round. The Kommandant would build her a greenhouse, and slave gardeners would grow her roses and orchids.

The Kommandant's wife wanted a guest room. Not that they had many guests, but Himmler was known to visit places like Judenstadt and Bergen-Belsen, Dachau and Sachsenhausen, for here was the full fruition of the concept he had himself in large part implemented: the neat, economical, functionally beautiful concept of the destruction of all Jewry — the Final Solution.

And if Himmler were to visit, he would sleep in the Kommandant's house, in the beautiful paneled bedroom that the Kommandant would have built.

The Kommandant could hardly believe his luck when he found out about Professor Bernstein. A Jew who had taught architecture, a *figure* who was one of the country's authorities on beautiful buildings. He called him into his study.

Ludwig listened to the Kommandant's plans with half an ear. He was involved in sensation, unusual sensation in that it was not, for the first time in many days, unbearable. He had been dressed in decent blue work clothes, three sizes too large, clean and pressed. He had even been issued underwear. The feeling of well-being was so acute that he nearly swooned. The Kommandant finished telling him of his plans for a walnut riding ring, and dived into the greenhouse. Ludwig, a scarecrow swimming in gigantic overalls, swayed back and forth on his feet, and waited. It did not occur to the Kommandant to ask him to sit down. This was a Jew, a useful Jew who would not be exterminated for the time being, but a Jew nevertheless. Ludwig concentrated on a thought that had occurred to him. If he could just open his mouth, he could ensure, he hoped, another few hours of this unbelievable warmth and cleanliness, this magnificent absence of pain and terror. The Kommandant dove out of his greenhouse, with a metaphorical orchid in his mouth, and plunged immediately into the bedroom which was to be built against the possible visit of Heinrich Himmler.

He was still talking of paneled walls and carved headboards and how large the bed should be, magnificently large, to accept the physique of Himmler, the rachitic chicken farmer who had become the third most powerful man in the Reich. To the Kommandant, Himmler appeared as powerful, as rich, as big and as superbly wise, as (he imagined) he did to this poor Jew.

Against his will, overcome by ease, Ludwig Bernstein began to faint.

The Kommandant halted his monologue. What was the matter with the Jew? He peered at Ludwig, and saw the lack of blood in the white face. Mentally, he snapped his fingers. The Jew was starving. The Jew must work, must draw plans for him. His brain must be in top shape, to accept and concretize his unusual ideas. Therefore, the Jew must be fed.

"Go to the kitchen," the Kommandant said. "Tell them I said to feed you."

"Yes, Herr Kommandant," Ludwig said. If he had dared, he would have said, Your lordship, your magnificence. He loved the Kommandant, he adored him at this moment. Out of his kindness, out of his virile and incalculable strength, out of the treasure of his wealth, the Kommandant had decided to feed him.

Ludwig saluted, a military salute with a trembling arm, and turned on his heel.

He smelled the kitchen before he entered it. A paradisiacal vision. The smell of food was so rich, so good, that he swallowed it like meat. It was almost too rich; he came near to vomiting on the smell alone. Eat slowly, he thought to himself with the operative part of his mind, or you will be ill. And you cannot be sick in the kitchen of the Kommandant of Judenstadt.

"Well, you mother-fucker? What do you want here?"

44

The cook was no Judenstadt inmate, but he had picked up the local lingua franca. His tone was not unkind, however.

"The Kommandant told me to come here," Ludwig said. "For food." But he did not believe it. At best he would get soup and wormy black bread. Still, it would be an extra meal in his one-meal day. He could save some of his bread tonight without fighting the deathly temptation to eat it all, every scrap, right away. He swayed again as he spoke, and some inconceivable temerity spoke for him.

"May I sit down?"

"Sit."

Ludwig sank onto a kitchen chair. He had not sat on a chair since Ludwig Bernstein had died, weeks ago. The chair was padded. The cook thrust a plate at him.

He picked the plate up and swallowed the hot soup. It was real soup, not flavored water, and the vegetables were deliciously crisp.

"Easy," the cook said. "Take it easy, you whoreson. You'll puke it up here in the kitchen and it'll be my ass."

Ludwig swallowed the soup slowly. When he was done, the cook thrust a strange dish at him. It took him some minutes to recognize the texture and the look of scrambled eggs. There were salt and pepper on the table. As much as he wanted. He ate the eggs slowly, and when he was half through, he stopped. His shrunken stomach could hold no more. He pushed the plate from him and began to cry. All that beautiful food wasted!

"Here, you bastard," the cook said. He put five slices of bread smeared with real butter into a paper sack. "Take it along with you. The Kommandant wants you to go to the library. You're to begin work."

Clutching his greasy sack to his bosom, tears of incredulous gratitude coursing down his cheeks, his emaciated body seeming to move within the elephantine proportions of his work pants twice for every step he took, Ludwig began his first day as architect-in-residence to the Kommandant of

45

Judenstadt, a job superior to all other jobs in the camp, a job that gave him almost enough to live on — for though he never again ate in the Kommandant's kitchen, he was allowed the pick of the soup kettle, down near the bottom where the good stuff was, and it was his privilege to eat as much as he wanted. He was the Prominent's Prominent.

For the first time in his life, Ludwig Bernstein was a rich man, one of the richest in Judenstadt. He lived. The others died.

It took time for healing. Life was no longer insupportable. But as he marched away at the end of the day, back to the nightmare of the barracks, back to the world of starvation, of dying and of pain, he found the contrast intolerable. All day he worked in the Kommandant's house. He made incredibly detailed plans of the walnut riding ring. He spent weeks on one section of the greenhouse. The paneled walls of the bedroom were to be richly carved, and every carving was executed in painstaking miniature, drawn to scale. He was unaware of the resemblance of his efforts to Chinese prison work, yet he would have found kindred souls in those long-dead prisoners who spent their lives carving one piece of jade, executing just one work of art. The difference was that if *they* stopped improving their work, the Chinese prisoners were put to death, whereas Ludwig's effort was to improve his *against* the wishes of a man who was slowly growing impatient, for when he was no longer useful, he too would die.

The Kommandant, luckily, was greedier for perfection than for speed. Every morning Ludwig would report to him in his home. The Kommandant's house stood on top of a small hill overlooking the camp. Work details of Jews who had been marked for extinction were always sent to the rock pits some two hundred yards away. Their job was to clamber down into the sixty-foot-deep pit and pick up the huge rocks with their hands. They would then lift them,

46

sinews cracking, to the edge of the pit, where they would immediately be bludgeoned into taking them down again. The purposeless work seemed extremely comical to the SS guards. Sometimes, in desperation, the Jews would join hands, five or six of them, and rush the pit edge, falling sixty feet and dashing their brains out on the rocks below. The guards allowed them to kill themselves whenever they wished: wasn't death what they were there for?

Occasionally, too, the Kommandant would indulge in target practice. He kept two beautiful dueling pistols in his study, works of art, long-barreled, fashioned by a great Berlin gunsmith. They were twenty-two-caliber weapons, as precise as a surgeon's scalpel. The bullets were half charged. On fine mornings, the Kommandant would often begin his day by stepping out onto his balcony with his dueling pistols and killing four or five Jews. As he would explain, it had to be a brain shot; otherwise the Jew would only be wounded slightly, not even enough to impair his efficiency. Even at extreme range, the Kommandant was a fine shot. He had much opportunity for practice.

Ludwig would wait through the target practice, and then the discussion would begin. The plans would be laid out on the Kommandant's desk. Ludwig would find endless ideas for improving them. He astonished himself with the fertility, the sincere worth of his elaborations.

Work began on the riding ring, and Ludwig became more indispensable to the Kommandant. The relationship between the two men was changing. The Kommandant was becoming more dependent upon Ludwig than was seemly. He enjoyed the Jew's company. Often he even forgot that Ludwig was the equivalent of an ox or a cow or a dog standing before him. He began to invite him to sit down. One morning he insisted that Ludwig share a glass of *kümmel* with him. Ludwig dared drink only a quarter-ounce; the liquor made him dizzy. It allowed some of the immense hatred he felt for the beast in front of him to leak from its sealed compartment. The violence of his passion frightened and confused him. The attack lasted only a moment and left him weak and trembling. He knew in some obscure way that he had won a battle — not only with himself, but with the Kommandant as well. He realized then his role was finally cast. He could, perhaps, do some good, even in this hell.

When he discovered Leah was still alive he had been four months in the Kommandant's house. The riding ring was still only half completed. The Kommandant, at Ludwig's suggestion, insisted on cabinet jointing and cabinet finish to this outdoor structure. This would take a long, long time, but it would, of course, be worth it. Ludwig had assured his master that he would possess the finest, the most original and beautiful riding ring in the world. Not to speak of the greenhouse and Himmler's bedroom yet to come.

He had been sent on an errand to the SS store. The way led past the women's compound, a way that would have meant immediate death had it not been for the Kommandant's pass and his phone call to the tower guard. The guard even shifted his submachine gun and waved in friendly fashion to Ludwig as he recognized him. There were a dozen women, dirty, wearing torn and unidentifiable bits of cloth as makeshift skirts, incredibly thin, their breasts pouches under their torn blouses. They could have been any age, and their eyes were deep-sunk in their heads. As Ludwig passed, one of the women began, for no reason, to pummel another. They went at it hammer and tongs, beating, kicking, and scratching, rolling on the dusty ground some twenty-five yards from the electrified fence. As the women fought, they yelled. The guard in the tower first cheered enthusiastically, and then lost interest in the pigs.

"Jochanan of Chelmno!" one woman would yell, beating her fists upon the slightly bloodied head of the other. "Tell him his sister is still alive."

This was old stuff to any Judenstadt inmate. This was the way the women could communicate. They were allowed to fight among themselves and yell. The messages were buried in obscenities.

"You filthy bitch!" the other screamed. "David Rabinowitz. His mother blessed him before she died. Burned yesterday."

Ludwig walked slowly. He would remember the messages, and they would get to the proper parties — if they were still alive, which was more than doubtful.

A third woman gave an inhuman yell and threw herself upon the struggling bodies.

"I'll rip your cunts out!" she screamed. "I'll tear your bubs off! Leah Seehligson is sick. Tell it to Ludwig Bernstein. You stinking woman-lovers. If I had a prick, I'd shove it down your throat till it came out your ass." Ludwig had paused imperceptibly, and now he continued his measured walk, his head correctly bowed, his hands in front of him in the proper gesture of subservience. Leah was sick. She was still alive. He would do something, he had to do something. He didn't even remember what she looked like. But he would try to help her. He felt something long dead stirring within him. He would take a chance for her. His first true effort for someone else. Under ordinary circumstances, the beginning of the end for any "old bird." But his position was different. Yes, he would try . . .

He tried the next morning. He waited in the Kommandant's study, as usual, while his master indulged in his morning sport. He had introduced a variation. His flaxenhaired daughter, a child of twelve, stood by his side. She would point and say, "That one, Daddy." Then, while she covered her eyes and turned her head away, the Kommandant would take careful aim and fire. He was in good humor when he finally stopped. His aim had been good; he had killed five Jews out of six. He smiled at his daughter's averted face. Her sentimentality pleased him; it seemed proper in a young girl. As the child brushed by Ludwig, standing at attention, she bumped his foot with her own.

"Oh, Ludwig, I'm sorry," she said. "I hope I didn't hurt you."

Ludwig blinked. "Not at all, little mistress," he said gently, thinking, If I could, I'd poke her eyes out with my thumbs. I'd quarter her and throw her carrion to the men below.

"Well, Ludwig," the Kommandant said. He sat at his desk. "What's the agenda for today?"

For some weeks the Kommandant had stopped thinking of Doctor Bernstein as a Jew. He used his Christian name easily now, with no self-consciousness.

By now, too, Ludwig was more than architect-in-residence. He was a butler, an odd-jobs man, fulfilling the functions of a majordomo in a great house. Even the Kommandant's wife, a plain woman with not much mentality, dedicated to the Hitlerian ideal of German womanhood and motherhood, liked him. He made life easy for her.

"Master, it's possible that the mistress is overtired?"

"How, overtired? Is she ill?" The Kommandant was uneasy. He had been carrying on a torrid affair with the head of the women's compound, a beautiful bitch with blond hair. She fucked like a rabbit, and did other things as well which the Kommandant had never imagined in his wildest fantasies. His wife had been shamefully neglected. Now conscience made a coward of him.

"She has not mentioned it," Ludwig said, "but she could use a personal servant. And you, master, another secretary." He hoped against hope that Leah could type. If not, she'd have to learn, goddam quick.

"Good," the Kommandant said expansively. "Don't bother me with details. I'll have someone sent over."

"Master, I know someone. Someone reliable."

This was it. There was a pause. Death minced into the room. Ludwig kept his eyes on the carpet before him, and waited. The Kommandant laughed, a barking laugh.

"Your mother? Your sister?"

"No, Herr Kommandant. A girl named Leah Seehligson. An expert typist. An obedient girl."

"I see." The Kommandant thought to himself, Well, Ludwig wants a woman. He felt a small sympathy for the man. Everyone, even a Jew, he supposed, wants a woman. It was important to keep Ludwig satisfied. Useful. At top form.

"All right," the Kommandant said. He picked up the phone and said briskly, "Women's compound."

"Greta."

"Greta. This is Josef. You have a woman there, a Jewess. Leah Seehligson. Send her to my house. My wife needs a maid."

He put down the phone, and the two turned their attention to business.

An hour later Leah, thin, weak, gasping with dysentery, her legs bloated, her breasts withered, was sitting in the Kommandant's kitchen.

Ludwig was sitting across from her. The cook fed her the same ceremonious meal he had fed Ludwig. She ate slowly and only a little. Her eyes were hard and vacuous. Her hair was filthy and tangled. Her flesh hung apologetically on her bones. She was a mass of welts and bruises. And she stank. Ludwig did not recognize her. They had not yet even said hello. When the cook turned away, back to his pots and pans, Ludwig reached over and took Leah's hand. It was scabbed and pussy, like the rest of her.

"Better?" he asked.

Leah nodded. She glanced around the kitchen. Her eyes screwed up and she began to cry, long racking sobs broken by snuffles. Her nose watered, and she blew it into the paper napkin in front of her. Ludwig watched her sobbing for five minutes. The cook kept his back turned, elaborately indifferent. If the Kommandant wanted a slut of a kike in his kitchen, crying over his table, that was his business. *He* would have ordered things differently.

"I knew you were alive," Leah said. "I thought you'd forgotten all about me."

Ludwig said nothing. In truth, he had forgotten her, as he had forgotten all life except the life-in-death of the camp. He owed her nothing. Who was he to be a gift-giver in the middle of hell? Yet he was fed better than most. He was warmer than most. The price he paid — intimacy with a monster — was smaller by far than most, for *they* paid with their lives, thousands of them a week now. Topft and Company had installed new ovens in the crematorium. Two huge gas chambers were in operation. The Kommandant had discovered Zyklon B. Every evening, the Jews lined up, naked most of them, pressed one to another in a long line, waiting wearily for their "showers." The line snaked back over the hill, almost into the big camp. The guards were efficient and calm. Calmness, it had been discovered, was the proper oil to pour on the troubled souls of people who waited to die.

For the most part, the Jews accepted their deaths with equanimity. The camp treatment had more than broken their spirit: those who were not reduced to the status of walking vegetables accepted the thought of reasonably painless surcease with joy. There was less suicide in Ludwig's barracks since the machinery of murder had swung into industrial gear. Ten thousand men and women and children a week were being disposed of. A specialist had come down from Berlin and had solved the logistics of burning so huge a number of bodies. The pyres were enormous — thousands of bodies stacked like cordwood, in scientific fashion, so that the melting human fat could add to the flames. When a fire went out and had to be started again, it was almost more than the Sonder Kommando — the corpse-carriers — could bear. As the Kommandant was fond of saying, these Jews lived on the fat of the land. All day and all night, in twelve-hour shifts, spurred on by

Sergeant Moll, who was completely mad, the blackened fire-singed Jews worked, hauling thin bodies from the crematorium to the pyres, where they burned with a writhe and a hiss and a crackle. At night, lit by the fire that fed on their brothers' flesh, the Sonder Kommando made the red, grisly evening even more awful with their gaiety. They drank, they capered, they sang, they made up playlets, lit by the death fires. And every two weeks they joined their comrades on the pyre. The SS wished to leave no witnesses to the Final Solution.

Even the Kommandant had been corrupted by the prevailing insanity. He called for figures every morning. An executive, he pored over lists, trying to increase production, trying for more efficiency, angered at the occasional slowdown of the complex machinery he had built. His talk was the same talk you could hear on the lips of the Krupp executives, who had built a huge plant nearby and manned it with slave labor from the camp. They produced chemicals and guns. Judenstadt produced only death. But the Kommandant had become so inured to this that he had forgotten what his product really meant. And if he had geared his camp to ten thousand corpses a week, and the figure was only eight thousand, he swore and was angered and slept badly at night, until production was increased. One of the troubles was raw material: there were fewer and fewer Jews. The Germans were scraping the bottom of the barrel. It had got to the point where the Kommandant would call for champagne every time a new convoy entered the camp. He would toast the newcomers, saying to Ludwig, ''Wait until we win the war, Ludwig. Wait until we go to America and South America. There will be work for us all, work for the next thousand years.''

Ludwig would sometimes be handed a glass of wine, and he would drink the toast to the convoy.

Looking at Leah sitting at the kitchen table in her stinking filth and misery, he wondered why one life was more important than ten thousand deaths. Then he gave up the problem, angered by this strange idea. His every emotion was wracked and strained with the effort of applying, even briefly, ordinary noncamp standards to a camp situation. He had saved her life. He had even managed to ensure comfort — incredible luxury, in fact — for her. Leah would live in, sleep on the kitchen floor. She would dress the Kommandant's wife, comb her hair. She would be given food and soap and clothing. She would be protected from the weather. She would live.

"I don't suppose you can type?" Ludwig asked her.

"That's what I was. A secretary."

Ludwig sighed "You're the luckiest Jewish bitch in camp," he said. The routine obscenity meant nothing to him nor did it hurt Leah. It was a programmed way of talking, nothing more, nothing less. The systematic degradation of human beings brought with it changes in language structure.

So Leah too would do some of the Kommandant's secretarial work. It never occurred to Ludwig or to Leah, until much later, that the Kommandant, over the years, had turned from a great Jew-hater into a man dependent upon his Jews, a man who almost loved them. For without Jews he would be out of a job. There would be no more walnut riding ring. The flowers in the almost-completed greenhouse would wither from lack of care. The paneling of the Himmler bedroom with its incredibly rich detail and its perfect jointing would never exist. No, the Kommandant did not hate his Jews. He needed them too much.

Away from the camp, Leah was able to forget the howling hell outside. But Ludwig still returned to his barracks every night, to new faces and new corpses. He still strode through the mussulmanity of the camp — the walking dead, emaciated to an incredible degree, no longer hungry, no longer thirsty, their own feces and urine threading the sticks of legs on which they walked ceaselessly, uncomprehendingly, uncaring. Sometimes these men would sit down, and it was the truncheon of a kapo beating upon a corpse which would discover their death. Their living was so little different from their dying that their passing was a trivial detail, merely the breaking of the poorest thread, of importance to no one, least of all themselves.

Both Leah and Ludwig had perfected their instinct for survival. While Leah made herself indispensable to the Kommandant's wife, Ludwig began slowly, with infinite caution, to exploit his relationship with the Kommandant, in an effort to alleviate some of the worse horrors of Judenstadt. He began with the children.

In order to do this, Ludwig had to subsume himself into the mad atmosphere which the Kommandant lived and breathed. He had to align his psyche with those goals precious to his master. He began his campaign one morning after target practice, when the Kommandant finally gave him his opening.

"You enjoy your girl?" the Kommandant asked. He had grown thinner and grayer over the months, as his raw material diminished and the war went badly for Germany.

"Yes, Herr Kommandant. Thank you."

"She types well, for a Jew." The Kommandant blew into the barrel of his dueling pistol and put it back in its exquisite velvet case. It lay there, the bright steel inlaid with gold, winking death to the room.

"Every man should have a woman," the Kommandant said with deep, sad conviction. His own romance with Greta had ended some time before. He was back to ploughing his plain, unsatisfactory wife.

"Some men," Ludwig said carefully, feeling the panic in his stomach, "do not like women."

"I will not have such in my camp!" The Kommandant was rabid on the subject of homosexuality. He didn't understand it, he didn't like it, it corrupted his men and his officers. At table, he would often state with much conviction how he loathed queers.

"There are a few, Herr Kommandant." Ludwig spoke softly.

"Who? Tell me their names." The Kommandant's voice was sharp. He looked at his majordomo's white face, realized that he had scared him. Jews, he thought to himself, cowards as well as beasts. "No one will harm you," the Kommandant said, seeing the varnished surface of his walnut riding ring sparkle in his mind's eye. "Who do you mean?"

"Schmidt, for one, Herr Kommandant."

"Schmidt?"

"Head kapo, Herr Kommandant." Ludwig explained about Schmidt's *pipels*.

"Four a month?" the Kommandant asked.

Ludwig remained silent. The Kommandant walked to the door of his study.

"Sergeant?"

"Yes, Herr Kommandant."

"Bring me a man named Schmidt."

"Head kapo, Herr Kommandant?"

"Yes, damn you. Bring him fast."

Ludwig made as if to leave.

"Stay here," the Kommandant said. "Schmidt is no Jew. Yet he allows himself to be profaned by the touch of Jewish bodies. The Fuehrer has plainly spoken on the subject of race defilement and perversion. I will not have these in my camp. Judenstadt is a clean camp. It is moral. It is dignified. It will remain so." Clearly, the master was disturbed.

Through the open window of the Kommandant's study, Ludwig heard the sounds of Schmidt's calvary before he saw him. The blows and curses of the SS sergeant resounded through the camp air. Under the thud of a truncheon Schmidt ran lumberingly, all two hundred sixty pounds of him sweating in his uniform, his epaulettes flashing gold in the sun, his crimson-striped trousers pumping up and down as he ran, his enormous hands clasped over the back of his neck. As he passed, the *mussulmen* stared with mouths agape at this impossible sight. Their world was, for a moment, turned upside down. But they forgot a minute later and began again their aimless meanderings, a snake dance winding inexorably to the crematorium door.

Three minutes later, Schmidt stood panting, hat in hand, in the Kommandant's study. His mouth was still greasy from his midmorning snack (Schmidt ate six or seven times a day, encouraged by the SS guards, who found his gluttony hilarious). Though the sergeant had beaten him with all his strength, irritated by the exercise Schmidt had forced upon him, the huge man was not even bloody. He was only vaguely aware that he had been beaten and forced to run like a Jew through the barracks lanes. He was concerned only with the fact that here he was, facing the one man in the camp he feared.

"Schmidt," the Kommandant said crisply, "You are a whoreson, a mother-fucker, a boy-bugger."

"No, Herr Kommandant." Schmidt was barely able to talk through his panting.

"I have been told all about your *pipels*. Little kikes. Disgusting."

"But Herr Kommandant, they're only Jews." He didn't understand. His job was to kill Jews, to maintain order. As for his personal life, no one had ever questioned his morality before. It wasn't anyone's shitting business, Schmidt thought, uneasy at the obscenity the Kommandant was throwing at him, knowing that the lingua franca of the camp applied only to Jews.

"They *are* Jews. Do you know the Fuehrer's attitude toward race defilement?"

Schmidt wondered what to say. Originally he was Ukrainian. He had lived the good life so long, he had forgotten his origins, the small village where he had been fated to live his life as a farmer's son, with hogs and sheep and cattle. Perhaps the Kommandant thought he was German. It was risky to say Yes to his question, death to say No. Schmidt said nothing.

"Come over here. By the window." Schmidt turned, and saw Ludwig. Something stirred in his slow brain.

"Was it him? That kike? Who said those things about me?"

"Never mind," the Kommandant said. "You can take care of him later. Go over to the balcony. Lean out and tell me what you see."

Schmidt's huge, blubbery, leathery face, with its crushed nose and wide shapeless mouth, worked uncertainly. But an order was an order. He walked to the balcony and leaned over.

"Further," the Kommandant said. "Now, tell me what you see."

"Jews, Herr Kommandant. Working in the rock pits. Picking 'em up and putting 'em down." A chuckle welled from the gigantic body. "It's funny, Herr Kommandant."

"I think you should take a closer look," the Kommandant said. He drew his Luger from his hip holster and shot Schmidt in the back of the head. Schmidt's head exploded in blood and brains, and the enormous body, kicked forward by the bullet's impact, toppled from the balcony and landed with a thud some fifty yards from the rock pit. No one even looked up. It was death to raise your head.

"Wipe up the railing for me," the Kommandant said to Ludwig. "Judenstadt needs a new head kapo." He paused, ruminating. "I would appoint you, but that's impossible. We'll have to see."

Cleaning bits of brain matter from the balcony railing, Ludwig was horrified to find that he had a killing erection.

A glow of well-being suffused him. He had seen one of them die, and he had been the cause. There would be fewer *pipels*.

The sinews of dependence strengthened. When the Kommandant put Doctor Bernstein in charge of the lists of the dead — those scrupulous compilations which represented the usufruct of the Kommandant's vast business — he finally had his chance to save lives. What he could do, he did. He doctored the lists, upping the daily total, the weekly total, by as much as he dared. He used the numbers of Jews killed in the early days of the camp. As the war progressed and the hysteria inside Germany began to be felt even here, in this world of killers and of killed, as defeat crept through the barbed wire and the watch towers, invading the camp as no enemy yet had, it became easier. The vigilance of the Kommandant relaxed. The war was going badly and so was his murder factory.

Over the years that Ludwig was useful to the Kommandant, he managed to delay death for countless thousands of people and to save, actually to give back to life, at least five hundred. His work was an open secret in the camp, but he was never betrayed. Though he returned every night to the barracks, he was under the protective shadow of his master, and no one harmed him. Nor was he much envied or hated by his fellow Jews. He was respected, regarded with awe, one who had gotten away with it, who kept fed and warm, who never forgot his brothers. There came and went many heroes in Judenstadt, but Professor Bernstein was the one who counted. He endured.

Somehow a part of him, of his luck, Leah endured also. When the Russian Army overran Judenstadt in January of 1945, the Kommandant, with his wife and child, had been gone for three weeks. The Kommandant's last act was to turn over his house keys to his faithful servant Ludwig Bernstein. Ludwig and Leah lived on, by the Kommandant's order, in the Kommandant's house, while destruction and death ran riot in the compound. The smoke from the furnaces, the greasy black odor of burning human flesh, created a ghastly, ever present smog. Enormous mass graves were dug, and the bodies of the Jews, hundreds of thousands of bodies, were interred deeply enough, the Germans felt, so that there would be left no trace of the Final Solution. There had been no time to burn these bodies, no time to do anything but kill and kill and kill.

The two were there still when the survivors of the camp were forced onto their last long march, a bloody winter's trek across Poland and into Germany.

They were there when the first red-starred truck arrived.

They were taken for Germans, at first. They were reasonably well dressed and certainly healthy. Only the testimony of some of the walking dead, whom Ludwig had tried to help in the confusion of the last weeks, saved them from execution. The incredulous Red Army captain, who spoke a broken and horrific Plattdeutsch, interviewed them casually in his ersatz office, a cleared barracks. His submachine gun was thrown onto a broken desk. To his left, their hands bound, some twenty SS guards awaited their fates.

"I wouldn't have believed it," the army captain told Ludwig. "Your luck has been incredible."

"Yes," Ludwig said. He looked at the SS guards, their manacled hands crossed at their waist, and his face twitched slightly. He moved with unexpected speed. He had the machine gun in his hands before the captain knew what was happening. He used it like a chauffeur hosing down a car, swinging it back and forth, his face softened and decomposed by pressures within . . . while he screamed. They had to knock him out to stop him. He had killed sixteen unarmed men.

At the hospital, they cheerfully informed him that as far as they were concerned, the incident had never happened. They did not tell the professor what he had been screaming.

"I want to drink their blood!" Ludwig had yelled as the machine gun stuttered. "Let me drink their blood!"

When Ludwig was able to travel, he found Leah in the temporary women's quarters, and they simply walked out of the camp and took a train back to Vienna. There, the academy where the gentle Herr Professor had once taught was helpful. A few months later, Leah and Ludwig were in America.

They had been married in Vienna. The night they made love for the first time as man and wife, they wept, through both foreplay and intercourse. The tears healed.

In New York City, Ludwig was appointed to an assistant professorship at Columbia University. He had his young men again, their faces round as ever. But now there was a ghost riding his back, weighing him down with awful, insubstantial weight. The ghost of five years, during which he had been protected, cosseted even, by a man whom he hated beyond imagining. Leah, full of Debbie physically, and then, after the birth emotionally, managed to forget. Professor Bernstein could not. One night he killed himself, politely but firmly and thoroughly, and so completed the work of Judenstadt and the Kommandant, who surely would have found his erstwhile architect-in-residence's suicide enormously amusing, fittingly obedient.

What Debbie did not guess, at her father's funeral, was what her mother was thinking behind her widow's veil. Had she known of Leah's anger, she would not have understood its cause. For Leah was furious with her husband; he had given in at last, when there was no longer any reason to. What she did not understand was that Ludwig Bernstein, gentle, cowardly, had finally come back to life, automatically killing the possessed man who had saved her so many years before. The two men could not live in the same body. Ludwig Bernstein killed himself as soon as he realized again who he was. There had never been any question of another course of action.

Debbie did not know about her mother's anger, but for the year of the stories, she borrowed her mother's anguish. Twenty years later, lying in bed with her lover beside her, her mind spinning more slowly now, like a dying top, she stopped re-creating her father's hell. A useful procedure, since in any case she could not imagine the complete truth. . . .

Debbie Bernstein, relaxed by love, facing an innocent future, finally slept. Her body was tucked around Jeff's, one of his arms was across her breast, and she clasped both hands around it, feeling its weight upon her with delight, and lapsed into deep sleep.

2

JEFF woke briefly several times during the night. He dreamed between wakings, slow pastel-colored dreams, formless shapes through which he floated. His sleep was tinged with anxiety. He woke to Debbie sleeping beside him. She snored lightly. He'd disliked that when he had first slept with her; it destroyed her fragility. Now, knowing her to be more than just delicate, he almost loved her tiny snores: somehow warm, ego-satisfying.

She didn't often allow him to stay the night. They had discussed the fine balance to be kept between two people who intended to marry. It had been Debbie's contention that if she gave herself unreservedly, there would be little to look forward to.

Jeff had guessed that she was afraid he would not want to marry her in January if she did not put some limits now to their relationship. His reaction had been not unpleasant — a warm, slightly smug feeling, mixed with tenderness.

He woke early in the morning. Debbie still slept, deeply, and when he moved close to her she murmured an inarticulate protest and turned onto her stomach, her nose pressed into the pillow. He lay on his back, half asleep, half dreaming. He dreamed of his boyhood — and, as always, of his father.

Jeff had never really known his father. It was difficult for anyone, much less a young boy, to know a man who had gone through five wives and three fortunes. Jeff's childhood was a blurred montage of hotel rooms, skiing resorts, summer retreats. Twenty-five years earlier, Jeff would have been familiar with Montreux, Deauville, Cap Martin, Wiesbaden,

65

Gstaad; his memories were of Lake Placid; Hot Springs, Virginia; the Plaza in New York. When he was four, his mother divorced his father; the act must have been rewarding indeed, for Richard Whitson was divorced by no fewer than six women before he was fifty. Dick Whitson was a sophisticated man — or so his friends, of which there were surprisingly few, had told his son. His complexity of character, his warmths and his defects, were all, unfortunately, beyond the ken of any child. He was an adult's adult. Of medium height, reasonably handsome, with dark wide eyes beneath two bushy eyebrows that gave his slim face with its small, well-kept mustache its peculiar attractiveness to women, Dick Whitson had been an enigma to his son while he was alive. His death had fixed him as a permanent puzzle, a secret which Jeff would never comprehend.

During the five years that Richard had spent with his first wife, Jean, his polite adulteries and suave cruelties had driven the wispy, pretty woman into a gentle alcoholism. Her breakfast was sherry with an egg whipped up in it. She spaced the burnt wine during the day, but by the time evening came and her husband was home, she was placidly inebriated. It was a commentary on their relationship that Richard Whitson did not notice his wife's almost chronic drunkenness for six months.

But Jeff, four years old, did. It was not so much that he noticed his mother's strange behavior as that his organism sensed a lack. He was weepy and given to fits of temper. He wanted what he wanted when he wanted it: with a grim hysteria, he would kick and scream until Miss Lorris, his English nurse, would lose her temper and give him a spanking. Whatever he wanted — a tricycle, sweets, a walk, a game — they all came down to his indignant demand for his mother, a frail slim woman with clouded gray eyes and shining brown hair who sat all day in a dressing gown sipping Harvey's Bristol Cream.

What had triggered Jean's drinking was the realization

that her husband was not only a confirmed adulterer but quite happy and carefree in his amorous adventures. He never tried to hide any of his mistresses from his wife; in fact, he seemed glad to parade them in front of her, often appearing with his latest girl on his arm in those few New York restaurants where his wife habitually dined with friends.

The year 1951 still carried with it some dwarfed heritage of puritanical America, and Jean Whitson was unable to laugh off her husband's adventures with sophisticated cynicism. She hurt. She would come home and cry. She made scenes, scenes in which Richard refused to participate. She confided to her analyst that there was something lacking in her husband's makeup. Not only was he impenitent, he was bewildered by the fuss she made. His reaction was to withdraw into himself and to come home less frequently.

She divorced him in 1952. She felt her heart turn over when he appeared after the divorce for the community property settlement.

He affected a slim walking stick in an age that had bypassed such niceties. He looked, Jean confided to her best friend, so damn successful and happy. It was his aura of success, his impregnable confidence, which broke Jean's psychic back. When the day was over, her ex-husband took both her hands in his.

"Come and have some wine," he said. This was no affectation. Richard knew and loved wine, as he despised liquor.

They went to the Colony. They sat at the small table where they had celebrated their engagement and all their wedding anniversaries, and Jean said to him, "Why are you doing this?"

"Surely," Richard said pleadingly, "we can still be friends." It was then, far too late, that Jean understood the reasons behind her husband's actions. He could not bear to have anyone dislike him. This vulnerability of his had led him to excesses of cruelty. So there was nothing to do but drink the Dom Perignon which he had ordered and toast the ghost of themselves in the waning afternoon light. When he handed her into her taxi, all emotion had left her. She was drained, a transparent ghost, a shell sucked dry, returning to an unreal apartment through a fine mist of spring rain that had the taste and texture of tears she could no longer shed.

That afternoon she discovered bourbon. Eight months later she was dead of too much alcohol, too little sleep, too little food — and too little purpose.

Had she lived, Jean would have had the satisfaction of knowing that she was not the only woman to divorce or be divorced by Richard Whitson. She had guessed the secret core of his actions, in her anguish managing to avoid the laminated surfaces of his deviousness that afternoon at the Colony; what she could not have guessed was how far his disease had progressed. Richard simply could not help himself; he felt that he would be damned eternally — he did not believe in God, but for some reason he had come to envision for himself a formless terrible hell, where he would agonize forever — if he did not marry the women with whom he was seriously involved. He married six of them.

The first three came and went while he was still successful. His life had always been that of an entrepreneur. He had been graduated brilliantly from Columbia, majoring in economics, and had made his first fortune by stepping into the presidency of a small company, a company which, everyone agreed, could not last another six months; it had been bled white, ruined by its former president and chairman of the board. Filling both functions, Richard weathered the half year, and with a nice combination of intelligence and ruthlessness, put the company back on its feet. When he finally left it, he picked up a quarter-million dollars in capital gains (originally the board of directors had been only too glad to give him stock in what they felt was a dying corporation). He looked about him and found new worlds to conquer. At thirty-six, when he divorced Jean, he was already worth some four hundred thousand dollars.

During the next ten years of his life, his luck swung back and forth like an erratic pendulum. He went bankrupt four times and recovered four times.

There clung to his neat figure the sinister yet attractive aura of someone damned. The despairs and successes of his life had put lines on his face and gray in his hair at an early age. He was paying eighty thousand a year in alimony when a double hernia sent him to the hospital.

It was a simple enough operation. He recovered easily, and two mornings before he was to be discharged, as he paced back and forth in his corner suite at Doctor's Hospital, he felt a violent headache. He put his hand to his head and stood for a few seconds, swaying, in his maroon silk dressing gown. He opened his mouth to call someone to help him, and crumpled dead on the floor, from an unpredictable embolism. His son was twenty-two.

Earlier, Jeff had lived a life of trips, of nannies, of extravagant presents and mysterious neglects. At ten he was a handsome child, very clean and currycombed, his coordination the result of swimming lessons, dancing lessons, tennis lessons, golf lessons and riding lessons. He was highly secretive and talked little. His education was the result of private tutors and dozens of interrupted beginnings in private schools throughout the country. He walked the floors of his hotel rooms or of his apartment — his father had bought and maintained a small but beautiful cooperative on upper Madison Avenue — with the contained movements of a sailor. Always there was about him the plaintive look of one who goes away; he was a perpetual, unwilling traveler, passing through a land of contented children and smug, dull families complete with snoring Sunday-afternoon daddies and overworked, shrill mommies. And how, in his heart of hearts, he envied them!

Once, when he was nine years old, he had taken a plane to Cap Martin on the French Riviera. It was his sixth overseas flight and he relaxed, the competence of the seasoned traveler sitting oddly upon a pale, muscular boy. He met his father that night for dinner. It was, as always, a highly emotional meeting. Richard was always physical with his only son, and Jeff had learned to respond with the professional emotions of a small gigolo.

The obligatory kisses and hugs over with (Jeff put his arms around his father with genuine despair, and his tears came from deeper within him than he knew) they all went down to dinner. The hotel was uncrowded. Sitting at the round dining-room table, Jeff was introduced to the twenty-two-year-old British starlet who was to become wife number four. Richard was over in France on business — he was organizing a European branch of his latest company — and this weekend, for which Jeff had been especially flown over, was the end of a week's holiday for his father and Pamela Brice. The two were exhausted. They had exploited to its fullest the ramifications of their physical relationship. Pam had been enthusiastically exposed to all of the physical variations Richard could bring to the act of love. She was brimming with a tired satisfaction, certain of Richard's affections, certain, now, of his proposal, and she'd been willing to be nice to his silent young son. In the noonday heat of their rut, Jeff felt left out. He sat, so to speak, in the shade, and watched the total absorption of his father in this young perfumed female, whom he compared unflatteringly to his last mother. He'd seen *her* at least ten times. She had been older, and riper, and therefore more like a mother than this adolescent girl.

He excused himself after dessert, while his father and the starlet buried their noses in huge glasses of Armagnac, and wandered into the hotel lobby. He was a specialist in lobbies. This was not an interesting one. There were no divans upon which to sit and watch the people as they strolled to and fro.

Nor was it large, with little odd-shaped rooms and mysterious corners and long corridors lined with transparent cases of jewels and leather goods. This was just an oval lobby, quite plain, quite clean. He wandered into the game room. There was a ancient billiard table, unoccupied at this hour, a good Swedish table-tennis table, and, to the right, the usual one-armed bandit. It was a new machine, reasonably expensive — a two-franc machine — and after a pause, Jeff pulled some change from his pocket and gave the lever a pull. The machine clattered and hummed, and three stars rolled up. Twenty-five francs cascaded into the metal cup beneath. He had won.

It was the first time he had ever won anything. He choked with excitement. He put in two more francs and pulled the lever again. Three more stars rolled up. The machine cascaded more francs into its metal palm.

It took him four successful tries to realize what had happened: something had gone wrong with the mechanism. The slot machine was broken; it could do nothing but spout francs. No one was around. The boy pulled the lever like one possessed. His rewards gradually decreased, until he was getting only three and four francs for every two he put in. But there were over four hundred francs in his pocket; he was weighted down with them.

Finally the machine no longer spouted its insane metal orgasm, and Jeff turned away. He could not have articulated what he felt, the warm bliss of a security that had cast a cloak over him. Tonight the world was rigged in his favor. Life had stabilized itself. He felt powerful, invincible, lucky. Wild with joy, he half ran back to the dining room to tell his father of his wonderful half hour, to show him the fruit of his labors, the result of his God-ordained luck.

The table was empty. Only his governess sat there, ill-temperedly drinking her third cup of after-dinner coffee, waiting for him. It was time to go to bed.

When he asked where his father was, Madame Sevigny

looked at him for a long moment and then said, with a touch of malice, *"M'sieu s'est couché. Il était fatigué. Il avait, certainement, l'envie de dormir."* Jeff's knowledge of French was minimal; he reacted to the emotion behind her words, aware somehow that something nasty was being said about his father. His disappointment was far beyond what the circumstances warranted. Luck seemed to fall away from him; he was peeled like an onion. As he rose to his room in the slow hotel lift, the weight of the coins in his pocket dragged him down.

That night he cried bitterly before falling asleep.

From that time on, Jeff became a conservative. He pointed his very existence toward two goals: security and love. Something within him broke; he became passive. He did not want to love: that was too risky. But he passionately desired to be loved.

He was sent, at twelve, to a prep school. The grounds were lovely; the dorm where he lived was properly ivy-covered. He went through six years of Connecticut winters and New York summer vacations. He was not unpopular at school; he gave away what he had, he bribed, in melancholy reflex, his enemies to be his friends, and his friends to continue their friendships. Deep down, he trusted no one, not even himself. Outwardly calm, his interior energy was consumed in a slow, perpetual plot to be respected, to be liked by everyone he met. His feeling for his father had been pushed into a tight, small place somewhere in the back of his mind. He had given up Richard much the way a loving woman finally gives up an impossible husband. He was courteous to him, even servile, when they were together, but he expected nothing from his father, and he discounted what Richard gave him. The two had never understood each other; Richard Whitson had for so long lived on the surface of existence that he had forgotten the depths that rolled beneath. To investigate these, either in himself or in his son, would have made him a different man; and to tell the sad truth, he often looked at himself and his life in the mirror of his remembrance, and found himself more than satisfied.

At eighteen, Jeff graduated from prep school with honors, though not high honors — which would have meant that he might have hurt some of his coevals — and found, a month later, to his surprise, that Harvard had accepted him. He was told by the dean of admissions, in circuitous fashion, that someone had helped him, and for a while he assumed it was Richard. But obviously it was not. Dick couldn't have cared less where his son completed his higher education. For some time Jeff tried to find out who his benefactor was, but with no success.

In his junior year he met Evelyn. He had managed to steer a middle course through the first two years of his college career. His marks were neither good nor bad. His dates were with girls neither beautiful nor unusually plain. He played some poker, he indulged in some bull sessions. He was mildly popular with his housemates. As always, he had a little more money than most of them, and he bought popularity where he could. He was more circumspect about this, though, than he had been in prep school. He had discovered that many people could not be bought directly, and he had obediently turned his talent for ingratiation to subtler ways.

Evvy Shirra had marked Jeff for her own from the first time she met him. She had struck up a conversation with him at a Pudding dance, and he had been amiable and amenable. On their first date he took her to an excellent Boston restaurant.

"You eat here often?" she asked him. The white tablecloths and the gilt menu were a trifle awesome.

"Not often. I don't usually have such a good excuse."

Evelyn was a tiny, dark girl with a sharp nose and brilliant black eyes. She came from a small Connecticut town where her father was a circuit judge. Everything about her was miniature. Her small breasts were delicate and firm, her throat was brown and rounded, her hands were in proportion to the rest of her. Had she been twenty percent bigger, she would have been a great beauty. As it was, she waited for some man who had eyes to see. Lately, she had stopped waiting. She had slept with a number of boys and found it interesting, though lacking in that violent final spasm she knew brooded somewhere in her. She had decided to sleep with Jeff. Only he wasn't responding properly.

He ordered dinner with a complete lack of ostentation. In fact, he seemed to be pleading with the waiter rather than telling him what he wanted. He ordered two filets mignons, medium rare.

The steaks came raw.

Evelyn cut into hers, wrinkled her nose, and said. "Tell him to take it back and put it on the fire. This animal's still alive."

"Try mine," Jeff said.

"Just the same. Call the waiter."

"Ev, let's not make a fuss." She looked at him. His tone was determinedly casual, but it was obvious that he meant it.

"Why not?"

"Well —" Jeff laughed. He said lightly, "We'll hurt the waiter's feelings."

"Nonsense."

"Let's not make a fuss. Please. I hate fuss."

"I don't like raw steak."

"Tell you what," Jeff said. "We'll pretend to eat it. I'll take you somewhere else."

"For God's sake!" She looked at him curiously. His face was pale. "It's not that important," she said gently, and dug into her steak. They ate silently and without enthusiasm. Jeff paid, and she noticed that he left a large tip.

"You're a big tipper," she said conversationally, as they got into Jeff's Volkswagen, and he said, "Not usually. Where to now?"

"I've got an overnight," Evelyn said. She put her hand gently on his knee. "Hi. You're my favorite aunt."

"Aunt?"

"My favorite aunt is taking me out to dinner tonight," Evvy said. "I'm staying overnight at her hotel."

There was a long silence.

"I haven't got a hotel room," Jeff told her.

"Try the Blackstone."

"I don't know. I thought we'd see a movie."

"Oh."

"But your idea sounds swell. Just swell."

"Thanks," Evvy said dryly. To himself Jeff thought, I've hurt her feelings. He put his arms around her. "I'm just shy," he said. "Men are shy too, sometimes." He bent and kissed her. Her lips were warm and her mouth was open. Her tongue reached out to him and probed his teeth. He put his lips around it, feeling the wet, live mobility, the beginnings of desire. She was light in his arms, her body like a bird's, her bones filled with air. Her movements were quick, her tongue danced in his mouth, and he had to hold her steady to kiss her again.

"Let's go," he said.

She waited demurely in a chair in the hotel lobby while he booked a room for himself and his "wife," for which he had to pay fifty percent more than he should. In the room they stood looking at each other.

"Should I send up for something to drink?" Jeff asked.

"No. I've had enough." Both their heads were buzzing slightly from the three martinis and the wine with dinner.

"I'm going to the bathroom," Evelyn said. Her small body moved lithely. The bathroom door closed behind her. When she came out five minutes later, her black hair swung free to her shoulders. She was dressed only in her bra and panties, and the bird bones of her breast cage shone white under her freckled skin. She looked at him coolly and said, "Why aren't you undressed?" She climbed into bed, and turned on her side away from him. He felt sure her eyes were closed.

He took off everything but his underpants — he believed in symmetry; somehow it was important that they should each be undressed to the same extent — and got in beside her. He put a tentative hand on her hip, and her fingers closed warmly over his. Then she turned to him, and they kissed for a long time. Somehow he unsnapped her brassiere, and her small breasts swung free. He covered them with his own chest and buried his face in her hair.

Her hands explored him. She stroked his testicles delicately; her fingers closed gently over his phallus.

"What?" he said. He had not understood her hot whisper.

"Gold," she said, stroking him. "Solid gold."

He took her nipple in his mouth, and she played with his hair. When he touched her, she was ready for him. "Let's make it," he said.

"Let me kiss you."

Jeff didn't understand, but when she slid down and took him in her mouth, it was as though she were repeating an act with which he was long familiar. It was the most exciting thing that had ever happened to him. He watched her work for a while, and then said huskily, "I'll come."

Evelyn nodded her head, up and down.

"Do you want me to?" he asked.

She said nothing, and a minute later he came.

Evelyn snuggled up to him, and sighed with satisfaction. His hand explored her wetness; he could feel the preliminary trembling. He was tumescent again almost immediately, and this time he rolled over on his back.

"That way?" Evelyn said softly. He said nothing, but his closed eyes spoke for him.

They made love with Evelyn on top. Now Jeff was sure she loved him.

They returned in the morning, in bright sunshine, full of their night together, the space between them crackling with their mutual physical awareness.

Evvy was no longer miniature. Her physical aura had changed, her femininity was awesome. There was power in her, power to affect him, to give him pleasure and pain.

They were together often thereafter.

They did not meet during summer vacations. Jeff went back to New York, to the unsatisfactory, febrile existence of the summer months, with no life, no real purpose of his own. The grayness of the New York summer was lightened by one dinner which he was offered, quite unexpectedly. The host was an uncle, James Whitson, Richard's elder brother. Jeff knew little about him except that he had disapproved of his sibling, and that the family ties were not strong. James had been a manufacturer of electronic parts, the owner of a small but essential plant that created tiny secret precisions under government contracts. He had been retired for three years now. He was fifty-five. Jeff was living in a one-and-a-half room kitchenette suite, made possible by Richard, in an unfashionable hotel on the upper West Side. He rarely had mail and spent the summer drifting in New York, drinking and dating as far as his week's pocket money could take him.

He was in when his uncle called, and the precise, flat voice on the phone was completely unfamiliar.

"Jeff?" the voice said.

"Yes?"

"This is James Whitson. Am I disturbing you?"

"No," Jeff said. It was ten-thirty in the morning, and he was slightly hung over. He was brooding over a cup of coffee, trying to mold his day.

"I'm your uncle. We've met several times, when you were small."

"Yes," Jeff said. "Of course. Uncle Jim." He didn't remember what the man looked like; he had only an amorphous memory of a large, comfortable house in Connecticut where he and his father had spent a few boring weekends.

"I'm in New York. Could we have lunch together?"

"I'd like that," Jeff said insincerely.

"Are you free today?"

"I could be."

"Good." His uncle suggested a small restaurant in the East Fifties. It was a medium-priced French place and Jeff had eaten there before without much pleasure. The best that could be said for the food was that it was adequate.

Between eleven and twelve forty-five, when he disappeared down the maw of the I.R.T. subway, Jeff regretted making the appointment several times. But, he thought, it *was* a free lunch, and there was little he could do about it. He knew he would be bored to tears.

He was early. The restaurant was hidden under a huge red and gold plastic canopy. Jeff sat at the small semicircular bar and sipped a dry martini. He kept a lookout in the soft gloom for his uncle. His face, in his memory, was ballooned all out of proportion, oversize, the face of a man seen through the eyes of a small child. He noticed someone checking his hat, and he recognized James Whitson immediately. The stiff, straight back, clad in dusty black, was astonishingly familiar. When his uncle turned around, Jeff could see his bald dome, with a fringe of gray hair circling it, shining in the dusty shaft of sunshine that speared the murk of Pierette's. The black suit, with figured black tie, was almost funereal. There was little resemblance between the elder brother and the younger.

Jeff had often noticed, without perhaps drawing any conclusions, the quick, mobile intelligence in his father's face. His uncle's face was impassive. No, Jeff thought, watching him approach, that was the wrong word; it was neutral, and closed tight over — what?

"Jeffrey. Have you been waiting long?" James Whitson's voice was of a piece with his appearance, as precise as it had been over the phone. In fact, Jeff realized, the voice was exactly the same. The telephone depersonalizes most voices, but it had neither added to nor detracted from James's.

Jeff felt his uncle's voice float about his ears, dehusked, like the dry wisp of a dead grasshopper's body, as light and impersonal as the brushing of moth wings.

"No," he said. "Nice to see you, Uncle Jim."

"A sherry," James Whitson said to the bartender. He sat down on a stool next to Jeff. "Tell me about yourself. It's been years since I've seen you."

"I'm at Harvard."

"Yes."

"That's about all, I guess."

James Whitson sipped his sherry. "Do you like college life?"

"It's okay. I don't like my marks."

"Oh?"

"I'm going to do better next term." Unbidden, the image of Evelyn naked flashed through his mind. He'd have to do less of that, and more studying. "The only trouble is" — Jeff hesitated — "I don't know why I should . . . study, I mean." He tried again. "I mean, I don't quite know where I'm heading."

"That," the older man said dryly, "is a dilemma which is shared by many people in this country. I might add that the large part of them are past college age." He finished his sherry. "Shall we eat?"

Sitting opposite his uncle, watching the massive bald head bent over the menu, vaguely curious as to what was going on behind the tight unlined face and thin lips, Jeff thought that James Whitson's formal manner and precise stilted speech became him. As the meal progressed, Jeff became aware that he was being interrogated; pumped was perhaps the better word. It was all vague, highly skillful, so gentle that he was unaware of it until he had responded almost too fully. By the time the dessert tray was passed, Jeff had confided that he was apolitical. He had even mentioned Evelyn — not by name, of course — and at the last he was speaking of his father.

The older man listened quietly. He did not smoke. His hands remained as still as the rest of him. The impression Jeff had initially formed subtly altered. By the time the bitter Italian coffee was served, Jeff no longer thought of his uncle as neutral; rather, he was responding to a feeling of controlled power. Mixed with this was a vague fear, unbased, irrational.

"I've never approved of the way your father handled you," James Whitson said at length. He sipped the dregs of the coffee. "As you're probably aware, I've never approved of your father. We've drifted apart over the years."

"What are you doing now?" Jeff asked. Shamefully, he felt that if the conversation continued on its present tack, he would break down completely and all of the loving hatred he felt for Richard would rise in his gorge, and he would spew it all out in front of this precise, controlled, vaguely formidable relative.

"I'm retired, more or less," Uncle Jim said. He beckoned a waiter and asked for a cigar. Jeff was noticing other things now: for instance, his uncle was known here, well-known, he would guess. And yet there was none of the ceremony, none of the commercial politeness usually lavished upon a valued customer. Everything was underplayed but the service. The meal had proceeded more smoothly than any meal Jeff had eaten here before. Even the food seemed better.

"Do you eat here often?" Jeff asked.

"The last time I lunched here was four months ago. I must say, the service has improved since then." But it hadn't — not as he remembered it, Jeff thought. It had improved only for his uncle. And he was left with the larger part of his question unformed in his mind, but there nevertheless. He sensed a mystery, an unimportant one, obviously, but even so he felt the meal had possessed a significance beyond its casual pretense.

"Keep your marks up," the older man said. He had

signed the check. "The better they are, the better for you. We'll keep in touch. And we'll talk again."

The hatcheck girl handed him his hat, and as he put it on he seemed almost to disappear. The singular force that Jeff had felt was abruptly no longer there, as though the hat had served as a huge black snuffer. His uncle patted him briefly on the arm — this was the only time he had touched him — and while Jeff blinked, dazzled in the sudden sunlight, James Whitson climbed into a small black battered Chevrolet sedan, and the car vanished into the midtown traffic.

The lunch, Jeff decided, had been oddly impressive, and the mystery of his uncle continued to tickle the back of his mind for some days afterward.

Dick Whitson died a week before Jeff's graduation from Harvard. Later, Jeff often wryly thought that perhaps his father just could not have borne the ordeal of attending his son's emergence into the world of men and money. Jeff had been sitting in his room, not doing anything but stare with an absent-minded sentimentality through his dusty small window overlooking part of the courtyard. He had passed through Harvard a wistful stranger, terrified of being unpopular, yet curiously passive. He did not want to leave. He had no idea what to do with his liberal arts degree; nothing in the past four years had convinced him that he was *meant* for anything. His romance with Evelyn Shirra was over, and he had decided against further sexual adventuring. Though his sexuality was strong, he was able with reasonable ease to refrain from any other entanglements, and apart from a few one-night stands — he repeated the same pattern always: dinner in a Boston restaurant, and then the Blackstone — he had stayed away from girls. His extracurricular activities had been minimal. He had managed to force his marks up to an A-minus average and be graduated cum laude, but none of this engaged him. He was aware only of a vague anxiety, a desire not to enter the outside world where he would have to bribe more people, more times, in other coinage than what he had to offer. He was afraid of bankruptcy.

When he picked up the phone, he had no idea who would be calling him.

"Jeffrey? This is James Whitson." Uncle Jim's voice was as flat as ever. "I'm phoning from New York. Your father died this morning. It was painless, an embolism of the brain."

There was a long pause. The only emotion Jeff felt was embarrassment.

"You had better take a plane or train to Washington. His ashes are being flown here."

"All right," Jeff said.

"You'll miss your graduation. I had intended to be there. Well," the voice paused, "I had better give you my address. You'll be staying with me."

"Oh." Mechanically, Jeff took down his uncle's address, and only later did he wonder why Uncle Jim had a Washington home. He'd lived in Connecticut as long as Jeff could remember.

Jeff decided to take a train to the capital. Somehow, he thought, the train would give him time to think. He told no one of his father's death. He was assured his diploma would be sent on after him. It took him twenty minutes to pack up four years of his life, and like a substantial ghost, he swung into the parlor car of the train that was to take him away from his small, bribable world into a large, incomprehensible one — a life that was starting off with a whimper and might well end, Jeff felt, with a bang.

He had thought that the train ride would allow him to grieve for his father, to begin to feel. It did nothing of the sort. He spent it in the dining car, drinking gin-and-tonic and flirting with mechanical persistence with an enameled young woman who was traveling alone and whose name was Marie.

82

He tried, between monotonous insincere sexual gambits, to think of his father's death, of his own life, of the funeral, of where he was heading. But his thoughts foundered in a black void. His head ached. He ordered another gin-and-tonic, his palms sweating, frightened of the formless future. After a while, rather snappily, Marie left him to himself. He continued to drink, but the liquor did nothing. His fear slowly altered to a gray, mouth-puckering depression.

The club chair was comfortable. He leaned his head back, his fingers around the cold glass, his eyes closed, and he tried to doze. He relaxed. His fear and depression dwindled to a small, manageable corner of his mind. He allowed memories (not so much memories as sensory impressions, forgotten, stored, but recallable in his moments of relaxation) to float behind his eyelids — a clear stream flowing now swiftly, now slowly, bearing upon its surface the traffic of his past. Jeff stood on the riverbank of his memory and watched his life pass by. The warmth of his daddy's arms (he must have been very little then) ; the few moments when his mother had held him tight, before sleep, bent over his bed ; the dreadful time (he was twelve years old) when he had discovered masturbation and his current mother had tied his arms to the bedposts, and the wonderful relief when Richard had discovered him crucified upon his bed, and with a decisive motion of his small gold penknife cut him loose. Jeff remembered how much he had loved his father at that moment, the man standing over him, releasing him from his humiliating martyrdom, never asking a question, never referring to the incident again. From then on, he masturbated in the bathroom, over the toilet bowl, swirling away the milky semen, eradicating any traces of his activity with toilet paper.

His thoughts ran into a soft dark tunnel, and he dozed. When he awoke the train was coming into the station, and there were tears on his cheeks. He had cried as he slept, cried for his father, as he could not do when awake.

83

There was no one to meet him at the station. He took a cab to his uncle's apartment.

It turned out to be a staid four-room affair, in one of the staidest and most decently shabby apartment houses in the city. When he rang the bell, there was no answer. He was about to turn away when he noticed a small envelope stuck under the loose-fitting front doorknob. He glimpsed his name, and opened it. "Key under doormat," it said. He opened the door, and the smell of his new life invaded his nostrils, stinging the very back of his head. He took a deep breath, switched on the lights, and entered, closing the door behind him. It swung to with a solid thud.

There was another note in the kitchen, and it said simply: "Home at five-thirty. Mix yourself a drink and relax." He found the liquor cabinet and made himself an iceless martini. Then he sat on the couch and sipped his drink. It was four forty-five. He had three-quarters of an hour to wait.

After a while, he began a tour of inspection, slowly, anxious to discover what he could of Uncle Jim. The apartment consisted of a small living room, two smaller bedrooms, a bath, and a kitchenette. As he prowled, he became more and more uneasy. The apartment was totally impersonal. He opened dresser drawers, found them empty except for three shirts, some neatly folded underwear and a few lonesome pairs of socks. The clothes closet held two suits. Kitchen shelves contained a dozen glasses, washed and shining. The refrigerator was immaculate, empty except for a half-quart of milk.

The apartment was sinister, and somehow phoney. It was hard to feel that anyone lived here. In spite of its small size, it gave the impression of large, empty space. And it became increasingly lonely. For a short while, Jeff walked an emotional tightrope between self-pity and irritation. Then, as his feeling of unease and apartness increased, he turned on the small television set in the living room, switching channels until he was confronted by a ten-year-old

Japanese girl singing, with repulsive perfection and a few inconsequential lisps, a popular love song. He sat down in front of the box and watched the show intently, losing himself in the easy idiotic rhythms, cradling his warm martini in hands that had now begun to sweat.

James Whitson came in quietly. Later, when Jeff got to know his uncle better, he managed to put himself on guard against the man's deft inconspicuousness. Whenever he expected Uncle Jim, anywhere, he honed his hearing and tightened his attention, for only by doing this was he able to notice him as soon as he came into a room. But now, knowing his uncle not at all, he was caught by surprise. His mind had moved into a dim and mournful room, hypnotized by the white screen in front of him. When his uncle touched him on the shoulder, he jumped.

"Are you all right?"

"Yes," Jeff said. His stomach felt queasy. The shock, for some reason, had been great. He had known, deep inside himself, that he was alone — and yet, there his uncle stood, his hat still on his head, bent over him, concerned.

"I'm sorry. I was daydreaming."

James sat down, cradling his hat in his hands. "I'm sorry I couldn't get here earlier."

Jeff switched off the television set. "I took you at your word," he said. He half raised the warm drink in his hands.

"Good. I should express my condolences." he said.

"Thanks," Jeff said.

"I dislike being the bearer of emotional tidings. I dislike it even more when the news is both emotional and unhappy."

"Of course," Jeff said patiently.

"Your father wished to be cremated. This has been done. He had the good sense to leave some money for his funeral expenses, in a savings account. He did not specify where he was to be buried."

The pause invited a comment.

"Where do you think?" Jeff said at last.

"His ashes have been flown to my office. We could bury him in Washington. It would save a trip to New York."

"You really never liked him much." Jeff observed.

"Not too much. I disapproved."

"Of him?"

"No." His uncle lit a cigarette. It was the first time Jeff had seen him smoke. He puffed inexpertly, like a schoolboy at his first prom.

"Few men wear their lives the way they wear their clothes," Uncle Jim said, a trifle pompously. "Your father had excellent taste in dress, perhaps a trifle vigorous. He was unable to extend his sense of what was fitting to his existence. A pity."

Well, Jeff thought to himself, that was neatly put, anyhow. If you thought about it, Uncle Jim hadn't really said anything of importance. But it had sounded clever and appropriate.

"I never really knew him," Jeff said. What a lackadaisical, what a poor and stumbling phrase.

He realized that tragedy could bring with it a bathos of clichés.

"I disapproved of the waste," James Whitson said, "Your father always underestimated himself. He thought he was a clever man. He thought, I don't know why, that he was *only* a clever man. Actually, if he'd given himself some courtesy, some due, he might have discovered that he was much more than clever." Uncle Jim paused. "He was a bright boy," he said in the dusk. "He was far brighter, far nicer, than he thought he was. He could have been anything, done anything." His voice was as precise as ever, and as emotionless.

"He was successful," Jeff offered.

"Not successful. He made a lot of money."

"Well — " Jeff let the silence frame his question.

"They're not the same thing at all. Perhaps for some.

But you have to be stupid to think they're the same. Or at least limited.''

Jeff said, ''You were in business.''

''Yes. I wished to establish a competence. I made money, I used it. And when I had made enough — no millions, I was never like your father — I liquidated the business.''

''And you retired.'' Jeff looked at the living room. ''I didn't know you had an apartment in Washington.''

''Not many people know. And it would be preferable if you didn't mention it.''

''Oh?'' Jeff didn't understand.

''The apartment is only *faute de mieux*,'' Uncle Jim said. The French phrase fell grotesquely from his lips. ''You know my home is in Connecticut.''

''I see,'' Jeff said, seeing nothing. The older man seemed to be trying to tell him something. A few minutes later, he thought that this was his imagination. Uncle Jim had begun to discuss the funeral arrangements. There would be a memorial service in this apartment tomorrow afternoon. Jeff's father had had no religion, but it seemed too cruel to this gay, fascinating, amoral, and pleasant man to let him sink back into nothingness without some sort of leave-taking.

At one point James Whitson paused in what seemed to be an endless series of phone calls, and said, ''You're wondering about the will.''

''Not really,'' Jeff said, lying a little, thinking it expected of him.

''There won't be much.'' Jeff looked at him unbelievingly.

''I'm sorry. Your father died at a bad time. His situation was always fluid. He owed or was owed. There will be enough left for a small income. But his debts were very large.''

Jeff had always known that he would work, but somehow he had never thought of himself as anything but reasonably well off. His father had always supported him; the money had always been there, without fuss. Now the money had stopped.

The best thing to do, Jeff thought to himself, while his stomach lurched a little, was to forget his own way of life: to start afresh, realizing that now and forever his standard of living depended upon himself alone. It was a bleak yet comforting sensation, a mixture of fright and relief. Now perhaps he would find out, for the first time in his life, who he was and what he was good for. Dimly, at the end of a dark tunnel, he caught a gleam of light. He held the future of Jeff Whitson in his own hand; with luck, he would emerge knowing himself, able to assess his weaknesses and his strengths. It seemed a tempting and worthwhile goal. The way was long and chilling. He decided he would discover his future day by day.

The first day was the day of his father's funeral. It dawned bright and cold. Eating his breakfast egg, he saw everything sharp and clear in the harsh morning light. He ate in his shorts, alone. His uncle, up at six, was long gone when Jeff had opened his eyes. He had left one of his notes. He would be back in the early afternoon. The service was set for four o'clock. The caterers would be there at three. And would Jeff like to write a short eulogy? There would be no minister. Everything, the note concluded, had been arranged. And, oh yes, the wives would be there.

The wives would be there. One woman, Jeff's mother, was dead. The other five were arriving from all over the country, leaving husbands and children and lovers and jobs to say good-bye to the man who had hurt them, irresponsibly thrown them over, one after another, as his fancy dictated. Five whims, converging upon the ashes of a memory. Jeff, shaving with care, wondered why they were coming at all. He sat down at the kitchenette table with a yellow pad and a soft pencil to write his father's eulogy.

And found he had nothing to say. He knew nothing about Richard. He found himself wishing that he could look up his father in *Who's Who*. Yet he had to say something.

He began. "Richard Whitson was . . ." Was what? And

to whom? His mind circled about nothing. His father was a vacuum to him. There was nothing he could do about it. He could write down his own frustrations, his angers, his long pain, his loneliness, and the eulogy would turn into a recital of Jeff Whitson's psychological ills. The only thing he really knew was that he was sorry, sorry his father had died; that his passing left behind an emptiness, a whirling stomach, and a gutful of fears. Again, nothing about the dead man; Jeff was full of pity for himself. Carefully he put down the pencil upon the yellow paper. His head ached. An hour had passed. He knew he could not write anything. Maybe Uncle Jim could contrive something. He wanted his father's memory hallowed, his life made to seem, for one final moment, significant and real. But someone else would have to do it, not he. He felt tears pricking his eyelids, and he knew he wept for himself, not Richard Whitson.

He was slightly high when the first guests arrived. His uncle had not yet returned from wherever he was. The caterers had come — two Italians, sour and silent — and they had tried to soften the living room. There were vases of flowers, and plates of small sandwiches spread out in the kitchenette. Something was warming in the oven. It looked, Jeff thought, as though there was going to be a party instead of a service. Even the two candles which were to be lit as the ceremony (if you could call it that) began, and were to be extinguished afterward, looked partyish. They were a royal yellow, with ivory spirals running through them. It would have been better, Jeff thought, finishing his fourth martini on the rocks, if they had been white. Or black.

A wake, he thought to himself, this is a wake. A subdued Episcopalian wake. As the doorbell rang, he wondered whether his father's ashes should have been present. They reposed somewhere in an aluminum cylinder.

Four of Richard's wives had met in the lobby. They all knew each other, a complex webbing of legal entanglements, alimony checks, indignant phone calls, and even a friendship or two. They were all on a first-name basis. And they all were wearing modified mourning, a spot of black somewhere.

They were relatively young and attractive. One of them, the starlet Pam Brice, was stunningly beautiful and astoundingly young. She had done her conscientious best not to look flamboyant, but her health and sexuality lit the room like a four-hundred-watt bulb.

Jeff didn't offer them a drink. He thought it might be in poor taste.

For him it was too much of a good thing. At one point or another in his life, he had called every one of these women "mother." He sat, surrounded by a matriarchal concentration that seemed to turn the air in the small living room to soup. Two of his father's ex-wives were in their late thirties. As they pecked him casually on the cheek, they murmured their condolences. The starlet patted him absent-mindedly on the shoulder, smiled a brilliant, vacant smile, and abruptly kissed him hard on the lips.

Jeff turned a dull red. The others laughed. Pam just patted his shoulder again and sat down.

At least the silence was funereal, Jeff thought. He would have to do something. No one was saying anything. Everyone was waiting for a cue.

"Are you still acting?" Wife number three, whose name was Clara, asked the starlet. She had good reason to dislike Pam, who had taken her husband away from her in something under two months. Clara was a dark-haired, bone-thin, bone-chic woman, remarried. She had protuberant black eyes that gave her face a somehow mournful, pleading look. She could wear clothes better than a fashion model, and in bed, as she would say herself, she was absolutely fabulous. No hundred-dollar call girl could match her, nor would they want to, for their hearts weren't in it, and hers was. She loved sex, and yet, and yet . . . there was this fragility about her.

"I mean, I haven't heard much about you lately."

"I've been around," the starlet said in chirping voice. "I haven't had to work, you know." Everyone present knew her alimony almost to the penny. It was by far the largest of the checks that had gone out, month after month, from Dick Whitson's attorneys.

"I do hope you'll stay with the cinema," Clara said. "They can do anything with anyone these days. Those makeup men are fabulous." Fabulous was her word. She pronounced it with tender loving care, sensuously; the word hung like the smoke ring of a five-dollar Havana.

"I may try Broadway," Pam said. Her eyes misted. A vision of a long play script floated in her mind's eye; page after page of complex dialogue, endless speeches, all to be imbued with a pseudo life, reinforced by hundreds of movements, of feelings. She knew she had to feel, feel on a wide range; that was acting, that was the theater. With the vision came a sense of panic, a sense of exhaustion before the fact. She remembered with affection her last director, and how those one- and two-line shots, repeated over and over until they reached his standard of perfection, had somehow cohered. When she had finally seen the completed film, it had nothing to do with the rushes or her work. She was overwhelmed, sitting in the dark of the projection room, with the perfection of her figure, the beauty of her voice, the excellence of her acting. It seemed impossible to her that she could have been this good. And when the director casually asked her to sleep with him, she did so without the slightest hesitation.

She had felt that through some sort of osmosis, some miraculous transference, she would share in his conscious control of perfection; she would know why she was good, what the acting bag was all about.

All that happened was that she forgot her pessary one night, and some time later she underwent an expensive, illegal, hospital-white, chrome-gleaming abortion.

That ended her romance with the director, who was married, anyhow, and under the thumb of his wife.

Six months later, she had met and married Jeff's father.

Now, seeing Dick's coltish reincarnation in front of her, under such affecting circumstances, she had felt the flush of a strange, melancholy desire, and had kissed the son-that-was-the-father on the lips. Jeff misunderstood the gesture completely. It was sexual, but in truth it was a good-bye kiss, and hadn't been meant for Jeff at all.

"Such an odd room," said one of the wives. They were all different, these women, but for a mad moment Jeff saw them as one corporate mother.

"The flowers are lovely," said another. The voices murmured and receded in Jeff's consciousness. All he wanted now was to go into the bedroom and lie down. He could feel the cool crispness of the sheets against his body, the texture of the pillow against his cheek. He would fall asleep and bypass this black comedy.

There was the sound of a key in the lock, and his uncle came into the apartment. Uncle Jim nodded to the ladies, smiled briefly at Jeff, and excused himself. He reappeared three minutes later. He walked to the center of the room, cleared his throat, and said, "Let us begin. Thank you for coming. My brother would have been touched. We are all here members, so to speak, of one family. We have gathered together to pay our last respects to Richard Whitson. Jeff, did you wish to say something?"

Jeff looked at his uncle and opened one hand on his lap. The fingers lay curled, defenseless, young.

"Perhaps," said his uncle, "you would prefer me to?"

"I'd like to say something." It was Pam Brice. The other women looked at her curiously.

"By all means," James Whitson said.

And so it was that Richard Whitson's eulogy was spoken by the youngest and certainly the stupidest of his wives.

When the short statement — it had been banal, surprisingly unemotional, quite standard — was over, Pam Brice sat down. Silence. The candles, which Jeff had lit, swayed in a tiny breeze. The silence continued for some thirty seconds, not unlike a pause for prayer. Then Jeff rose and snuffed the candles.

Pam alone ate some of the little sandwiches. Everyone but Jeff had a glass of champagne, almost furtively. Jeff could not drink champagne. It always, for some reason he never discovered, made him ill. And then they put on their various coats and pressed Jeff's hand and left, spacing their leave-taking so as not to have to talk to each other in the elevator.

Pam took Jeff's hand at the last and smiled brilliantly at him.

"Thanks for the eulogy," Jeff said.

"I said what I wanted." Pam took his face between her hands and kissed his forehead. "That one's for you. Keep well and have a good life." The apartment door closed behind her.

Jeff was conscious of a great weight lifted. He poured himself a stiff bourbon and stood in the center of the room, tasting not the drink so much as his relief. His father was dead; he could believe it now. And he would no longer mourn him, any more than Dick would have mourned his son. The time for remembering was over. It was time to act, to take up his own life, to do — what?

His euphoria drained. His future was a frightening gray wasteland.

He'd have to get a job.

"You'll have to get a job," his uncle said eerily.

"I know. I don't quite know how to start, though."

Uncle Jim sat down on the divan. He put a plate of sandwiches on a small table next to him and gestured.

"Have some dinner." Jeff ate a sandwich in silence. He hadn't known he was hungry. They munched reflectively.

"I could set up an interview for you," Uncle Jim said at length. "You might like the work."

Jeff looked his question.

"For me. For us, I should say. I've followed your college career with interest. We need young men like you."

"We?"

His uncle ignored him. "From the moment I was able to help to get you into Harvard, I'd hoped that you might want to work for us. In my section. Though I don't usually recruit."

"You work for the army?"

"Central Intelligence Agency," his uncle said. "I've been with them quite a long time, in fact."

"Oh." The puzzle fell into place. Yet, somehow, it was all so odd.

"But why?" Jeff asked. "I mean, why me?"

Uncle Jim looked uncomfortable. "I suppose," he said slowly, "that I feel I owe it to you. I told you I didn't get along too well with Dick. You were one of the main reasons."

"Oh?"

"Yes. In my opinion, he did not do for you what should have been done. What, perhaps, I would have done for my own child, had I ever had one. We had a number of arguments about that." His uncle leaned back, not looking at him. "Not that I'm doing you any great favor. Just a job, that's all, if you get it. It doesn't entirely depend on me."

Jeff felt warmed. In his fashion, Uncle Jim was telling him he liked him and somehow had protected him throughout the years. He looked almost with affection at the bald head gleaming under the lights.

"Thanks, Uncle Jim. Tell me, what do you do? I mean, what's your title?"

"Never ask anyone in this line of work what he does," Uncle Jim said, finishing his sandwich. "He may not be allowed to tell you. However, I'm one of the assistants to the director."

94

"Are you a — " Jeff found it difficult to bring out the word. "Do you spy?"

"No."

"That's one thing I wouldn't want to be."

"Well," his uncle said, "I doubt if you could become covert." He looked at Jeff humorlessly. "Have you any idea what the CIA is? What its duties are? How it functions?"

"No. Well, that is, I have some idea."

"You don't. What you've got in mind is an undigested mass of television nonsense."

"That's possible. I never thought very much about it."

"Think about it now. Let me give you some guideposts. Consider us primarily a pedagogical institution," his uncle said slowly. "As I hope you will see, our atmosphere is much like the one you have left — at its best, of course. We could easily staff a large university with the people we have working for us.

"We are, in point of fact, very much in the communications business. I could list at least twenty-two intellectual disciplines from which we draw our personnel. If you can disabuse your mind of cant, if you can shed those misconceptions which have been drilled into you by TV, you may find our work intellectually rewarding, even fascinating."

The picture limned by Uncle Jim was an odd one. Jeff was left with the impression of a vast educational institution, conservative, intellectual, far removed from the hurly-burly of the political power structure. It seemed that the CIA was an ivory tower topping all ivory towers.

He went to bed with his mind whirling, excited yet vaguely uneasy.

Still, it was a job.

It took Jeff months to realize how powerful his uncle really was in the organization. He was rushed through preliminary interrogation, evaluation, and recommendation with a minimum of discomfort and a maximum of courtesy. He knew he had been thoroughly investigated, but as the atmosphere of his job took hold, his ideas of his own privacy, and what that privacy was worth, changed.

But one thing his uncle hadn't warned him about was how boring his apprenticeship would be.

He remembered now, lying in the lightening dark next to Debbie, the first time he had met her. He had been working for only a few weeks, adjusting to a life that revolved around duties he found immediately boring, for a salary he secretly resented. He worked semi-exposed behind a glass screen that hid a reasonably large bare room divided into several smaller "offices."

He was on companionable terms with the three young men who shared his working space. They all had the same General Service rating; they had all started at seventy-two hundred a year. But though they spoke together in the mornings and shared a table in one of the two huge cafeterias that serviced the more than ten thousand employees who worked in the Langley complex, they never really *talked* together. Not that it wasn't allowed, but the calm atmosphere bred reserve, even secrecy, as a deliberate by-product.

The food in the cafeteria was good, but the room's immensity had an oddly illogical effect on Jeff: the rows of tables, the thousands of diners, closed in on him. He found himself suffering from a mild claustrophobia complicated by loneliness.

The CIA did not ordinarily hire blood relatives. It had taken every bit of Uncle Jim's influence to swing employment for his nephew, and it had put him for some weeks in a dubious, though not shaky, position with his colleagues. He had been owed small favors by compeers throughout the agency. The debts were wiped clean now. He had used up a part of his moral bankroll, and this loss mildly saddened him, much as another man might be miffed by a favorite stock suddenly losing a few points.

However, Jeff had the sense to work silently, to make no waves. Early in his employment, during his first week, to be exact, his uncle had asked him to stop by his office.

"One thing I wanted to tell you," Uncle Jim said from behind an impressive steel desk. The office was large and well furnished. A photograph, and signed, in color, of the President, and another of the director, also signed, hung on the wall behind him. On the other wall was a large aerial photographic blowup of the agency building itself, nestled in its immense wooded cockpit. It de-emphasized the gigantic scope of the complex, but when you looked closely at the thousands of parked cars, serried rows of ants, the size of the organization hit you with full force.

"One thing," his uncle repeated. "In this agency, if you wish to succeed, you must *not* stand out. The more anonymous you are, the better for you. Do your work as well as you can, and for the rest, melt into the surroundings. Depersonalize yourself during working hours. Remember that this is one of those jobs which do not end at five o'clock. Your off-duty attitudes and habits are as important to us as your work here in the complex. Don't rock the boat."

Jeff had felt like saying that it was a pretty big boat and he was a fairly light weight, but he had only nodded and withdrawn.

His long experience in humility, dwarfed as he had been by Dick for most of his life, stood him in good stead. He wasn't new to this game. It was just that it became increasingly difficult for him to keep rounding out the perfection of his mediocrity. Nothing, he thought occasionally, was as difficult as non-success. It needed an attitude quite different from that of clear-cut failure or accomplishment; it was more subtly demanding than either.

Then, the next week, he met Deborah, and his life took on a different coloration.

She had sat down next to him, quite by chance, during

lunch hour. Jeff wasn't at all hungry. He didn't really look at her until she brushed his elbow reaching for the salt.

"Sorry," she said. He smiled at her and took a quick, automatic male's inventory. Her dark beauty glowed somberly in the tiled light of the huge refectory. She took his breath away.

"Is there something wrong?"

"Why, no," Jeff said, embarrassed.

"Well, thanks for staring, anyhow." Debbie appraised him then, frankly, and with as searching a look as his. It was as though she were asserting her independence. With that look, Jeff felt a foreknowledge of what she would be like sexually: as forthright, as demanding, as a man. He turned his thoughts off in confusion.

"You're welcome," he said.

"Where do you work?"

"Third floor."

Debbie leaned forward and examined his badge, "Well," she said, "Mr. Jeffrey Whitson, I'm Deborah Bernstein."

Within moments Jeff found himself talking more than he had in months. Then Debbie finished her sparse lunch — he was to discover that she was often on a diet — and rose.

They walked slowly back toward the left wing of the building. The gigantic structure that housed the CIA was framed now in summer foliage. The trees formed a thick umbrella of green leaves, an umbrella many miles wide. The two walked in silence until they reached the steps of the main entrance. Stopping there, Jeff said, "Could we have dinner tonight?"

"Yes," Debbie said. "I'd like that very much."

They signed in at the lobby checkpoint and Debbie turned right, while Jeff continued on toward the elevators.

It took him a week to find out that Debbie was secretary to Simon Lee, and that Simon, as senior assistant to the director, was his uncle's superior.

98

It took him two weeks to fall in love with her.

It took him a month before he slept with her.

. . . And it had taken him almost a year to get her to let him stay overnight, in the warmth and intimacy of a double bed.

The dawn was now definite. It was time for Jeff to leave. He swung himself onto the floor. Debbie slept on. Silently, he flapped on bare feet into the kitchen and plugged in the coffee pot. He showered and dressed hurriedly. He had shaved the night before — Debbie couldn't stand bristle against her skin — and he looked fairly presentable. He would shave again in his own room before taking off in his battered car for Langley.

He turned, ready to go, for one last look at Debbie. He would see her again, in — he glanced at his watch — three hours, when he reported to Simon for final instructions. They would be bright and impersonal with one another. Not that they had to be circumspect — everyone knew of their affair and impending marriage, certainly Simon Lee knew — but because they were young enough to enjoy their shared secret; to remember, as they exchanged impersonal smiles and office chitchat, that they had held each other *so,* and the memory of their night together would lie behind their shining eyes.

Debbie moved uneasily, and then her eyes opened. Her face creased in a sleepy grin and she opened her arms. He kissed her and felt the pressure of her teeth on his lips.

"Today's the day," Debbie whispered. "Excited?"

"Well," Jeff said, knowing he was excited, knowing that perhaps this was the break, perhaps this was the beginning of that impossible jump from overt to covert status, from white to black, "not really. It's just an errand, you know. Nothing but a messenger boy."

"I think it's thrilling," Debbie said. She turned her nose

into the pillow. "I'm sleepy," she complained comfortably. "It's all your fault."

"Not so thrilling," Jeff said. He added bitterly, "Nothing will happen. Nothing exciting ever happens to me." And he turned and walked out, hearing Debbie's hiccup of laughter behind him, the echo of his words ringing a trifle shamefully in his ears.

3 ⚬

THE face of the young stewardess loomed above him. Her neck was still creased with baby fat, her lips scarlet in the dusk of her Latin skin. Even through the screening of the air conditioning, Jeff imagined he could scent her youth and her cleanliness. Her uniform was crisp, and she wore a pert little black and white hat.

"Would you care for a drink, sir?" Her eyes flicked to his left wrist. It was manacled by a slim steel loop to the attaché case he carried. Jeff quickly pulled his coat sleeve down.

"Scotch and water," he said. They had put him on a commercial airliner, in tourist class. He was entitled to two — or was it three? — drinks.

"Coming up," the girl said with a warmth Jeff hoped was not part of regulation courtesy.

She walked away, and Jeff eyed her trim backside as it swayed up the thrumming aisle.

With his unoccupied right hand, he touched a sheaf of papers in his inside breast pocket.

Simon Lee had spent five minutes with him, sipping coffee while standing by the window that overlooked the trees and the mountains in the background.

He spoke with his back to Jeff, and it had been difficult to hear him. Jeff had his doubts that this rudeness was unconscious; Debbie had told him she thought it was her boss's way of making sure his instructions were listened to with concentration.

"You'll transfer at Buenos Aires," Simon said, "for Asuncion. There's a room reserved for you at the Hotel Asuncion. The hotel will send a car for you. When you arrive at the hotel room, call the number you'll find in your procedures list. Your contact will be in your room in short order. He'll identify himself — you'll find identification code written down for you too — and you'll turn over your attaché case to him. He'll open it and remove its contents. He has the key. He will put into it at the same time what he has to put into it and lock the case. You will return the next day and deliver the case to me. That's all.''

A sixteen-year-old girl could carry out this assignment without difficulty, Jeff thought as he sipped his drink. The plane vibrated beneath his feet. It was only half full. There was the usual sprinkling of businessmen, two family groups with unusually well-behaved children, a rather ugly young woman traveling alone, and Jeff Whitson, a glorified Western Union messenger, manacled to an attaché case that probably contained the diplomatic equivalent of a get-well card.

He had been handed, too, a packet of guaranis for pocket money. Strictly accountable, Debbie had told him. He was to mark down everything he spent, and submit an expense account upon his return. The room was to be paid for in cash. He was to carry his raincoat over his left arm, to hide the fact that his attaché case was manacled to his wrist.

He spent the three quarters of an hour between planes in the Buenos Aires airport bar. It was a magnificent bar, actually, with a bartender who spoke good Brooklynese and who served him his drink with flair.

''You absent-minded?'' he asked.

''Nope.''

''Whyn't you take off your briefcase and make yourself comfortable?'' the barman asked, and turned away without waiting for Jeff's reaction.

Jeff flushed. His raincoat had been artistically draped over his arm. Obviously the camouflage hadn't worked.

The plane from Buenos Aires to Asuncion was propeller-driven, dirty, and frighteningly ancient. They broke through the clouds as Jeff glanced at his watch. Three forty-five of a Friday afternoon. He had been in the air almost seven hours. His muscles were cramped. His excitement had long since evaporated, leaving a sediment of irritation and discomfort.

He walked out onto the strip, roughly halfway between Luque and Asuncion, into a balmy seventy-eight-degree day. The soil was red and sandy. There were trees everywhere. The airport was primitive. A battered black Buick limousine waited patiently.

There were no formalities. Swinging his suitcase in one hand, and his attaché case in the other, Jeff climbed into the old car. It stank of moldering leather. He was the only passenger.

No one offered to take his bag. He placed it between his knees and relaxed. His head was still ringing from the noise of the obsolete plane. The driver of the bus fought the ignition. The ancient engine caught and the lumbering auto swung onto a reasonably well-paved road.

Jeff watched the countryside slide by. It was sandy, loamy country, tropical, dotted with fields and orange groves. There were herds of beef cattle but few people. The land had a luminous, deserted quality. Asuncion proper, however, had all the busy-ness of a port town, located as it was at the confluence of two large rivers, though six hundred miles from the nearest sea.

The Hotel Asuncion turned out to be a modern concrete and glass structure, rearing some nine stories into the blue air from a complex modern base. The porter took Jeff's bag and he walked into a ferociously air-conditioned lobby.

His fifth-floor room was modest, without a balcony. There was modern plumbing and a small shower. The reception clerk spoke good English, and the service was fulsomely elaborate in the Spanish manner, with much courtesy and little real efficiency. He tipped the bellboy, opened his bag, and lay down on his bed, staring at the ceiling. The air conditioning was beginning to give him a headache. It was centrally controlled, unfortunately, and he was unable to turn it off. The small room was as quiet as a coffin. After a moment he thought, The hell with it, and phoned room service. He ordered a pint of rum, and something called *yerba-mate*. When it arrived, he sipped the local tea and swallowed two ounces of the rum.

Then he took out his instructions and picked up the phone.

His number buzzed twice, and a cautious voice said, "*Sí?*"

"Jeffrey Whitson," Jeff said, feeling foolish. Surely they could have worked out something a little less dull than just announcing his name.

The voice said, "You are here?"

"Obviously."

"I will be with you shortly. Stay in your room."

There was a click, and Jeff hung up. He took another swallow of rum, and stared up at the pastel-colored ceiling. He half closed his eyes. After a moment he reached into his bag, took out an aspirin bottle, swallowed one, took some more tea, and then lay back again.

"Some trip," he muttered to himself. "Big goddam deal." Perhaps I can count flies, he thought, but there were no flies. The sound insulation was admirable. Jeff could hear the slow beat of his heart, and he turned his head, seeking a cool spot on the pillow. Time passed, punctuated by the hum of the air conditioner and the almost unheard sounds of life from beyond his closed, locked door.

Someone knocked.

Jeff swung to his feet, unlatched the door, and opened it. "May I come in?"

Jeff made a small gesture with his hand and closed the door behind his visitor, a young man about his own age who smiled at him. His teeth were white in his smooth, dark face. He was some inches shorter than Jeff, and he was undoubtedly one of the handsomest men Jeff had ever seen. His handshake was brief and firm.

106

"I am Ricardo Cordoval," he said.

He reached into his pocket, withdrew identification and a small key, and handed both to Jeff. "Please take off the attaché case." He smiled again, charmingly. "I will do what I have been sent here to do."

Jeff unlocked the case from his wrist and put it on the bed. Ricardo's English was excellent, spoken with a slight, noneffeminate lisp; that small softening that accompanies the speech of the upper-class Spaniard no matter what language he speaks. He was dressed in a neat dark suit with a deep red tie. Though the suit was cut a trifle tight for Jeff's taste, it did give a strong hint of his contact's powerful musculature. This was a man, Jeff thought, who kept himself in shape, who worked out, probably, every morning.

"I have to wash up," Jeff said. "I'll be some five minutes."

In the bathroom, he sat down on the closed john and waited, feeling vaguely humiliated, while Ricardo did "what he had been sent here to do."

When he reentered the room, his briefcase still lay on his bed, in precisely the same position it had been before. Yet Jeff knew it had been opened and the contents removed, while whatever it was that Ricardo had brought with him had been deposited. There was one change in the chamber. The electric lights had been snapped on, and the venetian blinds securely drawn.

The room was more tomblike than ever.

"So," Ricardo said. "You will put the briefcase in the hotel safe, unless you want to carry the damn thing around for the rest of your stay here."

Jeff nodded. The assignment was over. Mission completed for 007 Jeffrey Whitson. It was difficult to keep in mind that the *exciting* part of his trip had come and gone. Now he could relax.

Ricardo sat down on the bed and offered Jeff a cigarette in a flat black case. Jeff shook his head, and Ricardo lit the cigarette with a gold lighter. The action was stylized, formal, somehow un-American. Jeff began to realize for the first time that he was truly in Asuncion, Paraguay, thousands of miles from home. The thought cheered him mildly. His headache began to leave him.

"This is your first visit to my country?"

"Yes."

"It's dull, being an operative." Ricardo smiled. "Not like the movies."

"No." Was Ricardo laughing at him?

"I see you have already indulged in two of Paraguay's main products," Ricardo said. He pointed to the rum and the pot of *yerba-mate*. "All you need now is a large steak and you will be the complete consumer."

"Not a bad idea," Jeff said. He realized he was hungry, and then he realized he was being rude. He offered Ricardo a drink and poured the rum into two shot glasses.

"*Salud,*" Ricardo said. He tossed the drink down with a flick of his wrist, and Jeff thought, He needed that. Cordoval seemed at ease outwardly, but he was unable to hide his interior tension. His movements were a trifle tight. He was too conscious of his body; he sat with too much muscular control, and his eyes kept roving the small room.

He's frightened, Jeff realized, then let the thought pass. It was none of his business.

"Where can I get something to eat around here?"

"Well, there's the dining room downstairs. For extraordinary prices, you'll get a bad imitation of American food."

"My instructions were to stay in my hotel room, but I don't think I can stay here for twenty-four hours," Jeff said. "I'm booked to go back tomorrow evening, and I'm bored already. Perhaps you could show me something of your city?"

There was a pause. The rule was unwritten but there. Agents did not fraternize. Ricardo rose. "Rules were meant to be bent," he said, "but I am not good company these days for a walk around Asuncion." He spoke with sudden warmth. "Still there's no reason why we shouldn't have dinner together in the hotel."

Jeff rose and took the briefcase. "I'll get rid of this."

"Ordinarily," Ricardo said, "I wouldn't suggest the hotel safe. But there's nothing too important in there anyhow."

You have to rub it in, Jeff thought ruefully. He preceded Ricardo out of the hotel room and locked the door carefully behind him, hanging out the DO NOT DISTURB sign.

They began the evening in the hotel bar. They had two dry manhattans each, and the silence between them suddenly became noticeable. It was difficult to find suitable subjects for conversation. It was, Jeff thought, much like a first date with a girl. Yet even in the long silences Jeff found Ricardo more and more agreeable to be with. His face was mobile, his hands overfluent, but he seemed genuinely friendly and so willing to share his vitality that Jeff found himself relaxing for the first time since the beginning of his trip.

"The only trouble," Ricardo broke another long silence, "is that we're afraid to talk about who we are and what we do."

"It's silly, isn't it," Jeff said.

"So. Let's call a truce. Under the rose."

It was an odd expression, one that Jeff hadn't heard in many years. It smacked of things bookish.

"Where did you go to college?" he asked.

"Yale." Ricardo said.

"What's Asuncion really like? The country? The people?"

"Not all at once," Ricardo said. "Which do you want to know about first?"

"Well. The people. They're all that count anyhow."

"We're a proud country, but we're small — and poor.

We've been fighting wars ever since we can remember. We're hot-blooded, and when we're not at war with our neighbors, we're at war with ourselves. Revolutions, counter-terrevolutions, *coups d'état*. The whole shmear. It never stops.''

Jeff burst out laughing.

''What's funny?''

''Shmear. I had to travel thousands of miles to hear that expression. With a Spanish accent, yet.''

''I never thought I had an accent.''

''You do, though. Tell me about yourself.''

It was odd, Jeff thought. His involvement with Ricardo had grown almost independently of time and space. They had been together now barely an hour, and he felt as though he had known him all his life. The feeling of kinship, of recognition, was strong, so strong that he could not believe Ricardo did not feel it too.

''From my youth?'' Ricardo asked.

''If you care to.'' They were talking like Hemingway characters, reading between the lines, saying little and meaning much. The comradeship between them strengthened, and they spoke cautiously around it, testing it. Their speech was almost stilted.

''My family is rich,'' Ricardo said. ''I have no sisters, no brothers. In this country, you are either rich or poor. My father raises beef cattle. He has a thousand acres out in the Chacos. We have always had money, and always we have felt toward our country a strong sense of responsibility. Paraguay needs scientists, doctors, informed and educated men and women. We have too little of everything, too few schools, too few colleges. I was a bright boy. Even my father — I don't get along too well with him now — saw that. I was always asking questions. So he hired an American tutor for me and took me out of the local school.

''We lived in a big house modeled after a Spanish country house. A hacienda. There were always animals and servants and peasants and lots of noise. There was always meat roasting in the courtyard. I can smell the beef now — we take whole cows and let them cook slowly, in pits; once you're used to it, it is the only way to eat beef. It was a succulent atmosphere — very nutritious, like our peasant soup. I don't know how you remember your boyhood, but I remember mine through smells, and through noise.

"I was lonely. I almost never left the house. My father was constantly away, overseeing the land, for in a sense, he ran what was a small country within a country. We had — we still have, though I am now disassociated — six hundred people working for us. I was the young master, and the young prisoner.

"My tutor was only twenty-six. After four years he got involved with the daughter of one of my father's friends. He had to leave the country to save his life — " Ricardo broke off, seeing the lack of comprehension on Jeff's face. "Our women," he said gently, "are like our rich and our poor. They are either very good or very bad. The good ones are guarded like gold bullion. The bad ones are whores. I must admit, I prefer the bad ones. They haven't had their good sense knocked out of them.

"Anyhow, after Peter left, I had nothing to do for a long while. I tried to take an interest in Father's business — I was seventeen years old — but I found his 'country' was a dictatorship, and he the dictator.

"Then I went to North America and spent four years at Yale."

"But you came back."

"Of course. I had to. I was an investment." Ricardo looked sharply at Jeff. "The only real wealth any country has," he said slowly, "lies in its people. This holds true of any government: communist, fascist, democratic, socialistic. I was needed here."

He paid for the drinks. "I doubt if you have much of an expense account. I know how our friends work, out in

Langley." It was the second direct reference to the fact that Ricardo knew who Jeff was and what he did.

"Yes," Ricardo said, gathering in guaranis and leaving a large tip, "I was briefed on you. Thoroughly. A half page, single spaced."

"Don't rub it in," Jeff said, aloud this time. "You're always rubbing it in."

"I'm sorry. I am not important either." Which, if it was an apology, was certainly an odd one. Ricardo rose. "Shall we go into the dining room?" Before Jeff could answer he continued hurriedly, "Excuse me for a moment. I will return immediately."

Alone, Jeff realized that he did not want to eat in the hotel. Outside was a strange world, full of new sounds, new people. He would probably never be here again. He decided, The hell with it. He wanted to see Asuncion. And, as his friend had said, rules were made to be bent.

Ricardo returned and sat down opposite him. "I had to make a phone call," he said. "To break a date."

"Look," Jeff said, "couldn't we eat somewhere else? I'd like to see the town. I'd like you to show it to me."

Ricardo was silent for a long moment. "I cannot tell you any more," he said finally, "than that it is dangerous to do this."

"I like to live dangerously," said Jeff lightly. He thought, If he wants to talk like a spy movie, I know *my* lines.

"This is no joke," Ricardo said. "We are in sympathy. I would like to show you my city. But it would be a mistake."

Jeff stood. "Come on," he said. "I'm over twenty-one. I'll take the risk."

Ricardo shrugged. "As you say."

The night was temperate. The Hotel Asuncion rose behind them, a lighted finger pointing to the stars. It was seven-fifteen.

They turned right, onto a broad avenue, the Avenue of Our Lady of Asuncion.

112

"There is a good restaurant on one of our oldest streets," Ricardo said. He slipped his arm through Jeff's, and the gesture was inoffensive, casual. They strolled along arm in arm. Ricardo pointed out tourist attractions as they walked, and Jeff sensed his genuine pride in his city, in his country. They turned left, passed the Panteon and crossed the square dominated by Directorate General de Turismo. The building gleamed white and modern under the glare of spotlights. The streets were all straight and, except for the broad avenues, ill lit. Asuncion was a modern city, raw and new, somehow pathetic. They followed a small narrow avenue with the improbable name of Avenue de Juan E. O'Leari.

Eventually they came to the Street of Palms, lit with neon signs, a center of nightclubs, and small colonial houses that were either stores or brothels. Jeff couldn't tell which. The superimposition of a Times Square atmosphere upon the dignified colonial architecture of the original city only emphasized the vulgarity of the one and the quiet shabbiness of the other.

Here there was more action. The Street of Palms was crowded. Farmers from the country drove the wooden-wheeled carts which were the local mode of transportation. The spokes, some of them varnished, were fashioned by a craftsman's hand, and they picked up the light of the street-lamps and the electric signs, and tossed it back, fragmented and flashing, into the shadows of the streets. Businessmen passed by in North American suits of respectable gray or black. There were a few tourists, looking as tourists always do, Jeff noticed, and bands of young men, walking much as he and Ricardo were walking, arm in arm, talking and laughing, some singing. There were few girls. Those who passed Jeff were attractive for the most part, their dark faces alive with youth and laughter, conscious of and unembarrassed by the stares and comments of the men they passed. These, Jeff supposed, were the ones not guarded like jewels in their colonnaded houses.

The poor — and they were in the majority — bore their poverty as peacefully and as proudly as the well-to-do displayed their wealth. The theme was life, a running undercurrent of *joie de vivre* which was quite different, in intensity and direction, from that to be found in North American cities. There was dirt here too, and suffering, but none of it was dehumanized; all of it was compact of the life of the people and a measure of their heritage. Asuncion, unlike New York or Chicago, was warm and giving. Jeff decided he liked the Paraguayans.

The noise and confusion and laughter were permeated by a language which was not Spanish but Guarani, the immemorially old Paraguayan patois, the language of the people, sibilant as Spanish but more vigorous. Spanish, Ricardo had told Jeff, was the language of the upper classes. Almost everyone spoke it resentfully; almost everyone spoke Guarani happily and without reticence.

"It is a good language to make love in," Ricardo said, "and a good language to swear in. Which makes it a good language all around."

Ricardo was voluble. His words came in a spate, yet he had told Jeff nothing about his work, about who and what he was — or of what he was afraid. For frightened he obviously was. Even as he spoke and laughed and grimaced and flung his hands about, his eyes took no part in his ingenuous monologue. They were hooded, watchful. He was obviously intent on recognizing something or someone and on making sure Jeff did not notice his preoccupation. But Jeff did notice. He felt the muscles of Ricardo's arm contract in his, felt the rigidity of his friend's body, and he thought he smelled the acrid scent of fear. His friend's temples glistened with tiny drops of sweat. Yet it was cool and pleasant in the streets.

"We go in here," Ricardo said abruptly. He swerved on his heel, forgetting his hooked arm, almost dragging Jeff off balance.

The sign above the restaurant said simply CABALLITO NEGRO. Jeff thought, *Negro* was black, but was *caballito* a horse or a man? Or was that *caballero?*

The inside was semi-lit, noisy (what wasn't, in Asuncion?), the air full of good smells. It had been a long time since the lunch in the plane. They sat down in a relatively quiet corner, as far from the small band as they could get.

They ordered the local beer and gulped the first one down in silence. Jeff found himself a trifle dizzy and warm, blurry. He decided to take the *caballo* by the horns (maybe it was a bull at that).

"What," Jeff said, breaking a long silence, "are you looking for?"

"What?" Ricardo's voice was preoccupied.

"I said, what are you looking for? And why are you afraid of finding it?"

Ricardo stared at him for a long, uncertain moment.

"You have sharp eyes," he said finally.

"Well?"

"Let us order." They ordered rum and barbecued beef and Paraguayan *sopa*, which was no soup at all but a flat corn bread that came in long rectangles and which Jeff found terrible by itself but delicious when eaten with the beef.

By now they were both a trifle high, and Ricardo's nervousness seemed to have abated. He was listening to the band, which was playing a guaranias. The music was quite tender and lovely, and the instruments were a type of harp, made of highly polished wood, and a guitar which, Jeff knew, was being played by a master. There were strange, harsh, hard discords, as though the lilting melody was occasionally too much for the musicians to bear.

"They take off," Ricardo said. He had been listening, his eyes half closed, his profile almost Indian in the half-light. His facial balance would have been perfect had it not been for his nose, a hawk's nose, long and thin like the blade of a knife, with pinched nostrils; it broke up the symmetry of his cheekbones and allowed his good looks to become real, virile, instead of a model's mediocrity. "The melody is basically the same, but they introduce their own variations. This man is good."

Jeff took another gulp of rum, and at that moment the tenor of the night changed and began to move into nightmare.

A squat blond man materialized out of the shadows of the restaurant. He stopped at their table and glanced intently at Ricardo. Nothing was said. The man was obviously European and shortsighted. Having made sure he recognized Ricardo, he made a sudden odd gesture with his hands, smiled humorlessly, and passed on.

Ricardo looked intently after the man and then shrugged. His voice was weary.

"I've blown it," he said. "There was no way out. I've been stringing my luck along anyhow; it was bound to snap."

"I don't understand."

"I suggest you leave."

"Now?"

"The sooner, the better. Just forget I ever existed, will you? I was wrong, incidentally. Rules aren't made to be bent. They're made to be obeyed. I hope I haven't put your life in danger."

"Come off it," Jeff said. "What are you talking about?"

"Please go."

"No." Jeff meant it.

Ricardo turned to look for a long, uncertain moment at his companion. "After all," he said half to himself, "you *are* CIA."

"Yes."

"And I'm National Police."

"I figured something like that," Jeff said.

"You should go, you know. I don't believe you can help."

Jeff said nothing. Obviously, Ricardo meant what he said. On the other hand, if he'd been scared before, he was terrified now. Jeff summoned the waiter, and asked for two coffees. "It's settled," he said. He thought to himself, Never have I liked a man better, and I will not leave him now. He hoped with all his heart that he wasn't deluding himself, that he was not indulging in mock heroics. But even if he was, it wasn't important. He was not about to leave Ricardo alone with his fear.

"You let me know when we go," Jeff said. "Let me know what to do."

"There's nothing *to* do," Ricardo said quietly.

"Shall we leave?"

"Not yet." He took a sip of his coffee. "I don't want Schmidt to feel we've panicked. Besides, there's nothing to gain by leaving now. He's waiting outside. I know him. Give him time."

"He's German?"

"Y-yes." Ricardo was beginning to stutter slightly. The combination of alcohol and fear had made him twice as drunk, twice as fast.

"Would you like to tell me about it?"

"You should know a little." Ricardo took another sip of coffee and lit a cigarette. "As I said, I'm with the National Police. That's the nearest thing we've got to your internal security organization. We're much nearer FBI than we are CIA. Like everything else, there are too few of us for the job to be done. I work alone."

The band had begun a lively polka. Couples were stamping and shouting on the dime-size dance floor. The brisk tune was eerie enough, sustained as it was by the plangent notes of the harp and the musical trochaics of the guitar.

"You're covert?" Jeff asked. He was using the only slang he knew, trying hard to be competent and technical.

"You mean, am I an operative? Yes. At least, for my present assignment. Only — " Ricardo stopped and stared

117

down at his smoldering cigarette, "my cover's just blown."

"How long has this been going on?"

"I've been undercover for three months. I infiltrated an illegal organization. There are many of these in South America. Of all kinds. This is a special one. It has kept its secrets longer and more successfully than any of the others. It is well financed, which makes it of interest to our government, and, of course, highly dangerous. It is well organized. And it has a secret — a secret within a secret, so to speak." Ricardo paused. Then, in a rush, as though he had held in his knowledge for too long, his words stumbling over each other, he said, "Two weeks ago, I discovered something so fantastic that I could not risk telling my superiors about it until I had proof. I arranged to get that proof. Now they know who I am, who I work for."

"I see." Jeff thought, He's managed to tell me everything and nothing at the same time. "In how much real danger are you?"

Ricardo took a gulp of coffee. "I would say the prognosis is unfavorable." He looked at Jeff directly. "There's something in our favor. Their need for secrecy is greater than mine. They probably don't know you or what you are. They may think twice about killing me while you are with me."

"That's good," Jeff said ironically.

"On the other hand, they may decide it's worth it to them. To run the risk, I mean. And then — " Ricardo spread his hands in a gesture of finality.

"Well," Jeff said, "this joint has a phone, doesn't it? Call your people and let them know what's happened. They'll pick you up."

Ricardo looked at him quizzically. "That's impossible," he said. "I'm on my own on this assignment. I am under the strictest orders not to contact my office. Under *any* circumstances."

"Your control?" Jeff was talking out of his memory of spy literature read and half remembered. He was interested to find that such writers as Deighton and le Carré had indeed known what they were writing about. Ricardo understood him perfectly. Jeff thought, Tonight I am a spy.

"I have none. I cannot call anyone."

"I phoned you this afternoon."

"That was different. Insofar as this situation is concerned, I am an unperson. Believe me, Jeff, it would do no good to call."

"Well —" The coffee tasted strongly of chicory.

Jeff couldn't put his outrage into words. He had never before imagined what it would be like to be without human help, to be cut off, separated from the complex web of law and order that bound him and all of his fellow citizens together. Now he looked into the tight face of his new friend. He noticed that Ricardo's lips were white, and two lines had been drawn from the corners of his mouth halfway down to his chinline. He looked older.

"I think I'd better walk you home," Jeff said. The door of the café burst open, and six young men entered. Three of them held guitars. They stood in the doorway and began to sing a guaranias. They sang well, though only for a short time. The tables applauded and some paper money was tossed to the leader, who bowed low, smiled, waved his guitar in friendly fashion, and left. His band of singers trailed behind him shouting to each other at the top of their voices.

Ricardo called for the check, and they paid. The cost of the entire dinner was less than the price of the two manhattans they had drunk earlier in the evening at the Hotel Asuncion.

"We go," Ricardo said. He hooked his arm through Jeff's as he had earlier, and they walked out into the fragrant evening, smelling of oranges. There were still many people on the street; more, actually, than before.

"Two blocks away," Ricardo said, "there's a nightclub. The Monastery. There are always taxis there. Once we get a cab, we're all right."

119

"Won't they be waiting for you at your home?"

Ricardo shrugged philosophically. "Perhaps," he said. "If they want me, really want me, there's nothing I can do about it."

They were walking at a moderate pace. Jeff's own arm was caught in the vise of Ricardo's and was rapidly turning numb. Jeff tried to walk faster, but Ricardo slowed him down, applying a pressure he did not realize was brutal.

"We must not hurry," Ricardo whispered. "We must *not.*" They ambled. This nightmare, Jeff thought, is stretching itself out like a huge rubber band. No end to it. Ricardo's fear was so palpable it was catching. In spite of the temperate air, rivulets of cold sweat kept running into Jeff's eyes, half blinding him. He swiped at his face with his free hand as they walked. They crossed an intersection. "One more block," Ricardo murmured. He pointed. Three hundred yards away, an electric sign blinked. "Do you see the cabs?"

Jeff peered, blinking away sweat. There were two antiquated cabs, one with its hood open. Even at this distance, Jeff could see the cabbie bent over, probing his motor. Most of the private cars here were fifteen or twenty years old. The sight didn't attract one single onlooker — it was too common. The other cabbie sat in his vehicle, ready to roll.

Jeff lifted his right arm and waved at the cab. They walked slowly on, their leisurely gait in odd contrast to Jeff's insistently waving right arm. Passersby looked curiously at the norteamericano and dismissed him. The cabbie, still two hundred yards away, looked up from his newspaper, waved back cheerfully out of his window, and settled himself further in his seat, burying himself again in the latest news. If a man wanted to wave to him, he was not one to be proud. He would wave back.

Behind Jeff and Ricardo, there was a burst of song. They were now only some seventy-five yards from their goal.

We're actually going to make it, Jeff thought. His heart began to pound less heavily. Ricardo relaxed his iron grip about Jeff's left arm. Jeff could feel the tingle of returning circulation.

They were drowned in music. The same band that had interrupted their meal back at the restaurant was walking behind them. The guitarists were playing; the young men were singing. It was still a guaranias, or something like it, triumphant and tender, tuneful and infectious. They caught up with Ricardo and Jeff, and then, spontaneously, one of the band hooked his arm through Jeff's, smiling at him, blowing a breath sweet with wine close to his left ear. Another singer moved up beside Ricardo, and they were incorporated willy-nilly into the strolling group of singers. Their pace became even slower. The head guitarist led the party; his right index finger, banded with gold, flashed under the occasional brilliance of the streetlights.

They were all singing loudly. Ricardo pressed Jeff's arm. "Good," he said through the noise. "They will convoy us to the taxi." He threw back his head, and he too began to sing. Jeff hummed self-consciously under his breath.

They were at the cab stand. The first cabbie still labored on the engine of his ancient Chevrolet. The second still sat, absorbed, his newspaper spread open in front of him.

The singing was even louder. Jeff made a tentative movement to disengage himself. His arm was caught fast, and he found himself dragged along; he cried out, but now they were no longer ambling, the young men were walking at a half trot; he could hear Ricardo's labored breathing behind and to his left. He was being half-carried, and then they turned with military precision into a small dark, empty street. He caught a glimpse of a long black snout, a car purring loudly like a playful tiger, and the back door swung open, and he and Ricardo were stuffed into it. The men on each side of him drew down canvas blinds, the car snarled forward, and they were sitting there, out of breath, unharmed, bewildered, and angry. The inside of the car was black as death, and smelled of wet leather.

The whole maneuver had taken perhaps twenty seconds.

"What the hell," Jeff said. "What the fucking hell."

"Please. You must not talk." Jeff could not see the speaker's face. The canvas blinds were light-proof, and it was dark anyhow. The car vibrated faintly. He noted idiotically that the leather seat was real leather, English leather. He could smell it. An expensive automobile.

Every part of his body was vibrating. An enormous dose of adrenalin coursed through his system. He tasted iodine at the back of his mouth, and his saliva was copper-flavored. He had never felt more alive, and he had never been so frightened.

"But —"

"Truly, it would be bad for you to talk," said the smooth voice to his left. The English was unaccented, faintly foreign.

He heard Ricardo's slow breathing. Then he heard him whisper, "How much are they paying you?"

There was the sharp sound of a powerful slap. "You," the smooth voice said. "Shut up."

"How much?" Ricardo whispered again, his tone thick now with a blood more dreadfully imagined than seen.

"Let him talk," a voice on Jeff's right said hoarsely. "It is a long ride. I would like to be entertained."

"Five thousand?" This thick whisper was eerie in this black, small space, this dark world of violence and terror smelling of expensive upholstery, rushing silently through Asuncion with the windows shuttered, eyes closed upon its secret. "I will double it."

"There are six of us," the hoarse voice said patiently. "You are not only a traitor, but your ideas are unrealistic."

"Five thousand apiece," Ricardo said. His voice was

122

stronger. He moved, and Jeff, his eyes now more accustomed to the dark, guessed at the vague motion: Ricardo was wiping at his bleeding face.

"How do we know you would pay?"

"I am listening," said the smooth voice on Jeff's left. A mass of inky shadows moved uneasily in the tiny night. This was the third man, the one who had slapped Ricardo. He sat in front of them on a jump seat, and Jeff could smell him. It was a strange smell, medicinal, sweet, and unpleasant. Jeff decided he took drugs.

He was death in the shadows, violence waiting, terror personified.

"Listen if you want," the hoarse voice said. "I am entertaining myself."

"You know we would pay. Ten thousand apiece. That's sixty thousand. Dollars. Not guaranis. American dollars. In a bank of your own choosing, a Swiss bank under whatever name you wish. No one would know. You know I would not lie."

"Phooey," the smooth voice said. The expletive was fully pronounced, and Jeff thought it the strangest, deadliest sound he had ever heard. "Phooey. I cannot take your word. You fooled everyone for a time."

There was another sound of a blow, but different this time, meatier. The shadow in front of him had moved with convulsive speed. Ricardo's body jerked, he muttered something under his breath, and then he relaxed.

Jeff said, "You've killed him."

"No," the smooth voice said. "We did not kill him. Our orders are to keep him alive. But we have no such orders for you. You come from nowhere. Who are you?"

Jeff said carefully, "An American. How come all of you speak English?"

There was a chuckle in the dark. "We learned it almost twenty-five years ago. We had to. We have not forgotten it."

"Are we almost there?" the hoarse voice asked. Ricardo had begun to snore. He was unconscious, his body flaccid. There was the sharp stench of feces in the air.

"Ask the driver," the smooth voice said. The shadow in front of Jeff moved in the dark. He seemed to raise his hand to his mouth, the same hand that had just smashed Ricardo. He spoke in rapid Guarani, almost whispering. He was using a microphone, or an interphone system of some kind. The driver's partition was solid, wood or steel. The sibilance ceased.

"Any moment," the smooth voice said. As he spoke, the car slowed, veered, continued cautiously for some five seconds, and stopped.

"You pick bad friends," the hoarse voice said. "Get out."

Jeff made a preparatory movement.

"Slowly." There was a shuffle in the car. "Move slowly. First, I get out. Then you. Then we will lead you."

"What about my friend?"

"We will carry him. Lean forward."

Jeff leaned forward. He felt the sweet medicinal breath in his nose, and a bandage pressed against his eyes, too tightly. "Now," said the voice, "out. Move slowly. There is a running board."

He stood outside, gratefully sniffing the fresh air. There was the murmur of insects, the scent of flowers. This is the country, Jeff thought to himself, standing helplessly, his arms at his sides. We're somewhere in the country.

"The dog has shit all over himself," a voice said conversationally from behind him.

"You hit him too hard."

"You think he would have paid what he said?" There was grunting as the men shouldered a burden.

"No. Do not think of it. It would be disloyal."

"For ten thousand dollars apiece?"

"We would never live to spend it."

Jeff felt a hand on his shoulder. "Move forward."

Though he was not urged to walk fast, Jeff moved with the wind of unseen objects in his face. Sharp corners, furniture, anything might tear into him at any time, and he was defenseless.

A door closed behind him. He felt warm air. Hands fumbled at the back of his head, and then the light hit him. He closed his eyes for a moment and then looked around him.

Purple and gilt. He stood in the vestibule of a private house. The carpeting was scuffed and worn, red velvet. A gilt chandelier, its hundreds of dirty crystals winking a muddied light, hung overhead. Along the sides of the vestibule, reaching toward a twisting staircase, the risers of which were upholstered in the same velvet, there ran balusters of mahogany with broken ancient carvings. There were eight formal chairs, four on each side, unregenerated antiques, fragile and still beautiful.

"Upstairs," the smooth voice said behind him. "Do not turn around."

Jeff's head rang. He walked emptily and slowly up the stairs, hanging onto the slightly greasy wood of the balustrade, hearing the heavy breathing of men behind him carrying Ricardo's body. Or was it his corpse by now? The dark shadow had used something else for that second blow besides his bare knuckles.

"To your right," the smooth voice said, panting slightly now from his share of the burden. "Would you mind hurrying? We are tired."

Oh, Jeff thought, coming to a halt in front of a wooden door, what a pity. The weight of my friend's body is tiring. All you had to do, you bastard, he screamed silently, was not hit him so hard.

"Open it and walk in. It is not locked. Go to the other end of the room and stand there. Do not turn around. We will kill you if you do."

Jeff walked into a large bare room. It was ablaze with light, the walls a shiny white. It was almost empty of furniture. There was a small desk and a chair behind it. Another chair was catty-cornered to his right. No carpet. The room was clean, and not as shabby as what he had seen of the rest of the house.

Steadily he walked to the far wall and stood, his hands behind his back, staring at the thick shiny enamel, which seemed clinical and repulsive.

"When you hear the door shut," the smooth voice said behind him, "you may turn around. You will soon have a visitor."

There was the sound of receding footsteps. The door closed softly. He turned around.

Ricardo nodded in a chair. His eyes were closed. A thick trickle of blood had already coagulated on his left cheek. His hands had been arranged on his lap, his feet were turned out, his head drooped upon his breast. He still snored, but less now. Jeff half ran to him, then stopped short. There was nothing he could do: no warm water, no bandages, no bed.

He said in a loud, foolish voice, "Get us a doctor. Right away. We need a doctor."

As if in response to his command, the door opened and closed. A tall fair man stood there, looking at them both. His hair was cropped short. He wore an expensively tailored gray suit of English cut. His hair was silvery white, his face seamed and lined, and his eyes were a flat, light blue. The body under the tight suit was that of an athlete gone to seed. He carried his weight in a large, muscular belly, and Jeff knew that to hit him would be to hit a stone wall. His face was fair, almost pink, and his heavy jowls overlapped a tight collar. He wore a decoration on his left lapel, a large gold and diamond insignia that glittered in the overbright electric light.

"He does not need a doctor," the man said softly. He

126

spoke with a German accent, but his English was clear-cut and understandable. The overtones of his voice were harsh.

The man crossed the room and sat down at the desk. "If you wish to dump your friend to the floor," he said indifferently, "you may sit down. As you see, we have only two chairs here." Jeff made no move, uttered no sound. "I am named Franzl. Josef Franzl." Jeff did not twitch a muscle of his face. "And your name?"

"Jeffrey Smith," Jeff said reluctantly.

"So." Franzl leaned forward and straightened a pad of paper on his desk, frowning. "I have not seen you before."

"Nor I you."

"You are a stranger to Paraguay. Where are you staying?"

"Hotel Asuncion."

"Pleasant though expensive. You have a strange choice of friends." Franzl nodded toward the lolling body of Ricardo. "I regret that you have been involved in this vulgar adventure. You must be thirsty."

Jeff was immediately aware of a burning thirst; he swallowed convulsively. The door opened, and a small man entered. Like Franzl, he was over sixty, sharp and quick of movement. His small neat face was unremarkable, and his eyes darted restlessly to various parts of the room. He did not look at Franzl or at Jeff. He bore a covered tray in his right hand, which he carried like a waiter. He approached Ricardo, lifted the napkin from the tray, revealed a hypodermic and a carafe of water with two glasses. Deftly, he rolled up Ricardo's left sleeve and injected him. Then he put down the carafe and the two glasses on Franzl's desk, and withdrew.

Franzl filled one of the glasses and offered it to Jeff. It might be drugged, Jeff thought to himself, and as if guessing his mind, Franzl poured himself a half glass from the pitcher and swallowed it impassively. Jeff took his water in small gulps, and felt life return to his parched throat.

"Was he a doctor?" he asked. "What did he do to Ricardo?"

"He is no longer a doctor," Franzl said. "Did he seem bewildered to you?"

"Yes. Why?"

Franzl laughed for a moment, a short sharp hiccup. "He is not used to *reviving* men with his hypodermic." Ricardo stirred and moaned. "Your friend will be awake in a minute. I must ask you to stand again in the corner. Please do not turn around."

Ricardo's eyes flickered open. He said hoarsely, "I feel sick."

Franzl approached with the glass of water and held a fatherly hand under Ricardo's head as he sipped it. "Better?" he asked.

"Yes."

"Now," Franzl turned. "I have asked you to go to the wall," he said patiently to Jeff. "I do not wish to kill you. You must realize that by now. But we must have discipline here."

Jeff stood with his forehead pressed against the cool white enamel, the skin crawling on his back. He stood thus for some five minutes, while there was a rapid conversation in the local patois. Jeff heard his name mentioned several times.

"You may turn around now," Franzl said finally. His voice was cold and edged. "Your friend here assures us that you are unfortunately and innocently involved in this miserable business. We are inclined to believe him, even though he has systematically lied to us for months. We know you met only last night. We hope he has not talked."

"No," Jeff said.

"You are here on business contracts." So that was what Ricardo had told them, Jeff thought. "We would not wish to interfere with American business." Franzl's decoration glittered in the light. Jeff recognized it now. It was an Iron

Cross First Class — made, however, of gold and studded with diamonds. An ugly and pretentious piece of jewelry.

"I have to leave you gentlemen," Franzl said. "I will be gone for only a few minutes. You will notice the embrasures in the wall. There are several machine pistols trained on you."

When he was out of the room, Ricardo whispered, "Be careful."

"What now?"

Ricardo put his head in his hands. Then he looked up. "Did they put you through any training course?"

"No," Jeff said.

"Then you do not know how to kill a man without weapons?"

"No. I couldn't anyhow, I don't think."

Ricardo's face crumpled inward. He looked like an old man for a moment. "I had hoped that you might dispatch me," he said steadily. "I would prefer such a death." He sighed deeply. "I have no luck." He looked at Jeff. "Why they send a clerk on a man's job, I'll never understand." His voice showed intense irritation.

"You yourself said the job wasn't important."

"I know. They will kill me now."

Jeff was silent.

"Look up my father or write him a letter, if you can. Señor Juan Cordoval. Esperita Ranch, Asuncion. Can you remember?"

"Yes."

"There is a girl. Her name is Consuelo. I was to marry her. She will call you. I phoned her from the hotel before we left. I told her that if I did not call her by midnight, something had happened to me. Ask her to forgive me. And help her if you can."

"Yes. But you're not going to die."

"I only know what I would do in their place. I will tell you nothing about them," he said quickly as Jeff opened his

129

mouth to speak. "But in their place, I would kill me. There is much bitterness and anger." He added softly, "It may not be a pleasant death."

The door opened, and Franzl walked in, followed by two husky men who looked neither right nor left and did not speak. Jeff was certain that he was seeing Smooth voice and Hoarse voice.

"I telephoned," Franzl said to Ricardo. "Martin wants you dead. There is no other way." His voice was no longer clear, but husky and somehow warm. His mouth twitched slightly as he spoke, and Jeff could see his left hand clench and unclench. There was the merest whisper of a voice and exhalation of breath as Ricardo sighed. At that moment, Jeff jumped Franzl. The reason, he decided later, that he got as far as he did was that he himself had not planned anything like this. Had he, he would never have attempted it. But his body had taken over, and the next thing he knew he was on Franzl's back, clinging like a monkey, and his hands were on Franzl's throat and he was squeezing with every ounce of energy he possessed, feeling the iron-hard neck muscles under his fingers, knowing already that this man was far stronger than he, that he could not do him any damage in the time he had at his disposal.

The attempt may have been heroic, but the upshot was not. Franzl stepped back, his face purpling, and shook his shoulders. Jeff hung on. Then two steel hands circled Jeff's neck, and pulled. If he had not let go, his neck would certainly have snapped. He fell to the floor, and someone pushed him, rolling him to a corner with the flat of his boot.

"Do not shoot!" Franzl called out. "It is over. Do not shoot."

Jeff rolled to a sitting position. Franzl was readjusting his shirt and tie. Ricardo still sprawled in the chair. Jeff realized that his friend was badly hurt, that he could not move.

Franzl did not glance at Jeff. He motioned with his hand, and the two men with him bent down and hoisted Ricardo, making a chair of their interlaced hands. Ricardo's eyes were half closed.

"Sit down behind the desk," Franzl said. Jeff rose painfully. There were aches and bruises all over his body, but nothing had been permanently damaged. His moment was over. He walked to the chair and sat obediently.

The two men put Ricardo down against the far wall. He sat, his legs outstretched, and his breathing was noticeably raspy. "You shouldn't have tried that," Ricardo said. "I cannot help you. I am hurt. My head. I have no strength."

No one said anything. Franzl stood, his eyes looking nowhere, waiting stolidly. The two men opened a flat box — it looked a little like a gun case — and took out of it some round lengths of shining steel. These ended in two large suction cups. Jeff had seen something like them before; you could put the bar across a doorframe and use it to chin on. But the ones he had seen were for children. This looked professional, capable of holding the weight of a man.

One of the men fitted the steel rods together and snapped his fingers. The other crouched down, and with the suppleness of practice, the first man leaped onto his shoulders. The human pyramid straightened, lifting the bar. Held by the suction cups, the rods stretched across the width of the room, a stout steel bar. The top of the two-man pyramid shouted "Hup!" — it was the hoarse-voiced man, all right — and his partner stepped away. The hoarse-voiced man hung by his hands from the bar, testing its solidity, then dropped lightly to the ground. He wasn't even out of breath. The two stood patiently.

"All right," Franzl said. He turned to Jeff. "What now happens is your own fault. I would have let you go earlier. Now I think we had better teach you a lesson in manners." His voice was objective and flat, but something stirred in the back of his eyes. Jeff realized that Franzl was thoroughly enjoying himself.

Franzl nodded. The hoarse-voiced man reached into his

pocket and drew out two short lengths of thick new rope, each end of which terminated in a large cast-iron hook. He went over to where Ricardo was slumped on the floor, his back against the wall, and bent down.

"Excuse me," he said pleasantly, and tied the ropes to Ricardo's ankles, his fingers professional and agile, the knots tight and neat.

He and his colleague made a chair again and carried Ricardo over to where the bar formed a gleaming span across the width of the room. They stood there for a moment, the three of them. Ricardo had an arm around the neck of each man. Then Jeff heard another "Hup!" Between them, they managed to spin Ricardo upside down, and with two short accurate throws the hooks were caught on the steel bar, and Ricardo was dangling, twisting and turning slowly and aimlessly, his eyes huge and staring in his head. His arms thrashed the air, and then he folded them across his breast, and Jeff, who had risen to his feet, was pushed back down on the chair.

"Sit and learn," Franzl instructed him. He lit a cigarette. "It takes five minutes before discomfort commences. Within twenty minutes, much blood has rushed to the head of the subject, and he begins to feel the strain of his position. The heart must pump harder. But Señor Cordoval is a young man, and though he is somewhat weakened at present, he nevertheless possesses much endurance. They all die, sooner or later. But it may take many hours."

"This is monstrous," Jeff said, drawing the protection of formal phrases over him like a suit of armor. "You can't do this."

"Truly," Franzl said, "that is one of the most childish statements I have ever heard. We *are* doing it."

Ricardo moaned. His face dangled some three feet from the floor. He was constantly twisting his body back and forth, a slow, agony-filled movement.

"Why must you torture him so?" Jeff asked. No one answered.

Ricardo moaned again. His face was now suffused with blood.

"Shall we end this?" Franzl asked abruptly, as though speaking to himself. "Shall we end this now or shall we wait?" He reached in his pocket and took out a World War Two Luger, an ancient weapon that was nevertheless cleaned and oiled, so that it looked new. He hefted it in his hand, and said, still softly, "Do you want to die now?"

Soft as his voice was, Ricardo heard it, and he said, "Yes. Please."

"But not so easily," Franzl said. Lifting the Luger, he fired twice, and then twice more. The bullets smashed at Ricardo's ankles. The Luger thundered again and again. The acrid smell of cordite filled the room. Where Ricardo's ankles had been, there was a gout of torn and bleeding flesh. The bones shone through pink and white. The Luger never stopped. Then the left leg jerked free, leaving Ricardo's left foot still encircled by the rope but now no longer part of him. Franzl reloaded steadily, through Ricardo's thin screaming, and he aimed and fired, and finally the other foot was severed from its ankle, and Ricardo's body dropped softly yet heavily to the floor and he lay there conscious, the blood pulsing from his two terrible wounds.

"I had forgotten how messy," Franzl said to himself. He aimed again, and fired. Ricardo's neck jerked. His high, thin screaming stopped. He was dead.

Franzl gestured toward the body and said, "Clean it up." He turned to Jeff. "It would not have been so painful or so messy if you had not tried to hurt me. I am sixty-three. A number of people have wanted to kill me. They had better reason than you, many of them. They did not succeed. Now —" he stopped and lit a cigarette reflectively, "what you have seen will stay with you more effectively than any

133

threats I could have made. We will let you go. The Sons of Liberty are not killers except by necessity." Screw that, Jeff thought. I saw your eyes. "But believe me, it would be much better for you to forget everything that has happened here." He leaned forward and lit Jeff a cigarette. "But do not forget Señor Cordoval's death. It was pleasant, believe me, compared to the way you will die if you talk."

Ricardo's corpse had been removed. Someone was cleaning up the pool of blood on the floor with a bucket of warm water and a wet mop. Jeff felt dizzy and empty. When he looked at Franzl, still almost immaculate, white-haired and calm, he felt a rictus of fear distend his cheeks, a bubbling terror that started from the very pit of his stomach.

"I'm going to throw up," he said. The room stank of blood and cordite.

"Through the door to your right," Franzl said quickly. "There's been enough mess here. Let me show you."

Jeff vomited in the bathroom, his eyes watering. When he emerged, his head was still ringing and the dizziness had not left him. He kept trying to digest the huge fact that Ricardo was dead, tortured and murdered. It stuck like a large bolus in his throat. He had to breathe around it.

As he stepped out, the hoarse-voiced man held out a strip of cloth. "If you will allow me," he said courteously, and bound Jeff's eyes. He put a guiding hand under Jeff's elbow, and they walked together for a few yards. A door opened, and he was out in the fresh night air again.

There were others with him in the back of the car — it was the same automobile; he smelled the leather again — but the ride was shorter this time. No one spoke. The car stopped, and the door on his side was opened.

"A final reminder from SS Fuehrer Franzl," the hoarse-voiced man said. "Out."

As Jeff groped his way out of the car, a foot took him powerfully in the backside and he shot forward, landing on his hands and knees, waves of pain rising from his sternum. He heard a whinnying laugh, and the car door slammed. The car sped off, and he was alone.

Only then did he think to rip off his bandage.

It was an attenuated night, lit by a huge moon and a sky full of stars. He got painfully to his feet and began to walk, following his own forward motion, unoriented and uncaring, his body aching, his eyes smarting with hatred and unshed tears.

He walked mechanically, for almost a half hour. Then he found the main road and, fifteen minutes later, by some miracle, an empty cab. He gave the name of his hotel and sank back. He had been dropped seven kilometers from the heart of the city, near Marshal López Avenue, and it took some fifteen minutes for the ancient, wheezy vehicle to return him to the modern splendor of the Hotel Asuncion.

His suit was ripped, and his face and hands were grimy. He half staggered across the lobby, and the elevator operator looked at him with concern.

"Are you ill, sir?" he asked as the elevator rose. "May I help?"

"Just celebrating," Jeff said. His jaw ached too. "It got a little rough."

"You will sleep well tonight," the operator called after him.

In his room, Jeff ran hot water and lay back in the first tub he could remember taking since he was twelve (he loathed baths, and always took showers). Then he got into bed without brushing his teeth. He fell into a stuporous sleep.

His watch said eight-thirty when he awoke. It was Saturday, July twelfth. He lay in bed, his mind inactive. Then it all came back to him. He swung out of bed and into his torn and rumpled clothes.

He was to board a return flight this evening at six. He had a lot to do before then.

His body was sore. His bruises were not only exterior, for he kept remembering Ricardo's staring eyes, his face white and flat, somehow rounder than it should have been, as it dangled eight inches from the floor; and then, suffused with blood, his lips opening and closing, his cheeks purple; and the crashing sound of the Luger, and the blood. Jeff shook his head violently to drive away the memories.

He ordered coffee. Then he went to the front desk and asked for the address of the National Police building. The man who looked it up for him gave him a curious stare.

No, there had been no calls for him last night. An oasis of peace had been granted him. On the other side of it, he saw the shifting sands of the desert.

The usual ancient cab deposited him in front of a grimy, whitewashed building on the southern end of the Street of Palms. Inside it was dark and musty. The lobby was full of guards. The man who sat at the desk was armed. He spoke English. Jeff explained that he wanted to see the head of the National Police.

"General Díaz?"

"If that's his name."

"Impossible."

"Would you give him a message?"

"I could give a message to an aide. General Díaz sees no one."

Jeff tore a page out of a notebook handed him and wrote in large letters: "Ricardo Cordoval has been murdered by the Sons of Liberty. I was present. I must see you."

He folded the note twice over and handed it to the guard. The latter snapped his fingers. Another guard hurried over. The atmosphere, Jeff thought, was very military.

"Take this to Colonel Méndez," the aide said, still speaking English. He had a neat small face, with a pencil-thin mustache. The guard — tall, blond and lubberly, very

136

young — snapped a salute and took the paper with the tips of his fingers.

"You may wait here," the man at the desk told Jeff. He folded his fingers prissily together and stared at them with interest. It was quiet. Jeff waited. There was no chair.

He was conscious that he looked disreputable in spite of his shower and shave. His suit looked worse with each passing hour, and his shoes were scuffed and soiled.

The guard was back within five minutes. He shot a rapid stream of Guarani at the man behind the desk, and received a lordly nod. He crooked his finger at Jeff, and they crossed the small lobby to a dingy flight of stairs. The guard motioned up, and they began to climb.

At the top of the stairs there was a long narrow corridor with a scuffed wooden floor. Doors lined it to the right and left. They walked silently down the corridor, dimly lit by twenty-five-watt bulbs, and Jeff could not help but compare it to the inhuman glossiness and perfection of the CIA complex. Yet this was incomparably more sinister, and in some strange way, more professional. Americans, Jeff decided, do not make good spies. They have to be taught. These people were born to the convolutions of intrigue. They needed no billion-dollar monument to their discipline.

They stopped at the farthest door, and the guard knocked delicately. There was no sound from the other side, but he opened the door, stepped aside, and motioned Jeff to enter.

The man behind the desk did not look up as the guard closed the door noisily behind Jeff. The anteroom — for this was what it obviously was — was furnished in early-twentieth-century luxury. Its red carpet and rococo furniture reminded Jeff unpleasantly of the house where he had watched Ricardo die. The steel desk sat uneasily in the midst of all this faded opulence. The room smelled of floral perfume and tobacco smoke.

"What does all this mean?" The man at the desk did not raise his eyes. He was outsize, with enormous shoulders, painfully thin in his gaudy uniform. He had a long mournful face with a huge square nose in the middle of it. His hair was dark and brilliantined. When he lifted his eyes to Jeff's they were black and velvet soft, the eyes of a child in the face of a man who had seen everything. His mouth curved downward, gently sorrowful, and his teeth were stained. "Come along," he said. "Explain yourself." His English was excellent. Everyone seemed to speak English here, Jeff thought, at least above a certain class. This man didn't even have a Spanish accent.

"I will explain myself to General Díaz," Jeff said.

"You will explain yourself to me, or you will never see the general."

Jeff said patiently, "Ricardo Cordoval is dead. I know who killed him. He was tortured and then murdered. I want to see General Díaz."

"Who are you?" The colonel pushed at Jeff's note, open on his desk, with a white aristocratic forefinger.

"Jeffrey Smith. I was a friend of Ricardo Cordoval's."

"This — Cordoval person. You say he was murdered?"

"By a man named Franzl. Josef Franzl. Some sort of big wheel in a secret organization. He called it the Sons of Liberty."

"Why?" The word was shot out like a bullet.

Jeff shook his head. "I want to speak to General Díaz."

"General Díaz is an important man. He cannot see everyone with a tale of murder. Why did you come here? Why not the police?"

"Because as you very well know, Mr. Cordoval was a member of your organization, on assignment."

His statement seemed to agitate the colonel. Méndez's mournful face flushed, and he rose abruptly from his chair. "What organization? I do not know what you are talking about. All you foreigners who come here seem to get into trouble. Go to the police with your stupid story. Leave us alone."

138

"I will go to my consul," Jeff said carefully, and turned to leave. The door to the right of Méndez's office opened. A florid-faced man, squat and immensely fat, emerged. His face was a congested purple, and his eyes were shiny black slits in the folds of his skin. They sparkled now with a welcome and merry light. He strode forward rapidly and took Jeff's hand in both of his. His hands were small and soft, well cared for. "Mr. Jeffrey Smith," he said cordially in a basso voice. He said something rapidly in Spanish, and half propelled Jeff toward the door of his office as he did so. Colonel Méndez rose and accompanied them. He looked sadder than ever. "General Díaz does not speak English," he explained. "I will translate."

The office of the head of the National Police was immense. Nothing here was of indigenous origin. It was furnished in what Jeff might have recognized as Berlin modern had he seen it at its atrocious height in the early and late thirties. Díaz sat down behind a tremendous semicircular desk, thickly lacquered and polished, virginally neat. There was not even a sign of a telephone in the room.

Jeff sat next to Méndez. This was going to be more difficult than he had expected. What with the time lag for translation, he might be here a couple of hours.

He need not have worried. It all went incredibly smoothly. Méndez was a translator of professional ease and ability. He invited Jeff to tell his story. Jeff told it plainly, trying hard to keep emotion out of his voice, glossing over none of the details. It was the first such report he had ever had to make, and he was vaguely proud of his conciseness and objectivity. There was a short silence when he finished, and then the colonel launched into a flood of soft and liquid Spanish. Díaz listened intently. When the colonel finally stopped, he frowned and said something sharply.

"The general would like to know why you bring us this burden."

"Cordoval told me he worked for you."

"That is not so," Colonel Méndez said flatly. "The man — whoever he was — was lying. We have never heard of him."

General Díaz nodded at this, as though he understood it, and his fat face broke into a thousand laugh wrinkles. He'd make an excellent Santa Claus, Jeff thought to himself, except for the eyes. Buried in the flesh of his face, they were opaque, expressionless. Díaz spoke again in rapid Spanish.

"The general suggests that you take your story to the police. We know of no Cordoval and no Franzl. There is no organization in Paraguay called the Sons of Liberty."

"But — " Jeff said, and stopped. He could call their bluff. He could tell them who he really was, that Ricardo had been his contact. Then it occurred to him that they must know his real name; if Ricardo had known, surely they would know too. Why then all this stupid play-acting? Why, for that matter, had Ricardo been his contact? Wasn't it dangerous to take him off assignment, make him betray his real profession, when he was deep undercover? The events of the last twenty-four hours made no sense. He realized that Ricardo had told him far less than the truth, a truth he protected even when he faced a hideous death.

And he, Jeff Whitson, was involved, involved up to his ass in something . . . important. It had to be something goddam important. He knew, abruptly, that he wasn't going to get anywhere here. Doors were slamming shut everywhere he turned. Obviously he was supposed to do something — but what?

"Tell the general I am sorry to have wasted his time," Jeff said.

The general beamed. "Good-bye," he boomed idiotically. "So sorry. Good-bye, good-bye . . ." It was no doubt the only English he knew.

Outside, Colonel Méndez in a strange and unbecoming gesture put his arm around Jeff's shoulders. "Go home," he said. "Go home today, young man." If he had said, You are in danger, it could not have been more obvious from his tone that that was what he meant.

The door closed behind Jeff. Méndez hurried back to Díaz's office.

"You're sure he knows nothing?" Díaz asked in rapid Spanish. His face was grim, no longer jolly.

"I think not. He is totally inexperienced."

"Double the security guard the moment he gets that briefcase in his hands. Nothing must happen now. I want that case out of the country. It must all be perfect — we cannot afford for it not to be perfect."

"With God's help," Méndez said.

"And a security guard. I want him watched at all times."

"Yes, general."

"I hate working with Americans," Díaz said peevishly. "Why must they mix into our private affairs? I told the President to tell them to go fuck themselves. I hated to lose Cordoval. Why must the young ones be so enthusiastic? I shall go back to using agents without imagination. They will live longer." He sighed. "Myself, I would have had his report destroyed. But Washington wants it." He sighed again. "We are not inhospitable, here, to Germans. Has Mengele left Asuncion?"

"This morning."

"Let Franzl know it is too dangerous. Mengele and Martin must stay away. Nations have long memories. Now I've got to call those bastards." He reached down and took a phone out of his drawer. He dialed and said in perfect English, "Get me the director of the CIA. This is Díaz." Colonel Méndez nodded pensively, his long face sadder than ever. Then he closed the general's door behind him, stooping in order not to hit his head on the door stile.

Sighing in his turn he sat down at his desk and dialed a number. When the connection was made, he said in Spanish, "Señor Cordoval? I have some heavy news for you."

4 ❧

THERE was a phone booth in the lobby of the National Police building, one of the few Jeff had seen in Asuncion. He walked over to it quickly, angry and frustrated. A telephone book hung by a brass chain. The man at the desk watched with interest as he picked up the directory and riffled through its pages. He found what he wanted almost immediately, under Cordoval, Juan. There were two numbers, one of them obviously an office number in Asuncion. He went into the booth, deposited change, and dialed the operator. He gave the number in his feeble Spanish, and waited while the connection was made. The phone burred.

"Señor Cordoval," he said.

"*Momento.*"

Then the phone was picked up.

"My name is Jeffrey Smith," Jeff said into the mouthpiece. "Do you speak English?"

"*Inglés?* Yes, certainly. What is it?"

"I was a friend of your son's. I have something to tell you about him."

There was a pause.

"If you mean to tell me of Ricardo's death, I know it already."

"Oh." Jeff swallowed. The voice on the other end, rendered characterless by a poor connection, said, "Was there anything else?"

"I was there," Jeff said. "I saw it."

The silence stretched on.

"I mean, I promised Ricardo I would phone you. . . . Señor Cordoval?"

"Yes."

"How did you know? I mean, who told you about Ricardo's murder?"

"I have friends," the voice said metallically. "They did not tell me he was murdered."

"It wasn't an easy death."

"No death is easy," the voice said. "Had you known Ricardo long?"

"A short time. We would have been good friends, señor."

There was another long pause.

"Well," Señor Cordoval's voice said, "that is everything. You will be returning now to the States?"

"This afternoon," Jeff said, and it occurred to him that he hadn't mentioned that he would be going home.

"I would advise you," the voice of the other said emotionlessly, "not to stay here, but to go home as quickly as possible."

"I see," Jeff said. "It seems everyone's trying to get rid of me."

"Good-bye," Señor Cordoval said, and Jeff heard the click of the receiver in his ear. He was fuming. There's a goddam conspiracy here, he thought to himself. For Christ's sake, for Christ's sweet sake, are they *all* in on it? Including the old man? Death was riding the warm Paraguayan air, riding somewhere near him. He let his anger cauterize his fear and his awareness of danger, but the irritating ash remained. Suddenly he wanted to get back to his hotel.

Somehow, he thought, walking angrily down the street toward the Asuncion, somehow he was the world's prize sucker. Everyone was taking him. None of what happened made much sense, but he knew with certainty one thing: he was being used. He knew that he was responding to pressures, that he was dancing to an unseen piper's tune. The piper remained unknowable, annoying and sinister. Behind it all was a feeling of impotent anger, almost of shame. If this was some sort of complex game, surely he had enough brains to figure it out. Yet wherever he turned, there were those doors slamming in his face.

He walked on, grimly ignoring the ancient cabs, the peasants, the occasional woman riding a wheeled cart, a white and black striped umbrella held like a large strange flower over her head to protect her against the sun.

By the time he entered the hotel lobby he was sweating slightly and he was hungry. Remembering the dinner he had eaten with Ricardo, he reached into his pocket and took out his wallet. Of the twenty-five thousand guaranis the office had given him, some sixteen thousand remained. The rate of exchange was one hundred twenty-six to the dollar. He would treat himself to a decent lunch, pack quickly, get out to the airport, and shake off the dust of this mad place. "The hell with them," he said aloud. "They don't want me, I don't want them." Ignoring a curious stare from a matronly woman who looked as though she came from the Middle West, he lunged into the lobby.

"Señor." He was at the elevator before the clerk's call registered. He turned back to the desk.

"You have mail," the desk clerk said. He handed over two cablegrams.

They were in reverse order. Jeff tore them open and re-arranged them in his mind. The first said: ALL OK? WE EXPECT YOU HOME. The second was peremptory: YOU WILL TAKE SIX PM PLANE OUT OF ASUNCION.

They were both unsigned. Jeff had the impression of a hornet's nest buzzing more and more vigorously back in Washington. He turned to go to his room when the desk clerk said softly, "A young lady awaits you in the bar."

"Me?" Jeff said. "I don't know any young lady."

"She awaits you in the bar," the clerk repeated. "She is very beautiful. Not *inglés.*"

"You are a bigot," Jeff told him. He turned and went into the Asuncion bar. At this hour of the morning — he looked at his watch and was surprised to find that it was only eleven-fifteen — the place was deserted. The lights were low, giving the huge semicircle of mahogany a depressed and deserted look.

The bartender was a half-shadow behind the bar. The glasses were down from the interminable racks and he was polishing them in the half-glow. The room was deathly quiet. Jeff looked around and saw no one.

He sat down on a barstool. The false twilight annoyed him. The bartender continued to polish his forest of glassware, moving methodically, patiently. No matter how many glasses there were to beautify, you felt he would get to the end of them one at a time if it took him ten hours.

"Excuse me." Jeff said. The bartender didn't hear him.

"Mr. Smith?" a voice called softly.

He looked around but still didn't see anyone.

"Yes?"

"Over here," the voice said. An arm waved languidly, the fingernails flashing a deep coral in the half-light. It was a girl's arm, seemingly detached, floating eerily in the gloaming. Then a darker mass of shadows moved and Jeff's eyes, half accustomed to the gloom, made out the indistinct body of a girl sitting in one of the semicircular leather banquettes that lined the walls.

He walked over to her slowly. When he got to the table he stood waiting.

"Please sit down," the girl said. "Weren't you expecting me?" Goddam it, Jeff thought, they really all speak English. Some more, some less, but if you're in monkey business in Paraguay, you speak English.

"Yes," he said with sudden comprehension. This was Ricardo's girl.

"Please sit down," she repeated. "My name is Consuelo López."

"I'm Jeff Smith."

"Jeff Whitson," the girl corrected softly. She was drinking a ginger ale. The ice had long melted. She must have been sitting there for some time.

Jeff said nothing.

"I was Ricardo's *novia*," the girl said. Her voice was high, melodious. She moved in the half-light. Jeff caught his breath. Never had he imagined such hair. It gleamed blue-black, thick, crackling with youth. She wore it twisted in a large bun caught at the nape of her neck, and its mass moved with every movement of her head, trembling and swaying, lustrous and soft, groomed and yet wild. He felt a thickening in his throat, and he wanted to reach out and touch it. He imagined the texture of it; it would flow like water through his fingers, he would bury his face in its dry warmth, it would have the feel of silk, of sex.

"Of course," he said. "Ricardo spoke to me about you. He gave me a message for you."

"What?"

"He said, 'Ask Consuelo to forgive me.' And he told me to help you if I could."

It took Jeff a few seconds to realize that the small sounds she made were sobs. She cried without trying to hide her tears, staring into the bottom of her glass.

"Don't," Jeff began, and then stopped. Best to let her cry it out. Consuelo's face was small, the lips chaste, the cheek-bones high, the nose, like Ricardo's, long and winged. She had a small, determined, round chin, and her skin was dusky velvet. Her eyes were black, the whites without the slightest veining, as new as the eyes of a newborn child, huge eyes, the black lashes long and thick. Her ears were modeled close to her head, their lobes pink and perfect.

The rest of her was still in shadows. She stopped crying after a few moments, and hiccupped gently once. Then she lifted her glass and drank the ginger ale.

"You saw it happen?"

"Yes."

"Tell me about it."

"No."

"I was his fiancée," the girl said with dignity. She had a rather pronounced accent, much like Ricardo's, and she lisped her words slightly.

"It's not pleasant to talk about," Jeff said. "How did you know my real name?"

"Ricardo told me. He knew he was in danger, but he didn't know to what extent. He phoned me last night from the restaurant and told me to try to meet you if anything happened to him. You see, I am now in danger in my turn. And Ricardo hoped you would help me get out of the country."

Jeff felt the back of his neck tingle, as if the warm artificial twilight of the bar had turned wintry.

"You know Franzl?"

"Yes. Of course."

"Franzl murdered Ricardo," Jeff said patiently. It was all beginning to come untied. He was working on the outer edge of an immense fatigue. He thought for the first time in hours of Debbie; he wanted her badly, and his throat threatened to close on him. He felt very young and vulnerable. If someone had given him a cross word or a kind look, just then, he would have begun to weep.

"Yes," the girl said. "That's why I'm here. You see," she continued conversationally, "I have been a member of the Sons of Liberty for a year."

"Congratulations."

"When Ricardo died, I died." The line, corny, a cliché, carried its own dignity. "They had said they would not harm him."

"They harmed him," Jeff said. "They harmed him good."

"I did not know he worked for the National Police. When he came into the movement, five months ago, I believed his story."

"So did the others," Jeff said. "Or at least that's what

Franzl said. That's why they were so angry. It's a part of why they killed him."

"He was good at lying," the girl said, tossing her incredible hair. "It's not the only thing he was good at," she added, with a naive salaciousness that was, perhaps, a trifle disingenuous.

"Great spy, great lover?"

"Were you truly his friend?" Consuelo asked. She looked at him appraisingly in the dim light. "You sound so angry."

"I'm not just angry," Jeff said, "I'm furious."

"Why?"

"Because it was all so ridiculous. Ricardo's death and everyone lying to me. I tell you, if I didn't know better I'd swear I was in the middle of this. I keep thinking that I'm involved one minute, and then, the next, I know I'm not — I'm unimportant, I always was, I always will be. Unless," he added bitterly, "they fire me when I get home for botching up an assignment I didn't understand and on which I was improperly briefed."

"If we could continue this discussion in your room?" the girl said. "There is a time limit. It is running out. We have much to talk over, decisions to make."

"All right," Jeff said. He paid the check. He waited politely while the girl rummaged in her handbag, put on a pair of dark glasses, and rose. She was a small woman, coming barely to Jeff's shoulder. She was as exquisitely proportioned as a Sèvres figurine.

She walked ahead of him to the elevator. The gait itself was demure enough, but her tigress's vitality spread throughout the lobby. Not a specifically sexual effluvium, but rather the overspill of youth and health and beauty. Jeff thought suddenly, What a couple she and Ricardo must have made. But it was all too late for that, useless to think about.

He could sense the elevator operator's approval as he opened the doors for the girl with an almost operatic gesture.

151

When they were in Jeff's room, Consuelo locked the door behind her and sat down with a huge sigh.

"Would you have anything to drink?" She cleared her throat twice.

"Rum."

"Please." She swallowed the liquor neat. She put the glass down on the small end table beside her chair with emphasis.

"I must say," Jeff said softly, standing over her, "that I'm thoroughly tired of being pushed around. Everyone knows everything. I know nothing. First of all, how much did Ricardo know about me?"

"Ricardo phoned me yesterday from your hotel. Ricardo knew who you were and what you were doing here. He told me what he could, quickly."

Jeff said, "He knew more than I. I don't know what is in that briefcase, and I don't know what Ricardo put into it. Whatever it was, he said it wasn't important."

"But it is," the girl said. "Believe me. It is more than important."

"Then everyone is lying," Jeff said wearily. "Even my home office."

She looked at him with a puzzled expression. "You're not good for this kind of work," she said.

"Right now, I'm angry. Good or not, I want to know what it's all about. I need keys to all these closed doors." He passed his hand over his eyes and sat down on the edge of the bed. "I've got a hell of a headache."

"Could you tell me, in detail, what happened to Ricardo?"

Jeff sighed. "I don't want to talk about it."

"I do have certain facts," the girl said, lighting a long cigarette that looked vaguely Russian. "Perhaps I could give you one of those keys you are looking for."

Jeff swallowed some rum and leaned forward. He put his head in his hands, and in a muffled voice he told Consuelo all he knew. When he was through, he looked up. The girl

152

had stubbed out her cigarette and her eyes were half closed. She seemed carved out of meerschaum. Her right hand was clenched, and as Jeff watched, a drop of blood fell from her palm to the carpet.

She looked at him and followed his gaze. She opened her palm; five small wounds bled from crescent mouths. She reached into her handbag and withdrew a handkerchief. She held it clutched in her wounded hand and said, "Thank you for telling me. It was a difficult story to repeat."

"And difficult for you to hear," Jeff said. "I was going to give you the key," Consuelo said, "but only for the back door. Now I will give you the key to the front door, to the cellar, to the safe — to the heart of the matter. Only if I tell you all I know and if I give you proof, you must promise to take me with you."

"I can't do that," Jeff said.

"If you do not, I will be killed, just like Ricardo. Perhaps, so will you. They have let you live so far, but I do not know why. One thing I do know — they would not have murdered Ricardo so easily if the government had not let it happen."

"Well," Jeff said. He found himself thinking coolly but fast. He was unused to making important decisions, and he found it exhilarating. "I will promise you this. I will telephone my home office in one hour. If you have convinced me by then that what you know is important enough, I'll go out on a limb for you."

"On a limb?"

"I'll tell my superiors that you should come with me back to Washington."

"I have little choice." The girl shrugged and lit another cigarette. "Close the blinds. It will make it more difficult for them to shoot should they decide to."

History was repeating itself, Jeff thought. He remembered how carefully Ricardo had closed the blinds, in this same room, twenty-four hours ago. The blinds drawn, the room was in semidarkness.

"No," the girl said, "don't put on the light. Just sit and listen."

Jeff sat down again on the bed. After a while, as her voice continued, he swung his legs onto the counterpane and lay back with his hands behind his head, staring up at the ceiling.

"I am not a native Paraguayan," Consuelo began. "I was born in Spain, in a tiny town ten miles north of Madrid. My mother was English, my father Paraguayan. He was a businessman, very successful. They did not love each other much. There were many servants wherever we lived, and we lived practically everywhere."

"I know what you mean," Jeff said.

"Anyhow, mother died a year and half ago, and my father decided to return to Paraguay. He was going to revolutionize the beef-processing business here. I was to do nothing, just live and be happy and marry a rich Paraguayan educated abroad, or a rich American — someone rich, anyhow.

"My father died two months later. It takes longer in this country to settle an estate than it does in yours. So, while waiting, I went to secretarial school.

"Some weeks later there was an advertisement for a secretary. I had gone to secretarial school, and I knew something of such a routine by then. And I spoke French, Spanish, German, and English fluently. So I applied and got the job, as I knew I would. I wasn't too happy at first with my employer, but he was certainly fascinating."

"Franzl?" Jeff asked from the bed.

"He has charm for a woman. It took me a month to discover that I was working for a neo-Nazi organization, deep in the import-export business. The tie-ins with Switzerland, Germany, Italy, and Brazil were fantastic. I never got to meet the big boss."

"His name?"

"I never knew his last name. But they all called him Martin. And I guessed."

"You guessed?"

"Bormann. Martin Bormann. He and Franzl go fishing upriver quite often, along with the doctor. The little man with the hypodermic, remember?"

"Yes."

"Dr. Mengele. An SS doctor. A concentration-camp doctor."

Jeff shifted uneasily. "These are among the most wanted men in the world," he said.

"They're perfectly safe," the girl said. "I found that out quite quickly. Several are here, you know — six or eight of them, including party big shots you never heard of. All here and happy and fat-full of good living. Do you know what they call Paraguay, among themselves?"

"No."

"The Fourth Reich."

Consuelo lit another cigarette in the semidarkness. "Anyhow, I found out all about it, and then I went to Franzl and told him my suspicions. And instead of being angry, he laughed and told me who *he* was. He told me he was an SS fuehrer. Later he told me what his job was. Much later.

"I knew that these were among the most evil men in the world, but it had no personal meaning. It was an unusual job. Franzl kept raising my pay, and then he became — attentive." She paused, then said, "I've always been attracted to older men. He took me to restaurants, to casinos. The life of the rich and the self-indulgent can be quite exciting here; we took many trips to São Paulo, to Rio. And I felt very attracted to Franzl."

Jeff said nothing.

"Franzl is not a tender man, but he was efficient in bed, and he did take care of what he owned. He was careful of his possessions, and I became one of them. One of his most precious. And I liked it.

"He knew everyone. I met the President. I met General Diaz. I was on speaking terms with most of the powerful and important politicians, the people who counted. Not just in this country, but in Brazil and Uruguay too. No one seemed to hold Franzl's past against him. After a while, I went to live with him in the German colony. All his friends were good to me. He and I would go to work together and come home together.

"About the time Franzl asked me to marry him, I met Ricardo Cordoval.

"By now, I was involved in some of the activities of the Sons of Liberty that were not concerned with the export-import business. Franzl trusted me.

"I met Ricardo at a party meeting. Oh, they didn't call them that. But it was all there, all the trappings. There was beer, and they had flown over those tiny crisp little sausages that they call *wärme würstchen,* and in the room where all this went on, there was a portrait of Adolf Hitler.

"I was the secretary. I sat at Franzl's right and took notes. Drivel, for the most part. Solemn declarations that the Fourth Reich would rise again in time. That this time mistakes would be avoided. That East and West Germany would become one again . . . that sort of thing.

"Later, the real work they did was sometimes discussed. But only by a few, and I was not allowed to remain for these talks.

"I remember Ricardo as he sat there. He was low-voiced, unlike most of the party members, who half shouted everything. He did not speak German, only Spanish. He also managed to make me feel I was important — and a woman — something few of the others did. He would smile at me, and after the meeting was over and the drinking of beer and the eating began, he would come over to me and ask me if he could get me something to drink.

"His manners were easy. He did not bow or click his heels or talk in a loud strained voice. He was a touch of home to

156

me, a touch of a more subtle world I seemed to have left behind forever.

"Anyhow, I liked him. And when, one day, he asked me if he could take me to dinner, I said No, but I did tell him why — I told him I was living with Franzl. He knew enough about women to know that I had just told him I liked him.

"About this time, he became important to the party. He was asked to stay behind with Franzl and Mengele, to wait for the man they called Martin, whom I had never seen. Within a few weeks, Ricardo had gained Franzl's friendship, even his strong liking. Franzl told me one night that he considered Ricardo almost as a son.

"Finally, I met Ricardo by accident on the street, and we had a drink together and talked. That night, I took a terrible risk. I did not go back to Franzl's. Instead, I stayed with Ricardo.

"I was finally in love. Forever, with everything, the way I had always dreamed."

She fell silent, lit another cigarette. "Am I talking too long?" she asked.

Jeff moved slightly on the bed. "I presume all this leads up to something."

"I thought and thought of how to tell Franzl. My life became almost impossible. I was living as one man's mistress and sleeping with another. They were both demanding men. The situation was unbearably confusing and morally bewildering. When I spoke to Ricardo about it, I first began to wonder whether there wasn't something wrong." She took a deep drag on her cigarette. She said, pluming out smoke, "When I told Ricardo I wanted to leave Franzl, he wasn't enthusiastic about the idea. Yet I knew he loved me. He had given me positive proof of that, the best kind of proof, which is dragged out of a man against his will, or proffered when he does not know he is making you a gift.

"Ricardo was not the sort of man to let me be possessed by another. Yet he seemed to be not pushing me so much as allowing me to remain with Franzl. When I told him that I had to leave Franzl, he seemed disturbed.

"We argued about it for three weeks. At the end of that time, I was certain Ricardo wasn't what he had said: a young man with quite a lot of money who hated his father and found himself at home in the atmosphere of the Sons of Liberty. He had by then been hired through Franzl in one of the many party-controlled businesses, and was making a good salary. What else he was expected to do I don't know.

"Finally, I decided that I'd had enough. I went to Ricardo and told him that either I left Franzl the next morning or I would never see him again.

" 'All right,' he said then, 'but before you do leave Franzl, do me a personal favor.'

" 'What?'

" 'Ask him about the portrait of Hitler. Ask him why there is no crepe, no mourning around the frame.'

" 'Do you know something I don't know?' I asked.

" 'Yes. I'd prefer you get it from Franzl.'

"Then I began to work on him, and I didn't let up until I knew just who he was and what he was doing. It was worse than I'd dreamed. If the big shots, the *bonzen*, found out that Ricardo worked for the National Police, they would kill him, and it would not be a pleasant death or an easy one, for they trusted him, and they would have felt ashamed . . .

"From that moment on, I lived in terror. I went back to Franzl's that evening. I had made up my mind to give him one more night and then to leave in the morning. Ricardo had told me that I could go out of the country and wait for him, if I wanted. If I felt safer. His mission, he said, was coming to an end.

" 'There's just one more piece to the puzzle,' he told me. 'There's something that doesn't quite jell. And when I find out what it is, I can turn in my report, and they'll give me a month's leave of absence. They've already promised me that. Then we can go away together and get married.'

158

"I persuaded myself that it would turn out all right. That night, since I had promised Ricardo, I asked Franzl about the portrait of Hitler. I asked him why Hitler's portrait was not in mourning. I don't know what I expected, but all he did was laugh and say that an idea like the Fuehrer's Reich was immortal and did not die with the man. Then he rolled over and began to tell me about himself and about his life before Paraguay. He told me to listen carefully, because I would hear a story that only a dozen people in the world knew. He began to talk, and he talked throughout most of that night . . ."

Even this far underground, the walls shook. The explosions came from the Tiergarten, where the Soviets were advancing. The entire city of Berlin shook itself like a wounded wolf every time the bombs fell. The air outside was full of dreadful sounds, full of death, dense with hurtling steel.

It was the morning of April 30, 1945, and Berlin lay in ruins around the Chancellery. The Chancellery itself was a battered, broken, gutted hulk, bitten into by the steel jaws of Russian bombs. There was disorder everywhere, and everywhere the sweet stench of putrefying flesh.

It would have been a fair April day, but the smoke and haze of destruction literally obscured the sun, and the city lay sprawled under it, eviscerated, wounded unto death, in agony.

Deep underground, in the Fuehrer's bunker, there was still light and some order. Peace had vanished three days before. But at least, Josef Franzl thought to himself, there was the cushioning of tons of earth and metal and concrete above him. If the atmosphere was oppressive, the constant sound of Russian bombs, of Russian artillery, was muted here. You could sit, as Josef was sitting, on a folding wooden chair next to the corridor that led to the Chief's own quarters. You could know, as Josef knew, that you would still be sitting there five minutes from now, that the death raging outside could not get at you here.

Josef rose and stood at attention as Hitler's secretaries, dressed in light summer frocks, passed him, to lunch with their leader. Hitler had especially asked them to be his guests on what was to be the final lunch of the final day of his life.

Frau Junge, Frau Christian, and Fraulein Manzialy (the prettiest of the three, and the youngest) passed without even turning their heads in his direction. And they were usually so correct!

Their cheeks were still wet with tears. Frau Christian wept quietly into her handkerchief as they filed past.

They came to a stop outside Hitler's private quarters and waited there silently. Occasionally, one of them would sob and one or the other would shush her fiercely. Their invitation was for twelve-thirty. This was a day like no other day, for it had literally been years since the Fuehrer had been up in time for luncheon.

Overhead, the noises of the artillery shells reached them as dull thumps.

Behind the bolted door, behind the two SS guards standing there at attention, behind the door to the dining room, Adolf Hitler sat alone at the head of his dining-room table. Something had happened to the dynamo last night and all the lights were in mourning now. It did not bother the Fuehrer. He was beyond caring about such small things.

He had come painfully into the room some minutes before. Since his right hand had become almost as useless as his left, and he had found that his disease, whatever it was, made walking difficult and painful, he did not like to subject the women of his entourage to his ravaged shuffle. Sitting, he could still the trembling of his left arm with the trembling of his right, and he could still achieve some sort of composure, could still project some mask of power, of order and discipline.

160

He had said that this was to be the last day of his life, and it was up to him to make of it such a day that all who lived it with him would remember it for the rest of their lives, if they survived it, and pass it on to their children and their children's children.

He thought of all the comrades who had turned traitor when the pressure had become a matter of life or death. His teeth drew back from his gray, lined face in a grimace of hatred and contempt. Especially Hermann Goering, that fat sybarite, that gorged vulture. Martin Bormann had opened his eyes to what Goering really was. He had never done a better day's work than to strip fat Hermann of his power, of all of his titles and dignities. Now he's not even Chief Huntsman of the Reich, Hitler thought with grim satisfaction. There is nothing for him to do now but kill himself.

He sighed. He had recently had some dental work done, and the constant crump of the artillery shells seemed to penetrate even the dentures of the good Professor Blaschke. The nerves inside the repaired enamel responded to the constant bursts of artillery fire with small, agonized bursts of their own.

Hitler glanced at his watch. Twelve-twenty. Only ten minutes to lunchtime, only a few hours to his *götterdämmerung*. It would serve the cowards and the weaklings right, he thought to himself. If the German people would not prove themselves superior to these *untermenschen* out of the East, then they deserved to die like the dogs they had become. And *he* would not give the Russians the pleasure of putting him on exhibition in a Soviet *panoptikum*.

He sat in the massive chair at the head of the small dining table. His figure was quite frail, his hands trembled constantly. He stared straight ahead of him. Fragments of his past floated through his tired mind.

At least, he thought, I made Eva my wife. A good girl, he thought to himself, a good brave girl. Empty-headed

161

perhaps — she was always exercising and laughing at Berchtesgaden — but then, I enjoyed the sound of her laughter. After the day's work it was good to hear a woman's laughter in the air.

She will die with me, the Fuehrer thought emptily, she will die before me. I will see her dead before I go. In the end, it is the Fuehrer who must suffer, it is the Fuehrer who must always lead. He sank more somberly into meditation, thinking of himself in the third person.

The Jewish conspiracy cannot triumph, he thought. Hitler has lopped off too many of its heads. At least, in Europe, Hitler has settled the Jewish question once and for all. The kike is a hydra-headed beast, but Hitler has prevailed against him.

Damn the English! Can't they see, even now, that they have let loose a monster upon the world? Can't they see that they can no more trust Stalin and Bolshevism than they could trust Hitler and Nazism? Perhaps, he mused, his tired brain veering, perhaps there is still time. Through all the hopelessness and despair, he tasted a thin gold stream of honey: the British would attack the Russians and drive them from Berlin. What was left of Germany could regroup, and together Hitler and the Americans would drive the Bolshevik beast back into his vast, cruel, white spaces.

If only they had bypassed Stalingrad! That had been the beginning of the end.

And he had made such beautiful plans. Everyone always admired the technical beauty of his plans. Everyone marveled at his incredible memory. He could tell you just how many planes were operative, how many soldiers were in Army Group Vistula. Himmler had always said he was a genius, gazing at him with a dog's adoring eyes.

Because he *was* a dog, a dog of a traitor. Dealing with the English in that clumsy, ineffectual way of his, behind his Fuehrer's back. He would condemn him to death too.

Doenitz would take over. An incompetent nincompoop, like all of the generals.

He would die a German hero's death. The young Werewolves would remember him forever as a supernatural father . . .

The Fuehrer dreamed with empty eyes. His lined face twisted from time to time as the tenor of his thoughts changed, and most of the time it was not so much the face of hate as the face of Satan, bored, bored by his utter sterility and cold despair.

After a while, his chauffeur adjutant Kempka whispered in his ear, and Hitler roused himself from his grim reveries with a start. He composed himself, and the secretaries were ushered in.

It was almost a cheerful meal. The Fuehrer had let it be known that he wanted nothing changed. This was to be a meal with his *kinder* as always. The secretaries dutifully dried their eyes, stifled their fears, and chatted almost gaily with Uncle Fuehrer. The only thing was, it was difficult to know how to act when the Fuehrer would abruptly stop in midsentence and lapse into a muttering, twitching stupor, only to collect himself a few moments later and continue with the meal as though nothing had happened.

There was champagne on the table. This too was unusual, since the Fuehrer drank nothing but mineral water as a rule, and his dinner guests usually followed his lead. The girls drank as much as they could — anything was welcome that might help to relieve them of the choking oppression, the fear, the hopelessness.

The Chief talked less than usual. He launched off into his rambling World War One reminiscences only once. Then he caught himself up, shrugging as though to say, ''This is not the time.''

At the end of the meal, each girl received a little basket of chocolate and cognac. Then Hitler rose painfully to his feet, and the three secretaries curtsied and departed.

He sat again in his chair for a few minutes, then rang for Kempka.

"Tell them to come in," Hitler said. "All of them."

It took a little time but not too long, for the Fuehrer's bunker, though divided into many rooms, was actually not large. The only reasonable spaciousness belonged to the Chief. The others lived their lives underground in reinforced concrete boxes five by six or seven feet.

Franzl came with the rest. When he entered the blue dining room, he ranged himself on one side, standing at attention. Candles helped the dim lighting, and in their flicker Franzl found himself in a dream. He, the Fuehrer's head gardener, was actually standing in a room with such *bonzen* as Bormann, Goebbels, Krebs, Voss, Hewel, Naumann, Rattenhuber. The only person who sat, aside from the Fuehrer, was Eva Braun. Clad in a light silk dress, with silk stockings, and beautiful imported French shoes, her pretty mouth pouting, she was filing her long red nails. She seemed to concentrate on her manicure; a leather box studded with small gold instruments lay open at her left hand.

With some prodding from Kempka, the men and women lined themselves around the room, in a rectangular reception file. The officers of the General Staff came to attention as the Fuehrer lifted himself from his chair. He began to walk down the line, stopping by every man to shake his hand and wish him well. Outside, the sound of the artillery shells never ceased.

Eva followed behind him. She kissed all the women effusively on the cheek. "Good-bye, darling," she would say in a low sweet voice, and then pass on to the next. When she got to Magda Goebbels, the latter burst into tears and put her arms around Eva. The two women clung to each other, weeping, and Hitler turned and wagged an admonitory finger at them. Then he resumed his farewells.

He stopped in front of Franzl and gave him a limp handshake. "You will grow beautiful flowers again," he said

164

softly, "after this is all over." He sighed deeply. "I will not be there to see your work."

"My Fuehrer," Franzl said, his voice hoarse, choked with emotion. He felt the wind laboring in his chest, and his eyes pricked with tears. He blinked them back.

"Good-bye," the Chief said in a dead voice, and passed on to the next in line.

It was extraordinary, Hitler thought, how democratic death or the approach of death made one. He could feel no difference in the degree of his affection for his trusted advisers or his servants. Of course he had always relaxed among his personal servants. His relationship with Kempka, for instance, a prince among chauffeurs. A gifted mechanic. There was nothing about cars he did not know. The Chief always cherished a soft spot for the fifty-odd cars which formed his personal fleet in the Chancellery garage. After the terrible events of the twentieth of July, he had come to trust no one. His saturnine pessimism had proved all too prescient. One by one, as Germany disintegrated and the Third Reich with it, the Fuehrer had seen his friends and sycophants turn into traitors and opportunists. All except his personal staff and little Doctor Goebbels. He couldn't even be entirely sure of Bormann.

The Fuehrer was dressed, in this ultimate hour, in a civilian suit. This in itself was an admission of *götterdämmerung,* for had he not said that he would never change his uniform of SS gray-green for civilian clothes until Germany was victorious or he, Hitler, was dead? Today, in a suit with enormous lapels, a suit too big for his emaciated body, he stood making his final adieux. And if the crescendo of shelling outside the bunker was Wagnerian, there was little echo of it inside in the blue dining room.

Champagne was passed, and everyone raised his glass. It was good German *sekt.* There were over a thousand bottles of it in the Chancellery cellars. The Russians would drink it, Hitler thought bitterly, raising his glass. He had never really liked wine, but this was a special occasion and a special toast. Let them have everything, Hitler thought, overcome with self-pity.

Eva Braun and Magda Goebbels kissed again. Hitler sat down and watched them with a blank face. Then he moved painfully into the anteroom beyond the dining room, and sat there, on a bench. He had always liked Magda. He had been aware that she flirted outrageously with him — there had been a deep, bitter rivalry between Magda and Eva — but all that was over now.

He had married Eva yesterday. He had ended his many years of tacit hypocrisy. Now he would no longer have to greet her on the Berghoff stairs as though they were merely friends. Now, if he wished to hold her hand or kiss her on the lips, there was nothing to stop him. He was her husband, and she his wife.

"I am married to Germany," he muttered to himself, his lips barely moving. How many times had he uttered that phrase, using it as an automatic response to those hundreds of well-intentioned hero worshippers who, through the years, kept asking him why he was not married.

But he had now divorced his first wife, he thought to himself with sudden pity. He had divorced Germany. How else could he have married Eva?

She had been seventeen when he first met her at party-photographer Hoffman's sitting crosslegged on a worn red rug, surrounded by piles and piles of his photographs, drowned in black and white studies of Hitler at party rallies, Hitler at the Reichstag, Hitler talking to Hindenburg, to Goebbels, to Goering, to Hess. Even poor mad Hess looked handsome in those days.

He had trusted Hess, and Hess had betrayed him.

Bormann would do the same.

Best to shoot him now, before another traitorous act, before his authority was impugned once more by a little man.

166

He opened his mouth to call the SS guards before he remembered where he was and what the day would bring to him and to Germany. Again he felt the hot tears rise. Not for the five million dead German men, not for the nine million bereft German women and children, not for the utter devastation of Frankfurt or of Dresden, not for the pall of humiliation, shame, self-hatred that would now sweep over his conquered country. He sorrowed for a better reason than all these.

He was about to die.

Germany would lose its Fuehrer.

He felt the tears smarting under his eyelids, and he sat straighter on the bench in the anteroom of the blue dining room and sipped at his champagne without tasting it.

Someone sang ''Lili Marlene'' quite loudly.

Presently, others of the guests joined in, and then there was a respectfully insane little party with the artillery crumping outside, the world literally disintegrating above their heads.

Eva was standing now at his side. Hitler took her hand and pressed it to his lips. Then he said, ''Shall we go?''

''Yes, Adi,'' Eva said. She was the only one left to call him by the nickname of his early childhood. All the others were gone or dead. He had caused the death of most of them himself.

''Sit down by me a moment,'' the Chief said. Eva sat down. She was, as always, unalterably elegant. Her shoes were French, her dress came from Fraulein Heise's Berlin shop, her stockings and underthings were French silk. Somehow, in this dense world of damp concrete and of the acrid smell of shattered metal, she contrived to stay sweet and fresh. Her favorite perfume was behind her ears. She wore the necklace he had given her so many years ago, when they were young. Hitler looked down at his cuffs, projecting a proper half inch beyond the material of his suit, and he saw the flash of the diamond and gold cufflinks that she had given him.

Over the years they had made each other many gifts. For a while, Eva had been thrifty. As she became older and the habit of power grew, she began to charge personal effects to the party secretary. It had been nothing for her to spend ten thousand marks a month on clothes toward the end. The Chief shook his head slowly. He had never understood money, never! Power, that was something else. The exercise of it, the quenchless slaking of one's thirst for it — that was worth living for, worth dying for! But money? What could it really buy?

"You remember our month's bet?" he asked softly. Eva pressed his hand. Then she took out a cigarette, held it teasingly in front of the Chief's face, and lighted it. Only in the past two days had she dared to do this. Hitler noticed that for the first time in many years people smoked in front of him. He still loathed cigarettes. He remembered the standing arrangement he had made with the ladies of the Berghoff. If they could go one month without smoking, he would reward them with jewelry and some pretty clothes.

It had been Eva who told him, much later, that they had all cheated.

The Chief felt a gut-tearing anger within him. His head pounded with rage, he felt his stomach loosen, a bubble of nausea burst in his throat, and he belched. Even in this he had been deceived. No one was honest, no one was ever honest with him. Had there ever been an exception?

Perhaps Geli, he thought. Yes, Geli, his niece. For years her picture had hung in his bedroom. He remembered her high round cheeks and the curly dark hair. She had been sixteen, seventeen then, exquisite.

She had killed herself. There was no doubt of it. He had frightened her, he had bullied her, and she had killed herself. It had almost killed him. In those days, Hitler thought, he had not yet realized what his disapproval meant to people, to women particularly. Hadn't Eva herself tried suicide twice, and almost succeeded the second time? If he hadn't rushed to her hospital room with flowers, if he hadn't convinced her of his love, she would have tried again.

"We must go down to the lower level soon," Hitler said. Eva tightened her hand on his for a moment. Her round face was vacuous and sad. "The Stupid Cow," her elder sister Ilse had nicknamed her. It was true she was not intelligent. She would have been the first to admit it. But she was with *him*, and he had married her. She was Frau Hitler at last; he had made an honest woman of her. "You'll see," she remembered telling her enraged father seventeen years before. "You'll see. Hitler has an Achilles heel. He'll marry me."

It had taken all of those seventeen years, but he had finally married her. She remembered Ilse saying to her, "Sister, how does it feel to be a man's paramour?"

She remembered looking the word up that same night, and she could still feel the thrill in her heart when she discovered that the words meant literally "by love." Well, she had lived by her love, and she had kept her mouth shut. And, oh God, how difficult it had been, with Magda and with that English bitch, that breastless Mitford woman whom Adi had liked so!

She had managed to keep him. And now he would die, and she would die with him.

She gave Adi's profile a quick glance. It never occurred to her to analyze her strange mood. All she knew was that in a short while she would have her beloved Adolf permanently to herself. No other woman would be able to take him from her, ever. For he would be dead, and she would be dead, and they would be together, man and wife, for eternity.

And surely Adi would make a success of wherever he went. Valhalla, Eva thought, could well do with a Fuehrer.

Franzl found himself standing next to Bormann and Herr

Doktor Stumpfegger, the man who had taken over Morell's position as the Fuehrer's personal physician. Silently, still ensorcelled by the easy democracy of coming death, Reichsleiter Bormann handed Franzl a glass of champagne. The three men stood sipping wine, listening to the loud laughter and the singing and the smacking kisses of the orgy around them.

"Will he really do it?" Franzl asked at last.

"Yes," Bormann said slowly, "I believe he will. He has dictated his last will and testament. I have it here." He indicated the morocco briefcase in his left hand, the briefcase that never left his side, the briefcase in which he deposited all of the notebooks filled with his large sloping gothic script, as heavy and plain as the writer. For Bormann could well have been overlooked in a crowd. He was a stocky man with a receding hairline, a huge nose, and an aggressive fondness for women. In the ten years he had been married, his wife had never stopped being pregnant, and she had never even thought of using lipstick or makeup. She was safe, Bormann thought, safe from the holocaust around him, safe in the depths of Bavaria where the beast had not yet reached. Besides, the Americans did not war on women and children.

Meanwhile, Martin Bormann cast his eye about him. He was an experienced sensualist of the grosser sort. The hysteria of the dance of death; the fright and the stunned disbelief that had overcome the inhabitants of the bunker when the Chief had told them all was over, that he had been betrayed by everyone, and that he intended to die — all of this also meant to Bormann that a casual push from him in the direction, say, of a pretty young secretary, and he would have another conquered woman drugged by defeat and fear swooning beneath his tight buttocks and knotted muscles.

Perhaps he would write his wife about his successes, for they had long made their arrangement. As an ardent National Socialist dedicated to the theories of the Fuehrer,

there was no reason why Martin should not discharge his
seed into as many compliant young wombs as he could find.
His wife thoroughly agreed with the notion.

Herr Doktor Stumpfegger sat opposite the Chief on one
of the benches that lined the small anteroom, and looked
blankly into the palms of his hands. He knew perfectly well
what was the matter with Hitler — advanced Parkinson's
disease — and he knew too that the Chief was unbalanced.
He had taken over a half-poisoned, traumatically exhausted
patient from that quack Morell. It had been Eva who had
finally persuaded the Fuehrer to change doctors. But the
harm had already been done, done and compounded. Hitler,
in Stumpfegger's estimation, could live for a good many
years, but probably not as a reasoning human being.

His position gave the doctor certain privileges in the
bunker. He had heard, for instance, of *Odessa;* Bormann
had spoken of it once or twice. *Odessa:* the name stood for
Organization der SS-Angehorigen — Organization of SS
Men. The escape network, planned for years, planned and
furnished with secret funds spirited into Switzerland.
Odessa — an organization just beginning now, an infant
that would turn to a brawling burly youth, carrying upon
his back hundred of Nazi *bonzen,* wading with them across
the Styx of occupied Germany.

But the outline of the escape route was already delineated,
and Stumpfegger knew that Bormann intended to escape.

The main network which led to freedom in South America
was called *Spinne:* Spider. At the center of the web was
treasure. Millions of gold marks looted from the dead bodies
of countless Jews, created from the gold inlays ripped from
the gaping mouths of millions of dead *untermenschen.*
Money woven from the mountains of women's hair, mountains of black silk gleaming in the wintry suns of Auschwitz,
of Sobibor, of Maidanek. Who would have thought that these
Jews, these gypsies, starved, persecuted, subhuman slaves,
could still have managed to secrete so much treasure under

their polluted rags? Acres of diamonds, of gold watches, of gold lockets with blurred photographs of smiling wives and mothers, gold chains ripped from thousands and hundreds of thousands of women's necks — all this stained and shameful loot, sanitized and collected, was impounded in Swiss bank vaults. *Spinne* worked its web, and *Odessa* helped the friends and comrades. The *bonzen* disappeared into Chile, into Argentina, into Arabia, into Paraguay, into Uruguay, into white palaces overlooking blue tropical seas. There they lived comfortably, softly, happily, with mysterious bank accounts that replenished themselves as if by magic.

Dr. Stumpfegger licked his lips. If he could get out, he too might end up in South America. If the Chief had truly decided to die, then it would be every man for himself the moment Hitler became history.

Ten feet down in his special bunker, Hitler turned to Eva, his wife of less than forty-eight hours.

"Wenck will never come now," he said. "You know I wrote my last will and testament. As soon as I know these papers are handed over to Doenitz, we will die honorably." He beckoned to his valet, who handed him a round silver salver upon which there were placed, in rows, slim vials of green glass looking like lipstick holders. The Fuehrer handed the tray back to his servant. "See that all my guests get one, if they wish," he told him.

Holding the tray with the same grace with which he used to pass champagne and cordials after dinner in the Berghoff, the valet Werner Schwiedel passed among chatting groups of people, offering the ultimate in drinks: a vial of cyanide. Eva ignored him; she had tucked hers into her purse many days ago. General Krebs took the viaticum, as did several of the others. The conversation turned to the poison and the speed of its lethal effects. Ludwig Stumpfegger was much in demand. As a doctor, he presumably had the information they wanted. He reassured them.

"It works so quickly, there is no time to suffer," he said.

172

Magda Goebbels, who had been quite hysterical, took eight vials. Neither she nor her husband would outlive the Fuehrer. And her children . . . She would send them to sleep herself, with the help of Stumpfegger if her will grew feeble. She hugged the vials to her bosom and then carefully put them into a paper bag.

Very faintly, the sounds of the roistering on the upper level of the bunker penetrated the unholy noise of Russian artillery. The SS guards, having nothing else to do, foraged for women in the streets of their dying city. Women were being taken sexually everywhere, even in the Chief's barber chair, which could so conveniently be maneuvered into so many different positions.

The saturnalia, joyless, spastic, limped on. Hitler and his wife still talked softly together.

Bormann approached Stumpfegger. He beckoned the doctor into Hitler's war room, a tiny cubicle crowded with a large table covered with sweaty maps and littered with colored pins. The front was now two subway stops from the bunker. But Hitler, until only recently, had believed in Wenck's nonexistent army group and the insane possibility of its relieving Berlin. Only now did he finally admit all hope was as useless as the fourteen-year-old Werewolves' resistance to the Russian troops.

Bormann closed the door to the war room and faced Stumpfegger. The doctor quailed before the coarse, brutal face of the Reichsleiter — a man who had had, until only recently, power of life and death second only to the Fuehrer's and who, in this microcosmic Third Reich, this Hitlerian world of sweating concrete blocks, was as important as ever. Only the scope of his power had altered, not its degree.

"I would like to see the Fuehrer live," Bormann said quietly.

"Of course, Herr Reichsleiter."

"You agree with me that he is too important to Germany,

to the world, to die of a bullet in the brain, or cyanide?"

"Yes. Of course."

"Will you put him to sleep for me?"

"Herr Reichsleiter!" It had been for just this suspicion that Morell had been expulsed, literally hurled protesting from the Fuehrer's bunker, his (relatively) palatial suite given to the Goebbelses and he himself thrust forth into the death wind that whined and whistled still in the streets.

"We haven't much time. Will you help or will you die?" Ludwig Stumpfegger shrugged. He knew that Herr Bormann's threats were not idle ones and yet he was unimpressed.

"Death now or death later, Herr Reichsleiter. What's the difference?"

"The difference is that there need be no death for you. Do you not think a way has been prepared for the Fuehrer? That the route is not marked and hands ready and willing to help? That those who help the Fuehrer to escape will not share his retreat and his eventual rise once again to power?"

Stumpfegger said nothing.

"Of course," Herr Bormann said, "if you do not want to accompany us, then you may do as you wish. But all I want you to do, all you *will* do, is to make the Chief sleep. For three days if possible."

"I have something," Stumpfegger admitted, "but you would have to have someone along to reinject. The effects of the drug do not last that long."

"Good. Stand ready when I call you. Would you send in Franzl?"

"The gardener?"

"Yes. Thank you, Herr Doktor."

Outside he went to Franzl, who touched his hand with a pleading look before he could even speak.

"Is it the end, doctor? You know. You talk to them, to *him*. Is it the end?"

"The Reichsleiter wants to see you."

Franzl went rigid with fear. The less he had to do with the *bonzen,* the better. The Chief was something else; he was semidivine, always good, always thoughtful of his servants. He did not like or understand the Reichsleiter, a man who, until these last terrible days, had kept himself hidden. Some alcoholics imbibe invisibly; you never catch them in the act of drinking. Bormann had perfected the more difficult art of ruling invisibly; you never caught him in the act of power.

In the war room, Bormann closed the door and turned to Franzl.

"You wish to save the Fuehrer." It was a statement this time. Bormann knew his man.

The Reichsleiter looked with approval upon the burly form of the Fuehrer's head gardener. His legs were like small tree trunks, his arms bulged under the ersatz cloth of his cheap gray suit. "You will go outside," Martin Bormann said, "and you will go to the following address: Fourteen Charlottenstrasse. There you will find a Wilhelm Putzi. Tell him the Fuehrer has need of him and bring him back here, by force if necessary. When you have him, read what is written on this paper, and follow my orders *exactly.* That is all."

Franzl took the folded note, executed a party salute, and turned on his heel. He threaded his way through the long corridor that led to the Chancellery garden and to the half-finished concrete pillbox that formed an exit to the outside world. He paused at the lip of the exit and tensed himself for a quick run. The armored car used by the SS was standing by. For once it would be subverted from "whore detail" and used for legitimate purposes. Two SS stood in the haze and smoke of the day, waiting.

Franzl had been prepared for noise, for shells and screams. Instead, he found himself listening to a silence more horrible than the tumult of battle. There was a dead pause in the din and the death and the confusion. Through the quiet one could hear the groans of the city's agony. The smell of death was stupefying. From beyond, in the streets, the millions writhed and moaned.

Franzl, who was neither sentimental nor imaginative, did not choose to hear. He had smelled worse in his life. He recovered from his momentary hesitation and ran to the armored super-Mercedes.

"Fourteen Charlottenstrasse," he told the driver.

"Not far. With luck we'll make it."

They drove painfully through a monstrous world. When the Chief had created his gardens surrounding the Berghoff, Franzl had supervised the removal of thousands of tons of stone. The huge tractors moved boulders weighing a hundred and more tons, and he could still remember what the ground looked like after a week of work: an extraplanetary scene, acre after acre of torn gutted earth with the huge boulders resting half out of their age-old beds, monstrous monolithic shapes, knotted stone phalluses reaching to a fantastic sky. Now the whole city looked like the torn ground of the Berghoff eight years ago. The gutted, ruined buildings shed their stony blood upon the vast torn streets, rubbles of brick and masonry. The car moved slowly, skirting outrageous holes. As if by signal, the incredible, unbearable barrage started up again. The armored car crawled forward, its headlights hooded by slitted paper, pinpricks of light making it even more difficult to see. After ten minutes of incredible luck, the driver said abruptly, "Fuck it." He swarmed out of the car and removed the headlight screens. The road sprang into shape about them.

"Now we'll move," the driver said. Franzl said nothing.

They arrived at 14 Charlottenstrasse to find the building half demolished. Franzl hurried straight for the cellar. It was dark there and smelled musty. There were sandbags and coarse-fibered bags of loose stones blocking the entranceway. He shone the light of an electric torch into a small space; it seemed more like a cave than anything else.

In one corner, an indistinct bundle of clothing moved uneasily.

"Turn out that damn light!"

"Putzi?"

"Yes, yes," the bundle said. "Douse that light. Do you want to kill us all?"

"Come with me."

"Into that?" The noise of the shelling reached a pitch of utter terror.

"Or be shot," Franzl said. He drew his Luger. "The Reichsleiter wishes to see you."

"You don't frighten me," Putzi said. "I've spent more hours with the Fuehrer than Blondi."

Franzl swallowed. This man must be one of the inner circle. He knew the name of Hitler's Alsatian, the beautiful bitch the Fuehrer loved with such passion. He spoke of the Chief as though he knew him.

"Come along," Franzl said. "Hurry. There is no time."

He pushed the man out ahead of him. The armored car looked driverless. The chauffeur was crouched down, below the bulletproof glass and the armor plate. The shelling never stopped. An already gutted building abruptly swayed and collapsed into tons of brick and concrete. The disintegration was not instantaneous; the building died with awesome deliberateness. Then it was gone and you could hear the screams of those who were trapped.

"Inside," Franzl said, and the car began to move. Its headlights pierced the manmade haze. It seemed dusk, almost night, yet Franzl knew it was still the middle of the afternoon and that somewhere beyond all this the sun shone gold and warm.

In the car, Franzl looked at his prisoner and automatically stiffened. His suit was filthy, his face was covered with

177

bristles, his mustache and his hair were untidy, his nails were long. The whole man smelled of fear, of despair, of hunger, but in spite of all, he looked more like the Chief than the Chief himself. The resemblance was uncanny. Pitiful, too, for Hitler had greatly changed, and you could measure the real Fuehrer's disintegration by this human mirror, this scarecrow who nevertheless looked like a younger and more vigorous edition of Adolf Hitler.

Putzi chuckled. "Gets everyone," he said. "You don't know who I am?" There was a trace of injured vanity in his voice.

"No."

"I am the Fuehrer's double, and an actor. It's no great secret, really. The party found two or three of us many years ago. I was the best of the lot. I helped teach the Fuehrer how to speak in public."

Franzl said, his voice cold, "No one had to teach the Fuehrer how to speak. The Fuehrer is the greatest orator of the twentieth century."

"Yes, I know. I worked hard to make him that."

"I've never seen you on the stage," Franzl said. The car veered, avoiding a gaping shell hole, the rear tires spinning on the edge of disaster for several seconds. In front of them an old woman appeared. She dragged a bloody blanket behind her. She walked slowly and methodically, an old peasant woman with a vacant, wrinkled face. As she pulled, the blanket parted, and a human arm fell out. It was a gnarled and ancient arm, probably her husband's. She stopped, patiently put the arm back with the rest of the corpse, and began again her slow, aimless walk. She saw the armored Mercedes and gave the occupants a toothless grin, while she bobbed her head. Her eyes were mad.

"My God," Putzi said. "Did you see that?"

"Worse," Franzl said. "I said, I never saw you on the stage."

"No. I had to give up my career. The state subsidized me, but I couldn't act. You see, unless I'm made up, I look more like Hitler than Hitler."

"He is your Fuehrer," Franzl said.

"Oh, shit." Putzi hawked and spat.

Franzl struck him across the face with the butt of his Luger. He didn't hit him hard. He couldn't. The resemblance to the Chief threw him off. He opened the piece of paper the Reichsleiter had given him, and read what was on it. He grinned to himself.

Putzi held his face in his hands and then looked at the blood running between his fingers. He said nothing. Franzl decided he must have been a bad actor to give up a career in preference to being the living reflection of a great man. At least it wasn't as though he were a great doctor or a scientist who had helped to develop some of the secret weapons which the Fuehrer was constantly threatening to unveil.

The car drew up in front of the Chancellery gardens, trundled slowly into them, and stopped at the entrance to the bunker. The driver made an explosive sound with his lips.

"A miracle," he said in atrocious Plattdeutsch. "I didn't think we'd make it."

"We were lucky," Franzl said. He leaned forward and shot the driver through the back of the head. With an almost continuous motion, he shot Putzi in the left temple. There was little bleeding. The Reichsleiter's note had been specific. No witnesses.

He took the driver's body and threw it into one of the bomb craters that pocked what had once been the gardens of the Chancellery. He took the large, luxurious car rug and wrapped Putzi's body in it, wrapped it securely, leaving only the feet sticking out. Then he shouldered the bundle and vanished into the bunker.

He met only Magda Goebbels on his way to the map room. She didn't notice him. Death had become a part of life, and, besides, her thoughts were busy with the greatness of her moment to come, the moment when she would kill all of her children, an onstage Medea armed with vials of poison instead of a dagger.

In the war room, nothing had changed. The Reichsleiter still stood, leaning against the table's edge, his hands behind him, spatulate. His broad fingers rested on papers with the notation *"Streng geheim* — for the Fuehrer's eyes only," and you could see the extra-large type, the "Fuehrer type" which was used for the Chief's benefit. He hated to wear glasses and would not admit he could not read ordinary print without them. Franzl put down his burden and stood at quiet attention. Bormann nodded.

"We have ten minutes," he said. "I have persuaded the Fuehrer that I must speak with him one last time. He is quite ready to die. He has had Blondi poisoned in the bathroom. Her puppies have all been killed."

Dr. Stumpfegger entered the map room and closed the door behind him.

"It's an orgy back there," he said. Bormann nodded again. He had given orders that the remaining stocks of brandy and champagne be opened to all SS — in fact, to anyone who wanted to get drunk. This was everyone except Hitler. The intoxication was as much composed of despair as it was of alcohol.

"We will have to get rid of Gunsche," Bormann said. Otto Gunsche, an SS lieutenant, was one of Franzl's drinking friends. Franzl and the lieutenant had often engaged in beer-drinking competitions. Hitler's gardener was the social peer of any officer below field grade. He listened as the Reichsleiter told him what he must do.

"Quickly," said Bormann.

"Gorilla" Gunsche was a fine SS man. He looked like an ape, with his beetle brows and his thick bowed legs, his long powerful torso, and his massive neck corded with muscle. The submachine gun slung over his left shoulder looked somehow anachronistic. He should have carried a wooden club or, at best, a bronze longsword.

He was loyal, friendly, cruel, and stupid. Also, he liked Franzl, who had allowed him access to the Fuehrer's greenhouses when Otto was on personal SS service at the Berghoff. He was fond of grapes and apples, and everyone knew that the Fuehrer's greenhouses grew the best fruit in the world.

Between Gunsche and Franzl there had developed a convivial, brawling, beer-happy companionship that was uniquely German. If Gunsche had any friend at all, it could be said to be Franzl.

Now Otto stood, his submachine gun still slung over his shoulder, in front of the red silk hangings which screened off Hitler's study from the anteroom.

Hiding the empty vial of poison in his fingers, Franzl approached Gunsche. He slapped the man convivially on the back.

"You're not drinking?"

"No." Gunsche stood erect, his hands holding his machine pistol at port arms. Large tears ran down his expressionless, stubbled face.

"Here," Franzl said. "Have a glass of brandy. It'll help."

"I'm on duty," Gunsche said stiffly.

"Come on, man. These are not ordinary times."

"That is true," Gunsche admitted. "It is the *götter-dämmerung*."

"Even Siegfried drank mead," Franzl said. "To the Fuehrer."

"*Heil Hitler!*" Gunsche said in a loud voice. None of the fornicating, singing, laughing, sobbing people even looked around. They continued doing whatever they were doing.

Gunsche drained the poisoned brandy in one gulp.

Gunsche collapsed, sliding down the wall, his big round face vacant, his eyes closed. As Bormann had predicted, the bacchanal continued uncaring, unseeing.

There came the dull crump of an artillery burst directly above the bunker.

Franzl returned to the map room. He and Bormann picked up the rug-wrapped body and carried it into the study.

The Fuehrer was sitting on the right end of the sofa. On a low table in front of him, still holstered, was a 7.65 mm. Walther pistol. He was staring at the gun, his face pale, his eyes glazed. Eva Hitler half lay on the left end of the sofa, her head resting against the back, her arm outstretched toward Hitler. She was freshly dressed and washed, her hair immaculately set, her face expressionless. Her small pistol, unused, was lying on a pedestal table near a red stole. There was a smell of almonds in the air. A broken vial of cyanide had fallen to the floor.

Hitler, immersed in his brown study, did not notice the two men as they stood in front of him. His hand reached out to grasp the Walther pistol.

Stumpfegger entered, carrying a hypodermic. Hitler took up the pistol with a trembling hand.

"I promised she would die first," he said at last. "But who will give me my quietus if I fail?" He raised the pistol, and Franzl tensed to jump. Hitler's right hand trembled uncontrollably, and he covered his eyes with his hand. "Martin," he said, "I order you."

"No."

"I must be helped — it is only a physical weakness. Franzl."

"No, my Fuehrer," Franzl said. "But the doctor . . ."

"Not cyanide," Hitler said. He avoided seeing Eva's body. He stared straight ahead of him, in a posture of military attention. "If National Socialism is to rise again," he

182

said, and his voice took on its characteristically guttural, hysterical note, "then I must not die like a coward. Cyanide is all right for a woman. But for me . . ."

"This is painless, my Fuehrer. Quick. Unnoticeable." Stumpfegger held up the hypodermic as though in salute.

"Tell Gunsche," Hitler said rapidly. "He must use the pistol on me afterwards. No one will ever know then."

"Yes, my Fuehrer."

Stumpfegger walked quickly behind Hitler and bent to roll up the Fuehrer's tunic sleeve.

"No," Hitler shouted abruptly. "Give me the pistol." His hand had stopped trembling.

With a sudden motion, Stumpfegger pushed the hypodermic through the cloth of Hitler's suit and pressed it home. He withdrew the hypodermic, and Hitler sprang to his feet, his face uplifted. "Gunsche!" he screamed. "To me!"

None of the men moved. Hitler passed his hand across his face and collapsed half on the couch, half on the floor.

"Quickly, quickly," Bormann muttered.

Franzl unrolled the carpet-wrapped corpse. The entry hole in Putzi's temple was rimmed with blue, and the blood still trickled down his face.

Hitler was breathing heavily.

Putzi's corpse was still flexible. Franzl and Bormann worked now with maniacal speed. They stripped both the corpse and the unconscious Hitler, and exchanged their clothing. Then they rolled the dead actor back into the car blanket, covering his entire head. Meanwhile Stumpfegger bandaged the face of the unconscious Chief, leaving only small holes for the nose and the mouth. Hitler's thick shoes and dark trousers protruded from the blanket. Bormann picked up the Fuehrer.

"Will he live till he wakes?" Bormann asked.

"Probably," Stumpfegger said. "I can guarantee noth-

ing. But he is exhausted. Chances are the sleep will do him
good. You have forty-eight hours before he wakens.''

''Not much time.''

''Do we go?'' Franzl asked. He was carrying Putzi's
wrapped corpse.

''Yes.''

Bormann left the room. ''The Fuehrer is dead!'' he said
in a loud voice from beyond the hangings. ''Everyone for
himself now!''

He returned, picked up Hitler, and said quickly, ''I go
the back way. We meet in the car.''

Stumpfegger and Franzl carried Putzi's body out
through the emergency exit that led directly into the garden. There were wailings and screams from the drunken
crowd in the Fuehrer's bunker. Franzl returned for Eva's
body, which was carried unwrapped and placed by Putzi's
corpse, near a concrete mixer close to the observation tower
of the bunker.

Gasoline was poured over the bodies.

The funeral pyre flamed high. Goebbels, Krebs and some
SS generals stood at attention in the *Fuehrer-Grüss*. The
shelling became terrific. One by one, the witnesses returned
to the safety of the bunker. The bodies still flamed. They
took time to burn, and for hours the pale face of Eva Hitler
could be seen in the ceremonial fire of her suttee.

In the armored car, Bormann sat on the back seat. Hitler's unconscious body, the head heavily bandaged, lay on
the floor. Bormann put his feet daintily on the Fuehrer's
belly, and said, ''Let's go.''

Stumpfegger rode up front beside Franzl. There was a
pause in the shelling. The great moan of dying Berlin could
be heard again. The car moved ponderously forward, avoiding shell holes. In the bunker, the grisly party continued.
Magda Goebbels looked once more on the bodies of her
children. They were all dead now, wearing clean nightshirts

and pajamas, their toes crisped in agony. Then she turned to go into her husband's apartment to arrange for their mutual suicide.

The bacchanal continued. Hitler's barber chair was in constant use. Couples copulated everywhere. After a while they began to leave, some still clutching bottles of brandy and champagne, trying to outguess the bombardment and the heavy shelling.

Götterdämmerung moved with them.

September 27, 1945

The old inn in the heart of Flensburg, Schleswig-Holstein, had not changed for a hundred and fifty years. It was drafty; there was no electricity. The Allied forces had occupied it for a short while and had then left it in disgust to its owner, Herr Lipschutz. Johann Lipschutz, at fifty-four, had lived through enough wars so that the defeat of Germany had not disturbed either his health or his way of life. He had eaten well at his inn, feasting on the sausages and hams that hung from the beams of his attic. In a sense, war had passed by the Flensburg Inn. The bar was dingy, the guest room large and bare. It had proven to be uncomfortable for the SS who had gathered there to eat and drink, and they had gradually stopped coming, disgruntled by the poor fare and the host's obvious though naturally unstated lack of sympathy with the party. Herr Lipschutz was not a Nazi. He was merely a venal, loutish man interested mainly in money. He had slowly killed three wives with overwork, and he lived the life of a German peasant, a surly, unresponsive, greedy brute. He read with difficulty, and his cooking was atrocious. The inn had been in his family for generations, and he had never been able to sell it.

Now he put down a pot of soup and some brown bread in front of the three men who sat at the trestle table, shivering in the dim light of two oil lamps. They had arrived yesterday, and Johann Lipschutz was convinced that they were *bonzen* — rich, which automatically made them important people in these cataclysmic times.

The fourth man — a war casualty, obviously, for his face was covered with plaster-drenched bandages — was resting upstairs in the main guest room. His friends had said they would take him his meals.

Johann could have guessed much about his guests, observing them from behind his high oak bar while they ate in silence at the long table. But instead he reached down into his pocket and clasped again the diamond brooch which one of them had given him. Herr Klaus, he had said his name was. Whoever and whatever they were, they possessed the only currency of value at the moment in Germany: gold and diamonds. He was certain they had much more. He had lain awake for an hour the night before, planning how he might be able to murder them or at least steal their wealth. Johann, in his way, possessed a sense of history. He had lived through this before, after the First World War. He knew the Americans would soon be swarming over the country, and that American soldiers were rich and profligate. He intended to end up in the American zone and become a black marketeer. All he needed was capital. This was a beginning, a fine beginning. He gazed with satisfaction at his customers; they were ripe for the picking. He would figure a way.

At the table, Bormann, Franzl, and Stumpfegger ate and talked quietly. They had been incredibly lucky. Bormann was obviously following a carefully predetermined plan. He had even dropped a few hints, from time to time, that he was leading them to safety and comfort. No one had bothered them. The country was one vast ruin populated by dispossessed soldiers, returning veterans of all kinds, millions of wounded. Many moved aimlessly, finally finding their way back to their destroyed homes, staring with apathetic eyes at the wasteland that was the Thousand Year

186

Reich's final gift to its people. In the midst of these despairing millions, the four moved with a certain sureness, protected by misery, rendered invisible by universal poverty and hunger.

They had been hungry. They had been poor. They walked wearily. They did not hitchhike. Hitler had to be dragged on a board to which Franzl had attached roller-skate wheels; he had found them on a pair of red children's shoes. After a while the Fuehrer had awakened. He had demanded to be told where they were and what was happening. Bormann had told him, brutally enough, to shut up. When the Fuehrer threatened to become violent — he had begun to rant and rave about traitors — Stumpfegger had put him to sleep again.

Now he was quiet, apathetic. He had wandered through the ruin his regime had caused, had been forced to see it, to smell it, to hear it. He was no longer protected by an armored Mercedes or a special wagon-lit. He was literally faceless. No one paid any attention to him. His violence subsided, and Stumpfegger privately felt that his Fuehrer was rapidly declining into a catatonic state.

Bormann's reaction to this diagnosis was typical. "Good," he said. "The sooner, the better. He'll be less trouble then."

Johann tried not to notice too much, but there were many details too obvious to escape his attention. He noticed that Herr Klaus wore glasses. He noticed that every time Herr Klaus wished to read or look at something closely, he took off his glasses nervously, read quickly, and put them on again. The other three men with him had not been introduced. One was obviously a doctor; he carried with him a worn black-leather bag. The third seemed to act as some sort of general servant and muscular attendant to the sick man. He took orders. Herr Klaus gave them. Klaus had the money.

The man upstairs was an unimportant mystery. Johann dismissed him from his mind.

The men finished their supper. A bowl had been saved for the upstairs stranger, and after a while the man with the black bag disappeared, carrying soup and bread.

Klaus said something swift and low to the attendant and then beckoned imperially to Johann. It was a *bonzen's* gesture, and Johann approached respectfully. Klaus motioned him to be seated. They sat opposite each other in the wavering light.

"We are grateful for your hospitality," Klaus said dryly.

"Undoubtedly not what the Herr is used to," Johann replied, "but in these times . . ."

"All right," Herr Klaus said impatiently. "Do you know the country around here?"

"Like my wife's ass."

"And beyond?"

"And beyond."

"We wish to go to Austria. Or rather to the Austrian border. There is a small village called Nanders."

"I know of it. On the Austrian border, not far from the Swiss and Italian borders, mein Herr." Johann could sense Herr Klaus's hard eyes behind his glasses, and he did not like the feeling.

"Correct. Can you guide us there?"

"Probably not," Johann said after a pause. "We would have to avoid the Ami border patrols. It would mean walking through woods and across mountains. There is a high pass . . . Probably not."

"Why not?"

"It would be impossible for a wounded man. Difficult enough for well ones."

"Never mind about that," Klaus said. "We will carry him if necessary."

"It is dangerous."

"Well?"

188

"It would be very expensive," Johann said carefully. "Very expensive indeed. I might have to grease some palms along the way."

"We will pay you."

"Ah," Johann said, "you will pay me. I agree. But how will you pay me? And with what? Reichsmarks?"

"We do not wish to stop at Nanders," Klaus continued as though Johann had said nothing.

"Where, then?"

"In good time," the man said quietly. "You will know in good time."

"And why should I risk my neck for . . ." Johann caught himself. He had almost said criminals. ". . . for strangers?" he said.

"Listen, you!" It was the other man who leaned forward now. Johann measured his strength against the rock of a body close to him and decided that he would not be able to prevail physically, if it came to that. He felt his confidence slipping. It was always this way when he met someone stronger than himself.

"No, Franzl. Relax." Klaus lit a cigarette. Johann noticed it immediately. Only the *bonzen* in the SS had access to that brand. How many times had he seen them smoked, how many such butts had he picked up off the floor? His whole mind shouted warnings. "These men's shirts are not clean," he quoted a local proverb to himself. Better not to venture.

Klaus said, "You're in this up to your ass, my friend. You have given us shelter and already received payment. If you wish wealth, you will cooperate. We have wealth to give. We can mete out other things if we have to." There was a long pause. It was two against one, Johann thought, and one was the strongest man he had seen in months. Nor was this *bonzen* inclined to exaggeration.

The man called Klaus now opened up his tattered tunic and revealed a money belt strapped to his waist. He rummaged inside, and a small heap began to grow upon the table top — a man's gold watch with a gold band, a large diamond ring, two solid-gold cigarette cases, an eighteen-karatgold party badge emblazoned with rubies and diamonds.

"Your pay," Klaus said. "It is sufficient." He closed the money belt. "Half now and half later."

"Certainly, mein Herr." Johann reached tremulous fingers toward the glittering heap. The jewelry had come from different people; there were different initials engraved on the cigarette cases, for instance. But it could all be swapped for the beginnings of wealth and power. Frankfurt, Johann thought, staring at the gold and diamonds. Frankfurt, and himself eating in the Kaiser Kellar, surrounded by blonde whores, wearing a custom-made suit, laughing at the Amis, driving home in his Mercedes. He could do it. This was all he needed to get him on his way. He *would* do it.

"We start tomorrow," Klaus said. He pushed the two cigarette cases and the party emblem toward Johann and scooped up the remainder of the glitter. Johann picked up the jewelry and shoved it in his pocket next to the diamond brooch.

"We will start early," he said. "You will take care of the sick man? See that he keeps up. We will have to travel fast, and there will be cold and much snow over the high passes."

"We will guarantee him," Klaus said.

"Better turn in, then. It will be a long day. I will get the provisions together."

Both men rose. Klaus took an oil lamp. "Five-thirty tomorrow morning," he said. "Come, Franzl."

"Yes, sir," Franzl said. They walked up the steep wooden stairs to their bedrooms, and their shadows wavered, gigantic and distorted, before them. Johann felt the hard irregularity of the jewels in his pocket and opened the trapdoor to the cellar. He was already thinking of what would be needed: *schnapps* certainly, sausage, bread, knapsacks. He was lucky. He had them all. He looked once more around the bare taproom. Tomorrow he would leave. He knew he would never return.

"That was a bad journey," Franzl said, lying by his mistress's side. His body tensed at the recollection. "That was a very poor time, and I would not wish to do it again . . ."

Beside him, the girl listened quietly, so quietly she could hear the beat of her heart. She was caught up in a great curiosity, and an even greater fear. She put her hand to her breasts and crossed her legs under the coverlet, as though she were afraid of rape. Franzl's voice continued in a monotone, the story spilling out of him as water spills out of a broken pitcher, as if he had no control over what he was saying, as if his story were more an act of evacuation than a confession.

The woods were not the worst of it, Johann thought to himself. They walked in single file, he first, Franzl behind him, then Herr Klaus followed by the sick man, with the doctor bringing up the rear. As they approached high country, the soft floor of the forest, which had been covered with dried pine needles, became rocky and the ground uneven. Johann toiled onward, listening to the grunts of the laboring men behind him. They all had courage, he thought, all except the doctor and the bandaged man. The doctor kept whining to himself, a low-voiced monologue that never ceased except when Johann gave them a signal for quiet, knowing that here, somewhere, there were Ami patrols.

It grew colder by the hour. At night, they sat silently around a tiny fire and drank the water and ate sausage and bread. The sick man said nothing. His silence was at first blessed, then puzzling, and finally almost obscene. He would not eat the sausage, only the bread, and little of that. Johann knew most of the refugee huts strategically placed along the path. They had been there as long as he could remember,

191

small wooden edifices with emergency supplies and un-latched doors. They were always clean, swept out, ready for the next occupant. As the men toiled higher on their six-day journey, crossing the border into the Italian South Tyrol, it became colder and the snow cover grew thicker. Johann did his best to find shelter at night. But their pace was not the pace of a single man. Of the five nights they passed on their journey, the last two were spent in the open.

As the snow drifts grew higher and the temperature dropped, the bandaged man and the doctor began to falter. On the fourth night, as they sat around a guttering fire and ate in silence, Johann caught a hare — incredibly, with his bare hands. One moment he was staring abstractedly at the fire. The next, the hare, fat for the winter, was looking at him from a foot away, as though hypnotized. Then Johann's hands were around the little animal's throat, and there was the dry sound of neck breaking, and he was rip-ping at the carcass with a knife.

It was then that the sick man, the ghostly little man with the bandaged face who had said nothing for so long, reached for a branch near him and struck silently, with all his strength, at Johann's hands as they dismembered the hare. The blow hurt cruelly. Johann wheeled and lunged at the sick man. Franzl caught him from behind in an unbreakable grip.

"Enough," Herr Klaus said. "He will not try that again." He went over to the sick man, who was squatting silently, the bandages on his face now soiled and streaked with the filth of the journey, and slapped him smartly and coldly on the cheek. The man mewed.

"You will not do that again," he said, staring for a moment at the sick man. "This is no time for your vegetar-ian games." Then he turned to Johann. "If you lift a finger against him, we will kill you. It would be a waste."

That was all. The white silence of the snow and the cold possessed them again. In the morning, the sick man could not walk. When Franzl asked him to politely — Johann noticed that he was treated with ceremonious politeness by everyone except Herr Klaus — the bandaged head shook. Then the small figure lay down in the snow, one hand cupped behind his head, ludicrously at ease, as though lying on a feather bed. It was a gesture of complete resignation.

After a short pause, Herr Klaus said to Franzl, "Carry him." Franzl bent down and they arranged the sick man pickaback on his shoulders. Then they set out again, with the bandaged man's arms clasped around Franzl's broad shoulders.

So they toiled across the border, and Herr Klaus stopped often now to look secretively at a map which he drew from his money belt. Now *he* directed them. Finally, after some cogitation, he told Johann to take them into Vintschgau. There was an obscure Catholic monastery there, and that was where their journey would end. Their food had been eaten, the last of the *schnapps* drunk. They were weary, emaciated, and even Johann was tired and ill. Only Franzl looked about the same. During the last twenty miles of their journey he had carried the sick man. There was something almost regal about the calm acceptance with which the man allowed himself to be carried. Every so often, his feet would drum against Franzl's broad sides, and Johann expected Franzl to whinny and toss his head. Johann, who was anything but sensitive, grew to find the sight repulsive, though he did not know why.

It was a small, poor monastery, when they finally picked their way to it. The gate was wooden, unimpressive. They pushed a button which activated a shrill bell, and the sound echoed unpleasantly across the snow-covered waste that became the monastery's kitchen garden in the summertime. After a long wait, the door opened and a tonsured monk came out. He was thin, his face drawn.

Herr Klaus dug down into his money belt again and came up with a piece of paper which he handed the monk. The monk read, and vanished. He reappeared two minutes later, quite flustered, and beckoned them inside. The monastery observed certain rules of silence, and this was apparently a quiet period.

Herr Klaus gave Johann the rest of his pay and shook his hand briefly.

"You have done a wonderful thing," he said. "You don't know quite how wonderful. Now can you do something even more unusual?"

"What?"

"Keep your mouth shut," Klaus said. "As long as you do, you'll receive a check once a month, wherever you are, as long as you live."

"How will you know where to find me?" Johann asked, pocketing his jewelry as he spoke.

"We will know."

The sick man cleared his throat. He was on his feet now for the first time in many hours.

"I will never forget this," he began passionately, in a guttural tone.

"Quiet!" Herr Klaus's voice was a hoarse bellow. The bandaged man kept quiet.

"Good-bye," Franzl said.

"Good-bye," Johann said. It had been a long time since he had heard *Grüss Gott*. He preferred it to *Heil Hitler*.

The four men vanished into the monastery.

Johann made his way on foot to Frankfurt-am-Mein, where he soon lost all the capital his pay had brought him. He had no head for profiteering. But he was able to eat at the Kaiser Kellar and even at the Frankfurter Hoff, like an American, in spite of his bad luck. For every month, wherever he was, a check, always drawn on a different bank, would come to him. The amount was in Swiss francs, and it was generous. After a year, Johann came to expect it, in the way a retired pensioner expects his annuity. He kept his mouth shut about his trip, and he never found himself disappointed. The checks kept coming.

Until one night, in a beer cellar in Munich, fifteen years later, he finally told the story to an old friend, over too many schooners. The check did not come that month.

Six weeks later, he was found in a West Berlin alley, his throat cut from ear to ear.

At long last, Franzl had stopped talking. There was a hint of lightness in the warm air, and the morning sounds of Asuncion enveloped them. The girl got to her feet and fetched herself and her lover a glass of water apiece. Franzl gulped noisily and fell asleep almost immediately, purged of his story. The girl considered in silence, then dressed quickly, furtively. She closed the door behind her as quietly as she could. Once in the street, she began to run.

5 ❧

THE bottle of rum was half empty. Consuelo's face was indistinct in the gloom. The half-light in the hotel room had melted into darkness. The air was heavy with smoke. From time to time, as she talked, she had paced back and forth, waving her lighted cigarette in broad gestures, using her hands, her body, to illustrate her story. Her voice, Jeff discovered, had a husky, pleasingly monotonous quality. By now, the smoke in the room was almost tangible. Jeff still lay on the bed, his hands behind his head, his eyes half closed, translating Consuelo's words into quick, flitting pictures. It took him some seconds to realize she had stopped, that she was at the end of her story.

The pause filled the room.

"I ran to Ricardo," Consuelo said finally. "I told him Franzl's story. He had known about it for some time, none of it was new to him. He kept saying, 'I've got to get proof . . . I've got to make certain.' I told him, 'Please, forget what you know, what you think you know. Just come away with me.' But Ricardo wasn't like that. He was a man who saw a job through, no matter what it cost.

"He must have gone back to headquarters and then to Franzl's room. Because later that day, Franzl was terribly upset. Someone had broken into his apartment and gone through his things. He was murderously angry, but when I asked him if anything had been stolen, he said No. And then, when Ricardo didn't show up for the meeting that night, I knew they were onto him and that Ricardo knew too. He must have hoped against hope, but he was a dead man from that time on." She paused again. "It was unlike him. Ricardo was professional. Yet he made one mistake after the other, toward the end."

Jeff cleared his throat and sat up on the edge of the bed. "Yes," he said. "But you haven't told me the end."

"The end?"

"Hitler. Where is he now, where is his grave?"

Consuelo said. "I thought you understood. There is no grave. He is still alive."

"Come off it," Jeff said. He realized that he couldn't believe her because he didn't want to believe her. "No one could keep a secret like that. Not this long."

"Yes, they could. I haven't seen him myself. But I think Ricardo did."

"Where?"

"You were fifty feet from him yourself," Consuelo said. "The house where they murdered Ricardo. He lives there, upstairs, in a small locked room. No one is allowed on that floor. No one they do not absolutely trust."

"Ricardo saw him?"

"I think so," Consuelo said. "He never told me definitely. He didn't know I knew anything about it, and at the time, of course, I didn't. But he would hint at a deep secret."

"Yes." Jeff lit a cigarette. "He said something like that to me too."

"It was such a tremendous secret," Consuelo said, "such an enormous thing to know. Ricardo was so young . . ." She began to cry silently, as she had in the bar.

Jeff stared thoughtfully at his cigarette end. This is a totally unbelievable story, he thought. The girl's a good liar, an excellent liar. She mixes fact with fiction, she distorts as little as possible, as subtly as possible. He looked at his watch. It was six-thirty. He could catch a nine o'clock plane. He was already in trouble. He should have left hours ago. There is no room here for sentimentality, he thought. In this affair there is no room for false sympathy. It's none

200

of my business, any of it. Aloud he said, "You can prove all this?"

"Of course I can't, unless you want us to walk into that house and up to the top floor. I don't think we'd make it."

"Without proof," Jeff said, "there's little I can do officially. Personally, anything I can do, I will do."

"Will you take me with you?"

"No. I can't do that. I have no instructions."

"Do you always follow instructions?" Consuelo asked. There was no irony in her voice. It was carefully neutral. But the words carried a sting. That's what Ricardo had asked too.

"No," he said, "I don't always follow instructions. Agents aren't supposed to mix socially. I did. And look what happened. For all I know, I'm directly responsible for Ricardo's death."

"No," the girl said. "No. They would have killed him anyhow. Perhaps sooner. Did you have a good dinner together?"

"Yes."

"I hope it was a good one," she said. "I hope he had all of his favorite things."

"I don't know. All I know is, I'm collecting my briefcase and going home. I'm sorry. I wish I could help."

"When I leave this room," the girl said flatly, "I am leaving it to be killed. Franzl can no longer afford to let me live."

Goddam it, Jeff thought, it's a crock, whatever I do. "I hope whatever the hell Ricardo put into that briefcase is worth all this," he said. "Personally, I doubt it."

"Don't you know what's in it?"

"No."

"Why don't you find out?"

"Because I'm goddam well not *supposed* to know what's in it," Jeff said.

"You *do* follow instructions." There was another long pause.

"Look. I'm in enough trouble as it is."

Consuelo spoke rapidly, her words tumbling one over the other. "Ricardo said he'd written everything out. I was at his apartment shortly after twelve. I knew then something terrible had happened, and I wanted to take what he had written down, before Franzl, before anyone, could get it. I opened every drawer, I looked everywhere. There was nothing. I think he put his secret into that briefcase."

"He said there was nothing important in it," Jeff hedged. Or, he thought suddenly, had he lied? Was it his own conclusion that the briefcase contained something as harmless as a New York Central timetable? Again he felt the boil of his own impotence. The puzzle was still incomplete, the chess game unfinished; he was a pawn at the end of the board, almost queened, *en prise,* about to be taken, and still he knew nothing.

"I have to get it anyway," he said. "It's almost time to go. Stay here."

"I promise you I won't move," the girl said.

Outside, as he closed the door to the room, his perspective began to return and his confidence mounted as the elevator descended. There was no one at the hotel desk, and he had to ring the bell for the clerk. He handed over his receipt, and the briefcase was delivered to him immediately. He checked out and paid his bill. Then he returned to his room.

It had all been normal, easy, and rapid. As he opened his door, he was convinced that everything the girl had told him was a lie.

He put the briefcase down on the bed, noting that it didn't seem to have been tampered with. Consuelo was smoking a cigarette by the closed venetian blinds. A night-light had been turned on and then hooded with a towel. The atmosphere thus created was melodramatic. Jeff suppressed a desire to laugh.

"Here you are," he said.

"Open it."

"No. Besides, I can't. I don't know the combination."

"I think I do."

"You can't. Only Ricardo knew. And my people back home."

Consuelo went to her handbag and took out a black address book. "His private notebook," she said, flipping the pages.

"I thought you found absolutely nothing."

"Well, this was in his shirt drawer. I wanted something" she stopped and gulped, "something of his as a keepsake. I saw this." She held the open address book out to him. The numbers were scrawled and large: 30–74–66. "You know," Consuelo said, "Ricardo was always bad at numbers. He could never even remember his own phone number." She was practically prattling. "So I thought . . ."

"Yes." Jeff felt his anger mount. He took the girl abruptly by the shoulders, feeling her small bones and her softness through the material of her blouse, and shook her hard, with a cold enmity, as he might shake a man who had insulted him. "You had this all planned," he said.

"No. No, that's not true. How was I to know you would demand proof? And besides, I'm not sure it's there. I just think there might be something, anything, that would convince you to take me with you." The girl collapsed on the stiff, small chair that stood next to the writing desk and began to cry, violently this time. When she looked up, her lips were almost as white as her face. "I don't want to die," she said. "It's a chance. Please take a chance."

"The briefcase cannot be opened by me," Jeff said wretchedly.

Consuelo shrugged. "All right," she said in a dead voice. "Good-bye." She opened the door and walked out before

Jeff could think of anything to say or do. The door closed.
Jeff swore for a second and then opened it violently.

"Come back," he ordered. She was almost at the elevator.
She turned and looked at him in the harsh light of the hotel
corridor.

"Why?" She half shouted.

"Because I say so!" Jeff yelled.

Consuelo shook her head, turned, and pressed the elevator
button. Jeff ran down the corridor toward her. A door
opened to his right, and an anxious matronly face appeared.

"What's wrong?" the lady asked. "You're shouting so."

"Nothing," Jeff said. He gave a quick false grin. "Come
on back," he said to the girl, who was watching him ex-
pressionlessly. "I'll do it. Come on back."

They walked back rapidly, Jeff behind Consuelo. "Lover's
quarrel," Jeff said to the middle-aged lady as he passed.
"Nothing to be upset about." He gave her another glassy
grin.

He had left his door ajar, and he half pushed the girl back
in, closed the door, and locked it. His pulse was racing.
For some reason, he was now as convinced that she had been
truthful as he had been certain before that she was lying.
No one could invent such an involved story. It *had* to be the
truth.

"Open it," he said to the girl.

"No. You."

"Oh, no. Not on your life. If anyone asks me, I want
to be able to say that *I* did not disobey orders. Understand?"

"Considering what's happened," Consuelo said, crossing
to the briefcase, "I don't imagine anyone will think to ask
you."

"I hope not," Jeff said fervently. He turned his back
while Consuelo twirled the combination lock. I'm being a
complete hypocrite, he thought to himself. And then, Better
a hypocrite than a fool — or a pawn, queened or not. He

was filled with a sudden distaste for the CIA, for his assignment, for everything that had brought him to this land of Cockaigne; this topsy-turvy, nickelodeon, comic-strip position. "We should have balloons that come out of our mouths when we talk," he said as Consuelo opened the briefcase and took out a thick manila envelope tied with ribbon.

She opened the envelope and took out a manuscript and a paperbound book. She leafed through the manuscript, riffling the pages, stopping every so often to read. Then she gave a low exclamation.

"Here," she said. "Read this."

He read standing up. The report was in fact two reports. One was in Spanish, the other in English. It took Jeff a few moments to understand that one was a transliteration of the other. There was no indication of a person to whom it was addressed. It just started, and after a while it stopped. Each report was approximately fifty pages long. Enormously long for an agent's work. Home Office would boil it down, though. They had a number of specialists employed in what Jeff thought of as "succinctry." It was a private joke, that word, between him and Debbie. Private, semi-obscene. He longed for her abruptly, achingly, then turned to the page that Consuelo had given him.

"As for the subject in question," Jeff read, "he lives in a room ten feet wide by fourteen feet long. It contains a bed, a chair, and a hospital tray-holder on wheels. The chair faces a window which is boarded up. He sits there the whole day long. According to Manuela" — his informant, Jeff thought. He wondered how Ricardo had gotten to her — "he is very sick. And of course, he is very old.

"From Manuela's description, the subject is in an advanced stage of senility and Parkinson's disease. He has no control over his bowel or bladder functions and cannot feed himself. Manuela is often given the job of feeding him and she says that he has never uttered a sound while she has been in his room. He eats baby food, and little of that. He is quite emaciated. Neither the nurse nor Manuela look forward to the unpleasant task of cleaning him up. A minimal diet reduces this unpleasantness. He is blind, apparently, or nearly so. In fact, in the informant's words: 'He is a vegetable — a rotten old vegetable that stinks.' "

"He is unable to move from his chair. His life functions operate at a low level, and I am of the opinion — I have only seen him once, and then for only a moment — that he has not long to live. In any case, there he sits during the day, and there he lies at night. Sometimes, Manuela says, he moans. But that is all. Outside of his nurse and the servant, he is completely alone. No one sees him. No one knows he is alive."

What a ridiculously pompous style, Jeff thought. And then he thought, It's all true! Ricardo would not lie.

But Ricardo had lied to him. All operatives *had* to lie, sometimes it was their business to lie, if they had to.

In a report? he thought. Impossible. Yet this was not, after all, an American operative. His allegiance was to another country, and from what Jeff had observed, an unsavory little country at that. He closed the report.

"Now do you believe?" Consuelo asked.

"To tell you the truth," Jeff said, "I now believe that there is an old man in an advanced stage of decay living in a room in the house that is the headquarters for our acquaintances. But that is all I believe. This could well be a tailor, a cook, or anyone whom Franzl wants to keep prisoner for reasons of his own. Nothing here convinces me that he is Adolf Hitler."

"Ricardo believed him to be Hitler."

Jeff shrugged.

"He reports the same story I told you, but in more detail. How Hitler came here, how he has lived in that room ever since, how Franzl and Bormann have kept him a prisoner and a symbol. It's all in the report."

206

"Since I have come to Asuncion," Jeff said, "many people have lied to me."

The girl's self-control broke. With a scream equally compounded of frustration, anger, fear, and despair, she picked up the paperback and threw it at Jeff with all her strength. He ducked. The book hit the wall with a splat and fell at his feet. He picked it up. It was a copy of *Mein Kampf*, protected by a glassine envelope. Jeff looked at it curiously. Why, he wondered, would Ricardo have included this in his report? He opened it, ignoring the angry girl. There was an inscription on the flyleaf. He deciphered it slowly, with his high-school German, and glanced at the signature. The inscription was dated.

Suddenly his knees were rubbery. He sat down hard on the edge of the bed, the book still in his hands.

"I'm sorry," Consuelo said. "I lost my temper."

"It's all right." Jeff's voice was toneless. "I believe you."

"You do?"

"Yes, I do." He poked at the book with one finger. "Do you read German?"

"Naturally."

"Translate that for me, will you?"

Consuelo took the book. "To my dear friend and my second Goebbels, Josef Franzl. May the day come soon!" Her voice faltered.

"Yes," Jeff said. "Signed A. Hitler. And the date — March fifth, nineteen forty-six. Nineteen forty-six," Jeff repeated.

"It could be a forgery," Consuelo said, ironically.

"Perhaps. I can't take that chance. It looks real. I've seen Hitler's signature before. In any case, don't you see? It's checkable. Completely checkable. Ink, characteristics of handwriting — why, they'll test this the way no other signature has been tested in history. They'll know. They'll know for sure. They'll put a hundred experts on it if they have to."

"You don't have to shout," Consuelo said.

"Sorry, I didn't know I was."

Jeff picked up the phone. "I want to call Washington, collect," he said. And to Consuelo, "I'll insist that I take you with me."

It hadn't been a pleasant conversation, Jeff concluded ten minutes later, nor yet an unpleasant one. It had been full of pauses. The trouble was that he couldn't tell Simon Lee what had happened over an open line. He hinted that he had uncovered something unusual and that his informant had asked for political asylum in return for her information, that the information was in his opinion worth her price. Could he bring her with him?

"I see," Simon said, his voice neutral. "In your considered judgment, then, it is important that she be brought along?"

"Yes."

"All right. The tickets will be waiting for you at the airport in Buenos Aires. We'll see to it."

"Good," Jeff said. Simon broke the connection then, leaving Jeff vaguely uneasy.

"You don't have anything to pack?" he said to the girl.

"No."

"Once we're in Buenos Aires," Jeff said, "we'll be all right."

"I will be all right when I am in Washington," the girl said.

Ten minutes later, they were ready. Jeff manacled the attaché case to his left wrist and secured the combination. He hefted it. It seemed heavier than he remembered it, and the friction of the leather against his trouser leg was unpleasant.

Consuelo stood in the center of the hotel room, hugging

herself. She shivered. Jeff, for the first time in hours, was again aware of how beautiful she was.

"I'm cold," she said.

"It's quite warm."

"I feel cold — and frightened."

"Come here."

He sat down on the chair. Consuelo crept into his arms and nestled on his lap like a child.

He put his arm around her and let the briefcase rest on her lap. They sat there, in the half-dark, listening to the tiny sounds of the street outside, saying nothing, breathing lightly. The room was still.

After a while Consuelo kissed him, and he kissed her back. Her lips were soft, and he could sense her — excitement? No, he thought, she didn't want him that way. He cradled her head on his shoulder. She smiled faintly and whispered something in his ear.

"What?" Jeff asked.

"I said, thank you."

Five minutes later she was asleep in his arms. He sat still, drained, neither regretting the past nor fearing the future. It was as though this moment were carved out of stone. He wondered lazily why he had never before realized the tranquil joy of perfect quiescence.

It took him some time to realize he was strapped to the biggest story in the world. Inescapably, he thought, we are dead, Consuelo and I. If Franzl has his way. There was nothing that the Sons of Liberty would not do to prevent the extradition of their secret. He had already witnessed some of their determination. He wondered vaguely what Franzl would do to him.

His muscles stiffened under the rush of adrenalin that accompanied his thoughts. Consuelo moved once, and then woke. The next moment she was up, lighting a cigarette.

Jeff looked at his watch. It was time to go.

He phoned down for a cab. There was no use trying to

protect himself or his companion. Either they'd make it or they wouldn't. The only thing he could do was to narrow down their exposure time. He asked that the cab be waiting in front of the hotel entrance, ready to go. Thank God he'd already paid his bill.

"No elevator," he said as he closed the door of the room behind him. "We'll walk."

They descended five flights to the ground by way of the fire escape. When they reached ground level, Jeff said, "Wait." He opened the green-painted iron door and peered out. They weren't in the lobby at all. Sunshine blinded his eyes. It took him a moment to orient himself. The fire-escape door led, as all proper fire-escape doors should, directly to the outside.

They were both out of breath. The door opened onto the left side of the hotel. Jeff could see the ancient black Buick's exhaust pulsating in the bright air. It was obediently drawn up at the main entrance.

He closed the door. "Walk slowly," he said, remembering Ricardo's method. Was that only twenty-four hours ago? Perhaps it will work better for us, he thought, than it did for him. "Walk slowly and be ready to run."

They had some fifty yards to go. They hugged the side of the hotel, trying unconsciously to create some protective solidity around them. They walked slowly for the first twenty-five yards, but by the time they reached the cab they were half running, unable to help themselves, caught up in panic. They sank into the leather seats before the driver, who was expecting them to emerge from the hotel entrance, was aware of them. When he did see them he said something loudly and rapidly in Guarani.

"What?" Jeff asked.

"He wants to know where we sprang from," Consuelo said. "He says he's waiting for an American señor."

"Right," Jeff said loudly in English. "Let's go. Fast!"

Consuelo said something to the driver, and the car started off with a wheeze and a jerk.

"Can't you tell him to go faster!"

"Impossible." Consuelo crouched down on the cracked leather seat. "These taxis are all so ancient. Few can do over fifty kilometers an hour."

I'll be out of my goddam mind by the time we get there, Jeff thought fiercely as the cab turned right onto the road that led to the airport. It's at least a half-hour's drive.

They rolled along. Jeff glanced at his watch again.

"At this rate we should be there five minutes before take-off," he said. There was little traffic on the road. The flat countryside stretched out before and behind them. "Now," Jeff continued, "when we get there, I want you to go straight to the ladies' room and stay there until I knock." He rapped the leather seat three times. "Like this. Then get out and we'll run for the plane."

"Where will you be?"

"Next door. In the john."

"Oh."

"I'll be taking a long, long piss." Jeff grinned. "I hope they don't arrest me for soliciting."

Consuelo considered this gravely. "I don't think so," she said at last. "People here are quite worldly about things like that."

Jeff checked the driver's rearview mirror. The road stretched back, long and straight, for at least two miles. Jeff saw the blunt nose of an oncoming car, dwarfed by distance.

"There's someone behind us," he said tightly.

Consuelo glanced back. "We mustn't begin to imagine things," she said. "There are other cars on this road."

"He must be doing eighty," Jeff said.

The cab rolled sedately along.

"Ask him if he can't get some speed out of this miserable can," Jeff said. Consuelo leaned forward and spoke urgently. The driver grunted. Miraculously, the old cab began to pick up speed. Jeff couldn't see the speedometer — he couldn't tell if the car even had a speedometer — but the countryside was beginning to fly by in a more satisfactory manner.

The car behind continued to gain on them. It was only a few hundred yards away now. Jeff looked around for something, anything, with which to defend himself. Nothing. Consuelo was crouched in a corner of the cab, her hands over her head. Jeff heard his breath whistle between his teeth. He hadn't realized he'd been holding it.

Faintly, he heard the peculiar sobbing screech of the Paraguayan version of a police siren. He looked back and he thought, My God, it's the Keystone Cops. Behind the car a huge Harley-Davidson motorcycle, complete with attached cab, was overtaking the car as fast as the car was overtaking them. The motorcycle must have been doing a hundred. It gleamed in the sun, its 4,500-cc engine snarling at the wind of its passage.

The motorcycle drew abreast of the car and began forcing it to the side of the road. After a short while, the car slowed down, and as the drama dwindled in the distance, Jeff could see the car stop and the motorcycle swerve across to block its path. Two policemen jumped off and started toward the stopped auto. Then a bend in the road hid the scene from view.

"That," Jeff said aloud, "was a satisfactory sight." He could feel his hands trembling. The driver muttered something, and the old cab slowed down again to its original wheezing pace.

"He said," Consuelo spoke hastily, "something like 'The damn bastards think they own the road.' "

Then they were both laughing hysterically.

"I'd like to have seen his face!"

"Whose?" Jeff gasped.

"When he was stopped."

"If it *was* Franzl."

"Yes. We'll be seeing them under every stone pretty soon."

"Probably just some poor guy trying to make time."

"I don't think so," Consuelo said. "As far as I know, there is no speed limit here."

"Are you sure?"

"No. But I've often gone faster than that with Franzl at the wheel. Ricardo drove carefully. Besides, there aren't that many policemen in Asuncion or that many cars to police."

The rest of the ride was as uneventful as Jeff had hoped it might be. They arrived seven minutes before plane time. Jeff paid the driver and added an enormous tip, which brought an embarrassed smile to the man's face. He'd been obviously prepared to argue with the rich American, and now he had nothing to argue about.

They raced for the small airport building, and Consuelo vanished into the ladies' room. In the men's room, Jeff, feeling inexpressibly foolish, unzipped his pants and stood for some five minutes at the urinal. No one bothered him. Outside at last, he rapped three times sharply on the ladies' room door, and Consuelo hurried out. They held hands and ran to the trimotor. Inside the plane there was a small delay while Jeff confessed to the stewardess that he had no tickets, that they were waiting for him on the Buenos Aires–New York jet. Finally, he paid for the tickets in cash. The plane was half empty. A stroke of luck.

The half-hour flight was so uneventful it was boring.

Until they touched down. Then odd things began to happen almost immediately.

The first thing was the young blonde woman in a hostess's uniform, waiting by the landing incline. She seemed anxious, Jeff noticed, as he helped Consuelo down the landing stairs. As their feet touched ground she hurried over to them.

"Mr. Whitson?"

"Yes?" Jeff felt a touch of panic as he admitted who he was.

"Will you and your friend step this way? Cross American Airlines welcomes you."

Consuelo took his arm and they followed the trim figure of the stewardess. Consuelo did not even look questioningly at Jeff. She was — every step of her walk proclaimed it — only too accustomed to this privileged treatment.

Jeff had never been in a VIP lounge before. It was situated at the very summit of the Buenos Aires airport, a small room almost completely glass-enclosed. There were two or three couples sitting at tables, sipping drinks. The stewardess shepherded them to a table near a window, where they could overlook the entire landing area. The planes lifted and fell, their wings gleaming silver and gold in the sunlight. Consuelo ordered rum; Jeff, scotch and water.

The drinks were in front of them before Jeff could light Consuelo's cigarette. The scotch, though Jeff hadn't specified, was obviously the best. A smoky, tangy liquor that tasted the way he had imagined scotch would taste before he had ever had any.

The stewardess approached them with two tickets. "You have the first-class lounge reserved," she said to them. "As your office instructed, sir."

Jeff took the tickets. If Simon had decided to do this, it must be for some reason. At any rate, it certainly beat tourist class.

Jeff looked at Consuelo and saw again how beautiful she was. She felt his look, reached over and squeezed his hand.

"I have had no time to thank you," she said. "I know how hard it must be for you to trust me, to trust anyone from *there*."

"I was thinking that you are a very beautiful girl," Jeff said.

"Are you married?" Consuelo's tone was idle.

"No. Engaged."

"What is she like?"

What was Debbie like? Jeff wracked his memory, but he realized that, enveloped in the haze of their sensuality, he didn't know the answer to the question. He didn't really know what Debbie was like.

"I don't know," he said. "I'll find out later."

"After you're married?"

"I guess so. She's beautiful too," he added loyally, knowing that what Debbie had was uniquely her own. Physically, she could not compare to this small dark perfection. He felt obscurely disloyal and triumphant, all at the same time.

"I like you," Consuelo said gravely. "I like you very much." She looked at him. "I will sleep with you in Washington if you wish."

Jeff blushed.

"You wanted me in the bar," Consuelo said.

"You did not want me."

"No. But Ricardo is dead. I've got to begin again." She measured him appraisingly. "You would make a good start." Her hand clasped his. He could feel the cool pressure of her fingers. "Perhaps a beginning and an ending too."

"Well," Jeff said lamely, "we'll certainly be good friends." He blushed again and finished his drink. Another appeared, served by a young woman who seemed dedicated to the proposition that no one's glass ever be empty. She presided over a small portable bar set up in a corner of the room.

There is a distinct dividing line in any human relationship when an acquaintance becomes a person. For the first time, Jeff looked at Consuelo López and truly *saw* her. Her reality blinded him for a moment, and suddenly she was *there* for him, every inch of her, and the atmosphere between them had cleared and recharged itself. Jeff felt a sense of both loss and gain as he looked at her with new eyes.

At this point the stewardess told them that they were ready to board. They walked down a gangway and into the Jet Liner. The first-class passenger compartment could seat eight people, but it was all theirs. They were opposite the bar and the ship's galley, and near an endless amount of service.

The compartment was equipped with sliding glass doors, and these Jeff closed. The effect was that of a drawing room on a luxury train, something that Jeff had never experienced, though he had heard his father talk about them.

The plane took off on time. As it arced upwards, a silver bobbin reeling in an invisible thread, a purposeful feather in the blue of the sky, Jeff felt an almost painful sense of relief. They'd made it. Consuelo returned his grin, and they both put their heads back on their pillows (extra-fluffy), and Jeff felt his brain swim. He had been under enormous strain for too long.

He was too tired to sleep. His head buzzed unpleasantly, and he refused the stewardess's offer of a drink. It seemed as though VIP treatment consisted of making the distinguished passengers as drunk as possible, as quickly as possible. He asked for coffee instead, but it tasted acrid, though he dosed it liberally with sugar.

Consuelo turned her head to look at him. "Why don't you sleep?" she asked. "I shall sleep too. We will sleep together."

Jeff closed his eyes, and gradually the dizziness subsided. He reached out his hand, and Consuelo's fingers rested, curled and cool, in his palm. He imagined he could feel her pulse, the coursing of her blood through her body. She had become more important to him than he wished to admit.

He was too tired to pursue the idea. He let the encroaching darkness envelop him, and the rush of the jet through the rarefied atmosphere became distant, and then he heard nothing.

He awoke, feeling much better, and checked his watch,

216

which he had reset. By Washington time it was three A.M. He had slept two and a half hours, and Washington was only a short space away. The great ship was quiet. Through the glass doors, he could see small overhead reading lights spangle the dark interior like stars. Jeff stretched. Consuelo awoke at his movement, and rose.

"Be right back," she said and headed for the bathroom. The ever present stewardess entered the compartment and smiled at Jeff as she sat down. She was an extremely pretty girl.

"We've been waiting for you to wake up," she said. "We're only an hour and a half out of Washington. The captain sends his compliments. Would you like to visit the cockpit?"

"I don't think so," Jeff said tiredly. "But thank him for me."

"A small snack? We have some special sandwiches on board for you. You missed dinner, you know. But you can have anything you wish."

"Is this usual?" Jeff asked.

"Hardly. You're two very special people." The girl smiled mysteriously. "I'll prove it."

She ducked out and returned in a moment with a champagne bucket from which protruded the neck of a bottle. "Everyone else gets California champagne," the stewardess said. "*This* is for you." She held up the dripping bottle. "Dom Perignon, fifty-nine. The best in the world."

"Very nice," Jeff said. He loathed champagne. Consuelo returned and resumed her seat. She had freshened herself. Every hair was in place, her cheeks were delicately powdered, she smelled good, and she looked more beautiful than ever. "Look what we got," Jeff said, indicating the champagne bucket. The stewardess returned with a silver plate of hors d'oeuvres and little thin sandwiches.

"All comfy?" she asked, and then, nodding her head in

approval, withdrew, Jeff closed the sliding glass doors behind her.

The sandwiches, Jeff thought, were delicious. Consuelo shook her head when he offered her some.

"Some wine?"

"In a little while," Consuelo said, "when my stomach settles. You have some."

"I don't drink champagne," Jeff said. "Makes me sick as a dog. Hadn't we better talk?"

"We are talking."

"We're sitting on top of the biggest story of the twentieth century. Have you ever been to America?"

"Of course. But not the United States."

Jeff accepted the rebuke. "I meant that, of course."

"No. I'm looking forward to it."

"You're going to be quite famous," Jeff said, "when this gets out."

"Famous?"

"There'll be photographers, and with your looks I don't think you'll need to worry about money or — or anything else."

"What about you?"

"I don't know. I think I've made a mess of everything."

"You are not a good operative," Consuelo said gently. "I told you that." She switched the subject. "Are you uncomfortable about Hitler being alive?"

"Yes, I suppose I am. Or rather I feel I ought to be. It's as though Attila the Hun were still alive. The whole business is pretty remote."

"Yes, but it's very real to Franzl. And the others. They go on thinking their horrible thoughts, caught up in a time that won't let them go, still in love with an evil that is long past." Consuelo lit a cigarette. "What do you think the United States will do, once they know?" she asked.

"Probably take him in. Give him a trial and hang him."

"There is no extradition from Paraguay."

"For *him?* He's the greatest criminal in the history of the world. They wouldn't dare keep him."

"I wonder. However, you may be right. Tell me about the United States."

"You're asking the wrong person," Jeff said. "I wasn't really brought up there. I wasn't really brought up anywhere," he added. He began to tell Consuelo something of his boyhood. She listened, and he could see she understood. He had talked about his early life to Debbie many times, and her maternalism had been aroused by his conviction that he had suffered. But Consuelo was also the product of Europe, of an expatriate internationalism. She understood what lay behind his words, understood in a way that Deborah Bernstein, product of the despairs of West Manhattan, never could. Occasionally, Consuelo squeezed his hand. Once she smiled, and Jeff, who thought he was being particularly poignant, stopped his monologue.

"What's so funny?"

"Nothing. It is a touching story about a lonely little boy. I am sorry for the little boy. But tell me, don't you think the man is feeling a little sorry for himself?"

It was a barbed question. Jeff felt unable to answer it. It was obvious that Consuelo did not expect him to. "I didn't intend to talk so much about myself," he said stiffly. "I'm sorry."

"Darling." It was the first endearment Consuelo had used. "I loved it. You will find I remember every word. And more than that," she smiled at him, "I'll act on it. Now. Tell me about American politics."

So Jeff told her what he knew. His political opinions were unformed for an adult. He knew that the United States was the best country in the world. He mouthed all of the Republican, middle-of-the-road opinions which he had heard all his life. His college training had given him grounding in politics and sociology, but little had been digested, absorbed, or colored with rational and intensive thought.

219

"It all sounds too good to be true," Consuelo said at last.

"It's the only system I know of that works," Jeff said sagely. "It's not fashionable to love your country anymore, but I do. If only because there is no other place that's any better, no other system in the world that works half as well."

"Please, I'll have some wine now," Consuelo said. As Jeff removed the gold foil and worked at the cork, she added, "I think I'll have to find out about the United States myself, my own way."

"Possibly," Jeff said. He worked the cork slowly out of the bottle's neck, waiting for the explosion of trapped gases. There was none.

He poured the wine into a chilled champagne glass, picking it up off the cracked ice in the bucket. The wine was clear gold, but there was no foam.

"Flat," Jeff said.

"Never mind. It's the most beautiful white wine in the world."

"I can't drink champagne," Jeff said. "Flat or not. It makes me deathly ill. Every time. Have fun."

"Never mind," Consuelo said, again.

She raised her glass to him. "To what will happen," she said. "For it will happen."

It was a strange toast. The girl drank her wine off in a gulp and motioned for him to refill her glass. Jeff did so and signaled to the stewardess.

She appeared immediately.

"This wine is flat. Could I have a scotch and water?"

"Oh, I'm so sorry," the stewardess said. "The man who gave it to us for you was so proud of it."

"What man?"

"The man from your Paraguayan office, Mr. Whitson."

"But . . . " Jeff turned to Consuelo.

She shrugged. "It's all so mysterious," she murmured. "I never asked you why all this attention. Are you so important?" She had half drained her second glass of wine.

Jeff frowned. "No," he said flatly, "I'm not. And I have no office in Paraguay."

"They had the bottle brought to the plane especially," the stewardess said. "I'll bring you your scotch and water." Her tone implied that she considered Jeff a boor.

Consuelo said sleepily, "I'm dizzy and tired again." She curled under her blanket until only her face was visible, and closed her eyes. "I think I'll sleep a little."

"You drank too fast," Jeff said.

"I know. But it makes me bloom . . ." Consuelo stirred faintly. "You make me bloom, too," she said, almost whispering.

She closed her eyes and slept. Jeff leaned back in his seat. There was something wrong here. The entire VIP treatment, the large compartment to themselves, the wine, the sandwiches. None of this fitted in with what he knew of his office. He looked at the briefcase manacled to his wrist. He had taken all this for granted, since he was bringing home such important news. But, he realized, Simon didn't know that. Or his uncle. For them, back in Washington, he was an enigma. They had trusted him enough to let him bring the girl along with him, but that didn't mean that they would arrange or pay for the kind of service he had been receiving. He took a gulp of his scotch and turned to look at Consuelo. She was sleeping peacefully and he decided not to disturb her. It will all unravel itself soon enough, he thought, sleepy now himself. I shouldn't have had that drink. He put down the glass and closed his eyes. Sleep came . . .

He woke with a start.

There was danger, he could smell it. He had forgotten something, he hadn't added things up correctly. There was a smell of danger all about him. He shook Consuelo.

Then he stopped shaking her.

Her face was supernally beautiful. The bones shone softly under the transparent skin, and there were delicate blue shadows under her closed eyelids. The lines of her throat were poetry, and her head moved loosely on her neck. Her small hand was heavy, and the fingers uncurled quite naturally as Jeff watched.

Then he was shouting, and shaking her again and again, and her head arced back and forth on her slim neck, and her arms moved gracefully in their sockets. And she was dead. She was dead.

Someone said, ''Stop shaking her.'' The compartment was full of people: three stewardesses, the captain, and a young man with heavy spectacles who was a doctor. Jeff let Consuelo's body drop. The doctor examined her rapidly. He stood up, shaking his head. ''Some sort of poisoning. Not natural, that's all I can tell you right now.''

The stewardess who had been taking care of them with such solicitude turned white. ''Oh, my goodness,'' she said loudly and emptily, ''oh, my goodness.''

Jeff gripped the doctor's arm and yelled, ''The wine! That was why it was flat! Don't you see! They had to remove the cork and then put it back in! That was why it didn't bubble! They couldn't put the bubbles back in!''

Someone slapped him smartly across the face. The doctor was backing away from him.

The captain, trim and magnificent in his uniform, said sharply to Jeff, ''Get hold of yourself now.''

Jeff said, ''Excuse me,'' and rushed for the lavatory. There, two miles up in the air, he leaned over the toilet bowl, and for the second time in twenty-four hours, he vomited. Then he put his head against the small metal washstand and wept. Only now did he begin to realize his loss. Only now did he begin to feel rage, impotent anger at the men who had murdered Ricardo, who had murdered Consuelo, who had tried to murder him. For a moment he wished fervently that he too had drunk the wine and was now beyond reach, unable to feel or think.

When he returned to the compartment, he was calmer. The captain touched him on the shoulder, and said, "I'm sorry, there's no place to put her. We'll be circling Washington in fifteen minutes. I've radioed for an ambulance."

Jeff said nothing.

"Would you like to sit up front with me?" the captain asked. Jeff shook his head. He stared numbly at his clasped hands. The champagne bucket had been taken away, the champagne saved for analysis. "An alkaloid poison of some sort," the doctor had said. "She obviously didn't suffer at all."

Consuelo was curled up as before, only someone had pulled the blanket over her face. The plane buzzed with the news. The stewardess, still numb with shock, had been comforted by her co-workers and sat limply in the galley, where Jeff could see her. Her head was in her hands, and she was weeping.

Jeff just sat there, staring at nothing, thinking as little as possible. Consuelo, under her blanket, seemed to sleep. The plane lost altitude rapidly, and Jeff's ears popped.

It's going on, he thought to himself, the nightmare goes on and on. He wanted desperately to sleep. He wanted to be drunk. He wanted Debbie, now, this moment.

6 ❧

EVEN this early in the morning, it was hot. Washington sweltered. Jeff was dazed with grief, with the lights, with the questions. There had been two sleepy young men from the agency, ready apparently to take Consuelo in tow. The ambulance had roused a curiosity which had not been satisfied. Reporters had been warned away.

Consuelo's body had been put quickly and methodically into the ambulance. Next to her, in a metal container that looked like nothing more than a huge mailing tube, rode the poisoned wine. A wisp of Consuelo's blue-black hair had escaped the blanket. A young man in white carefully tucked it back in and smoothed the wool down with a proprietary gesture.

Jeff unlocked the briefcase from his wrist. The convulsion of relief was so intense that a muscular spasm passed across his face. At the same time, involuntarily, he yawned.

He picked up the briefcase. It didn't seem to weigh so much now it was no longer part of him. He held it carefully by the handle and lifted his overnight bag with the other hand. I can get four hours sleep if I hurry, he thought.

The CIA took care of its own. By tomorrow Consuelo's death would be hushed up, reduced to a two-page summary. But he would be in the hottest water of his life, untouchable, a mess-maker. He didn't know what the reaction would be to his news. But he was certainly the bearer of bad tidings. No one would like him for that. Don't rock the boat, his uncle had said. Well, the boat was all but capsized.

He hailed a cab and gave his home address. The briefcase lay on his lap. He was used up, his head was spinning, his eyes kept filling with weak tears, his hands trembled. There was the bitter taste of vomit in his mouth.

Halfway home he changed his mind and gave Debbie's address. In for a penny, in for a pound, he thought. I've had it, anyhow. As long as he was still a courier — and he would be an operative until this morning around nine-twenty — he was not supposed to vary his routine. But he had to see Debbie, had to see her right away.

He was ringing her bell twenty minutes later. There had been the freshening scent of dawn in the air as he paid for the cab. His watch said four-thirty. He pressed the button, two short sharp rings and then a long one — their private signal. He felt he'd been away for years. He could hardly remember what she looked like. It seemed as though the signal were someone else's intimacy; he felt removed from himself.

It took Debbie three minutes to answer. Her face was puffed with sleep when she opened the door, after carefully asking, "Who is it?"

She took Jeff by the hand and pulled him inside. He could hear the double lock snap.

"You're not supposed to be here," Debbie said. "Oh, Jeff, for God's sake, what went wrong? Everyone's in an uproar. I've never seen Simon so upset in my life."

"Fuck them," Jeff said. He sat down on the couch. "Let me have some coffee, will you?"

Debbie snapped on the lights in the kitchenette. She hadn't kissed him hello, he noticed; she was all business, all efficiency. She made some instant coffee, and Jeff sipped it.

"Now," Debbie said. "Tell me what you can."

With some part of his tired mind, Jeff noticed her careful phrasing. He told his story disjointedly, in spurts, out of sequence, sipping coffee. His voice was hoarse.

He left out the fact that he had opened the attaché case. He did not mention the copy of *Mein Kampf* or the horror in the small room. But he told her everything else, as, he supposed, he would tell Simon Lee four hours from now.

For Debbie it was a question of listening with more than her ears. Jeff looked exhausted, she thought. There were new lines in his face. She tensed when he mentioned Consuelo, and the careful neutrality with which he described the girl bothered her. There were gaps in his story. The discovery of yet another neo-Nazi party in South America was not enough in itself to have caused all this furor. When Jeff finished, Debbie found herself uneasy and dissatisfied.

"How terrible for the girl," she said at last.

"Yes."

"But why didn't they just let her go?"

"I don't know," Jeff said irritably, and Debbie thought, You do! She was aware of something hidden. Then, with an almost muscular contraction of her heart, she knew that there had been something between Consuelo and Jeff.

"Did you sleep with her?" she asked casually.

"No."

"But you were in love with her?" The question was painful, and Debbie realized that it made no difference what Jeff answered. She knew the answer.

All he did was put his head back on the couch pillows and close his eyes. Within seconds he was in the deep sleep of utter exhaustion.

Debbie dressed, brushed her teeth, fixed herself another cup of coffee. During all these familiar actions, she was groping her way to a conclusion. Not rationally, but with the fingertips of her mind. She was all feeling, delicate and questing. Nothing hung together. She looked once more at Jeff, snoring on the sofa. In the pale light of the coming summer day, he looked absurdly vulnerable. She wasn't sure how, but she felt he was headed for trouble. After all, she told herself, she was partly responsible for all this. If she hadn't intervened, hadn't begged Simon to give him this assignment, Jeff would never have gone. Her bowels yearned towards him; she felt an overwhelming surge of protective love.

Then, not having thought about it at all, not knowing why she was doing so but aware that she had to, she went over to the briefcase and took it into the kitchenette. There she made herself some soft-boiled eggs, and she opened the attaché case and sat down to read.

It took her fifteen minutes to assimilate Ricardo's report and thirty seconds to examine the paperback edition of *Mein Kampf*, to take in the inscription, the signature, and the date. She was unaware that her mouth had opened in profound shock, that her face had turned bone-white. She was unaware of knocking over the eggcup so that it shattered on her immaculate floor. She was unaware of the strange sounds that issued from her throat. For she was back in the past, listening to her mother's voice, a terrified little girl listening to horrors during the day, and dreaming of them at night. She looked at the signature again and closed the book. Her mind screamed, *He's alive! The beast is alive!* The beast who destroyed my father, who destroyed my mother, who destroyed part of me.

With the clarity and vividness of a dream, she saw herself

as part of a huge throng in Times Square. People pressed against her, and she moved slowly, pushing them out of her way. As she neared the edge of the throng, she saw a cage. It was hung from a smartly colored crane, its steel bars glittering in the afternoon sun. At the innermost fringe of the crowd she stopped, breathless, and looked about her. The men and women who had pushed their way to an unobstructed view of the man standing in the cage all had the same faces. The men were all her father. Their eyes were dead under their spectacles, their mild faces graven with intolerable memories. The women were all her mother, haggard, their hair in disarray. The men and women chanted a strange song, an old intonation half remembered. It was the Kaddish *they were chanting, Debbie remembered, and she found herself chanting with them. Then the sea of faces behind her were no longer her mother or her father. They were all indistinct, pallid faces from beyond life, Lazaruses exhumed from huge piles of stinking corpses, all of them waving their bony fists and chanting in unison.*

The man in the cage gibbered with fear. He had the same umistakable mustache, and though a very old man, it was unquestionably he. Next to him in the cage was a wheelchair, but in his fear his paralysis had left him. He was standing up in his uniform, shouting above the moan and tumult of the crowd, his guttural voice alternately pleading and threatening.

Her father to her left unzipped his pants. Out of the corner of her eye, Debbie noted all her fathers, all the ghostly people, unzipping their trousers at the same time. From a thousand phalluses, there fountained great, glittering, golden streams of urine, to splash upon the metal cage. Debbie screamed in frustration and hatred. Now she realized that she too had a penis, a huge penis, longer and thicker than any of the others around her. She aimed it like a gun, pointed it at the old man in the cage, and urinated. The jet arced high into the blue sky overhead and landed on the cage, spattering it. Where it fell the bars hissed and turned red. The man in the cage was no longer shouting. He was screaming with fear as Debbie's urine spattered around him and upon his clothing. Where it touched him the uniform smoked. Under it, the man's skin charred. He now screamed in fear and hideous pain. Slowly the urine rose, enveloping him. Deborah continued to spout forth her acidic stream of death. Then, still urinating, still holding her phallus pointed at the old man who was now writhing hideously, she felt her mouth fill, and she spat a huge, smoky, iron-hard glob of saliva that sped like a bullet through the sunlit spaces and hit the man in the cage full in the face with stunning impact. It smashed his bones and turned his nose, his lips, his mustache and his forehead into a red crushed mass. Still the man screamed. He would not die.

She could hear police sirens in the distance. The crowd moaned in anger and frustration. They had not yet killed him, and the police were coming to save what was left of him. The sirens sounded more and more loudly. To Deborah's horror, she felt her penis wither and finally retract, curling back into her vagina. The streams of urine thinned out, wetting the square in sparkling droplets. The sirens were louder now, intolerably loud. . . .

And the phone was ringing in the bedroom.

The waking dream had been so vivid that Debbie found herself physically disoriented as she staggered toward the mechanical shrilling. The pieces of herself that she had sorted out so many years before and put tidily away into separate little pigeonholes, were whirling kaleidoscopically through her head. She felt fragmented, empty. Underneath it all was an irrational conviction that she was soiled, totally awry. Her hands made small patting gestures in the air. She tried to rearrange an invisible dress around her. She wanted desperately to cleanse herself and comb her hair.

And oh! how she mourned for her lost phallus, for the power she had had, gone now.

The world snapped back into blurry focus as she picked up the phone. Somehow, it was six forty-five in the morning. Her daymare had lasted longer in real time than in her mind.

As she spoke into the mouthpiece, a wave of fear for her sanity washed over her and receded.

"Hello," she said in a dry whisper.

"Deborah? This is Simon. Is Jeffrey there?"

"Yes," Debbie said.

"Oh. I left instructions that he go directly to his apartment."

"He'll be in at nine," Deborah said mechanically.

"He hasn't had much sleep. Let's delay the debriefing

an hour." Simon was straining to be casual. "Would you please bring his attaché case with you when you come in?"

"Why, yes," Debbie said. Her mind was fierce and cunning. "Is it all that important?"

"No. We know what's in it," Simon said, "but it's still sensitive material. Routine but sensitive."

"I looked," Debbie said. "I opened it and looked."

There was a long pause, and then Simon said quietly, "You shouldn't have done that, Debbie. You know that's forbidden."

"I know. Since you know what's in it, what are you going to do about it?"

"Come now." She had never known her boss's voice to be so cold before. "This is an open line."

"What are you going to do?"

"Nothing. For the time being."

"There's proof in there," Debbie said. "If it's so, it's incontrovertible."

"I'm sending someone right over," Simon said at last. "You don't sound well."

"I'm not well. Are you going to see the President?"

"The President?" Simon said. "Why, for God's sake?"

"To tell him. To send over and get that — the —" Debbie choked.

"Well, now," Simon said, "you know me pretty well. You've been my secretary for some time now. When do I ever get to see the President?"

"He'll see you on this."

"I don't know what you're talking about," Simon said coldly. "I'll see both of you at ten. I'm sending someone over to pick up the case. Until then you are officially ordered not to move."

"Yes," Debbie said.

The phone clicked.

She moved now like a sleepwalker. This, she thought, was not her secret, or Simon's, or the United States government's. It belonged to everyone, everyone who had been affected by this man. And that was almost everyone in the world. For a brief moment her fantasy, still sharp, obtruded itself upon her memory. She packed it up and stowed it away, afraid to look at it, knowing that she might have to unpack it later, knowing that if she did, like something old and forgotten in an attic, it might well stink. But there was no time to think.

She removed the contents of the attaché case, hesitated, put back Ricardo's report, tucked the paperback under her arm, picked up her checkbook, put both book and checkbook in a large leather carryall, and left the apartment.

Jeff slept on. She did not so much as glance at him. He would have to take care of himself, she thought as she closed the door behind her. The rage that filled her left no room but for what she must do, and do quickly.

In the cab, she leaned forward and said, "Airport." She glanced at her watch. She could catch the eight o'clock shuttle to New York. Once there, lost in that surging anonymity, she could stop and think and decide. But first she had to get away — fast — before they caught her.

The thunder of insistent pounding on Debbie's apartment door brought Jeff out of his stupor. He stumbled to the door and croaked, "Just a moment." The pounding ceased. He went to the kitchenette, almost slipped on a smear of egg yolk and toast that had landed near the cupboard, and doused his head under the cold-water tap. Gasping, he went to the bathroom, dried himself, combed his hair, and then went to the door.

Two men brushed by him. One of them said briefly, "CIA. Stay where you are."

"You don't say," Jeff said. The man who had spoken was over fifty. He had iron-gray hair, a plump, pleasant face, and a small brown and gray mustache. His eyes were round and black. The other was a well-set-up young man with a

234

crew cut. Jeff had met his twin at the airport. He passed dozens of them at work, every day of his life.

Jeff said, "Debbie?" There was no answer. The young man came out of the kitchenette, carrying the attaché case. "It was on the counter," he said accusingly.

"I'm sorry," Jeff said. "I should have put it in the safe. Except there's no safe."

"Save the funnies." The young man didn't seem sympathetic. "You're in enough trouble. Better take things seriously."

"Where's the girl?" the older man asked.

"Her coat's gone," Jeff said. "She's probably left for the office."

"Office?" the older man said. He sat down on the couch.

"Yes," Jeff said patiently. "Her office. Your office. She's Mr. Lee's executive assistant and secretary. Remember?"

"I didn't know," the older man said equably.

"What's your name?" There was a pause, and then the man rose.

"We'd better go," he said. "Come on, Whitson."

"Listen, I'm hungry. Let me make myself some breakfast. I haven't had much sleep."

"We're supposed to take you in. Orders from Mr. Lee," the young man said.

"Am I under arrest?"

The older man moved uncomfortably. "Take it easy, Larry," he said to his partner. "He can make himself something to eat. There's time for that."

"I'll fry up some eggs," Jeff said, "and shave."

"Watch him," said the young man named Larry.

"I'm watching." The old man lit a cigarette. "My name's Fred," he said then, belatedly answering Jeff's question. "Larry takes himself a mite seriously."

"You tamper with this?" Larry held the briefcase in front of Jeff's face.

"Nope." Jeff shouldered past him into the kitchenette

and broke two eggs into a pan, adding butter as an after-thought. The smell was delicious.

He sat down to instant coffee and fried eggs. And found he couldn't eat.

Jeff rode down in the usual nondescript CIA automobile, picked at random from the car pool. He sat in the back next to Larry, who held the attaché case carefully on his lap. At one point, the young man asked idly, "You live there? Where we picked you up?"

"No," Jeff said. "It's Miss Bernstein's apartment."

"Pretty soft."

"We're getting married next month." Jeff kept his voice neutral.

"That so?" Fred, who was driving, said into his rearview mirror. And to Larry, "Shut up, kid."

"Okay," Larry said. "Keep your hair on."

The rest of the drive was silent.

They walked straight to Simon's office. He was standing in Debbie's small anteroom, looking over some papers, when they arrived.

"Hello, Jeffrey." The older man was freshly dressed. His face was calm and talcumed.

Jeff said, "Hello, Mr. Lee," and looked around him. The two men put the attaché case down on Debbie's desk and left without a word. "I don't much like the way I'm being treated," Jeff said loudly. "Where's Debbie?"

"They were acting on my orders," Simon said. "Blame me. I thought Deborah was with you."

"She left early. Hasn't she shown up?"

"No." Simon picked up the attaché case. "Come into my office."

There, he sat down and poured himself a cup of coffee. He did not offer any to Jeff.

"Report," he said.

Jeff tried to keep his facts straight. Most debriefings, he had heard, were recorded. There was no sign here of any equipment. He told the entire story, everything. Simon listened without interruption, sipping his coffee. When Jeff was finished, he pushed a cup over to him.

"Have some coffee," he said.

Then he rose and walked to his window. He stared out, and when he spoke his back was turned to Jeff.

"All right," he said. "You realize this'll have to be bucked all the way? All the way up?"

"Yes."

"Some of the most powerful people in the country are going to take a hard look at what you've told me."

"It's all recorded," Jeff said. "I'm willing to back up everything. Besides, the proof is in the briefcase. Ricardo's report and the book."

"We'll check the signature," Simon said. "My God, what a hornet's nest you've stirred up. I'll have to speak to the general about this. The Secretary of Defense. The Secretary of State. Perhaps the President." He turned. "It's a heavy briefcase," he said, eyeing it.

"I know," Jeff said. "I felt that way coming home."

"Well. Your responsibility ceases as of now. Only one thing. I want you to listen to what I'm saying, and listen carefully. You are to mention this story to no one. No one. Ever. Until," Simon added, seeing the look on Jeff's face, "until it is declassified. This is not even top secret." He spread his hands helplessly. "There's no real classification for it. Let's call it 'need to know.' And you do not need to know, anymore."

Jeff sat stunned. "But it'll be in the newspapers," he said. "Everyone will know. You can't keep the fact that Hitler is alive a secret, Mr. Lee. People have a right to know."

"*If* he is," Simon said. "*If* he is. We have no substantive proof of that at present."

"Just look at the book. Look at the signature and the inscription."

"Yes," Simon said. "Believe me, I will." He sighed. "And so will others." He looked at Jeff. "I don't know how you feel about this, but I think you ought to pray that your proof is a forgery."

"And Ricardo's report?"

"Unreliable. We trust only our own operatives."

"You sound," Jeff said slowly, "as though you're hoping that this is all a farce. But Consuelo *was* murdered. They tried to kill me. They wouldn't have gone to the bother if they hadn't felt they had to keep us from talking." He stopped because surely Simon knew this; a child would have known it. He felt foolish explaining self-evident facts in this austere office.

"We don't yet know if she was murdered. The doctor thought so, as Ricardo thought Hitler was alive. But there is still no substantive fact in any of this."

"Except for the book."

"Yes," Simon said slowly, "there's that." He sighed. "Well. Let's take a look."

He had the combination memorized, Jeff noted, and he opened the attaché case.

"Lock the door, will you?" he asked.

Jeff locked the door. Simon withdrew the manila envelope and unfastened it. He took out Ricardo's report.

"There's no book here," he said.

"There must be." Jeff rose. "I left it there when I went to sleep on Debbie's couch."

"It's not here," Simon said in a sick voice. He unlocked the door and went to the anteroom. "And still no Debbie." He came back and sat down on the office couch. He looked white and tired. Even his freshly pressed suit looked crumpled.

"We've got to get it back," Simon said.

"But who knew? Who would take it?"

"Debbie had the combination. She set it, as she always does."

"She wouldn't do that."

"It seems improbable," Simon said. He lit a cigarette and, after a pause, offered one to Jeff.

"We have to go by the facts," Simon said. "She's the only one who could have taken it."

"There's no motive," Jeff said. "There's no reason."

"She sounded . . . strange when I spoke to her this morning," Simon said softly, half talking to himself. "Did you know her mother and father lived through the Judenstadt death camp?"

"Yes," Jeff said. "She never told me much about it, though."

"It's one of the reasons I hired her," Simon said, "but sometimes these things backfire." He took a deep drag. "What's she going to do with it? Sell it?" He answered his own question: "No. She's incorruptible. I'd swear to it. We've got to get to her. She's carrying an atom bomb, booksized."

"Now look," Jeff said, "you don't even know if she's guilty. I'm going back to her apartment to wait for her."

"You are going to your office," Simon said slowly, and his words were cold. "You will sit there and forget this ever happened. The whole thing is out of your hands."

"If she calls me?"

"Let me know immediately."

"I don't want her hurt or frightened," Jeff said.

"Don't be ridiculous."

"I didn't think it so ridiculous this morning."

"What must be done, one does."

"*Befiehl ist befiehl?*" Jeff's German was barbarous.

Simon flushed a little. "Entirely different," he said. "And I'm not on trial in Nuremberg." He turned away. "That's all," he said. He picked up a phone by his desk. It was the yellow phone. Jeff had never seen him use it before. "Get me the general when he comes in," Simon said. His voice was strained. "Urgent."

He nodded to Jeff.

"You can go now," he said. "I've got work to do."

In his office Jeff held his head in his hands. His brain swam. I'm on the edge of collapse, he thought. I'm getting older by the minute; I haven't had enough sleep or food. He was ragingly sorry for himself. When he thought of Debbie, he felt resentment, for he was scared. For Debbie to do something like this was so totally out of character, so completely at odds with everything he knew of her! His hands sweated. He realized he didn't know her at all. Or himself.

On the New York shuttle, Debbie shared a seat with a half-asleep bald man who kept trying to read his morning paper and dozed off every few minutes. His siesta was interrupted only when Debbie pounded the seat beside her in despair. "What's happened?" she asked aloud, "what the hell's happened to me?" She pounded the seat again. "I've lost me," she said. Then she began to cry, striking the seat harder and harder, again and again. The bald man grew alarmed. He said nothing but looked around nervously for another place to sit, away from this hysterical girl.

In a pseudo-modern room in the Hotel Times Square, near the Times building, Debbie sat with her handbag on her lap. She tried to control her rebellious body and her rebellious mind. She had developed a rash on one cheek which she was constantly fingering. Sometimes she sobbed. Mostly she just sat, quivering with tension, and tried to think.

She had little idea of where she was or how she had gotten there. Her mind functioned only sporadically. She knew that she was running away with a secret. But for long moments at a time she would forget just what the secret was or why it was so important to let everyone know immediately. She opened her handbag and combed her hair straight down around her face. Her eyes were hooded. Deborah Bernstein, Jewess, sat rocking and wailing in her chair for her lost spiritual virginity. Fragments of a crushed, suppressed inheritance floated through her mind.

She shook her head violently. She was Deborah Bernstein, and she had nothing to do with those people in Maidanek, with the bony corpses of Judenstadt, with the robust fanfaronnade of Israel. All this had happened in another country before she was born; it was no part of her.

She knew it wasn't true. Her Jewishness had been dormant inside her, waiting. It would have stayed quiescent forever, had it not been for this . . . thing inside her handbag. She had had her share of parties where she had laughed at the insular society Jews made wherever they went, wherever they lived: tight little groups of God's chosen. She had always thought of them as very different from her — vulgar and loud. She had paid lip service to their intelligence, to their ethnic tragedies, to their loyalty and courage, but inside she had known always that she, Deborah Bernstein, was not one of them.

Now she knew she was. She had been blind all her life, that was all. She wondered fleetingly if her anti-Semitism had been the main reason for her attraction to Jeff. He was everything she was not: white, Protestant, aseptic. The world belonged to him, not to her. And she had accepted that world, the laundered, chromed, push-button American Dream. It had swallowed her up, and the irony was that while she felt she was living, truly living, she had actually been dying, truly dying.

Now she knew who she was: she was nothing; neither Jew nor Gentile nor atheist, nor supermodern and superbright, nor chromed and gleaming, nor happy and confident. She had no place to turn. She had lost herself completely. It was terrifying to think of the long dark road down which she must now wander, to find herself at the other end, a dwindled, changed person, a person she might not even be able to live with.

Debbie gave up. She curled up on her chair and fell asleep.

When she woke, she was rational again. She knew what she must do.

When his phone rang at eight o'clock that Monday night, Jeff somehow knew it was Debbie. He picked up the receiver and said quickly, "Where are you, honey?"

"New York," Debbie said. Her voice sounded remote.

"What the hell are you trying to do?" Jeff asked. "You realize you could go to jail for what you've done?"

Debbie laughed, and her laughter was unforced, natural. "That's where I've been," she said. "In jail. You've got to help me, Jeff. You're the only one I trust. I don't trust Simon or even myself. Just you."

"Okay," Jeff said.

"How soon can you get here?"

Jeff calculated. "An hour to get to the airport . . . I can catch the nine o'clock shuttle."

"I'll meet you in front of 1501 Broadway," Debbie said. "At eleven. That'll give you plenty of time."

"Right," Jeff said. "Where are you now?"

"Good-bye." Debbie broke the connection.

Well, Jeff thought as he checked his wallet and turned out the apartment lights, Simon had it all figured out in advance. He had known Debbie would call.

And now I'm supposed to call him.

Then, as a wave of rebellion seemed to surge from the very tips of his toes, Jeff thought, Fuck him, I don't like him, he doesn't like me, and I don't give a shit. Thinking the short, brutal words gave him a peculiar pleasure. He straightened his shoulders and locked the apartment door behind him. He would find Debbie and bring her back himself. He didn't give a god damn what Simon would say or think or do about it.

He was whistling as he waited for the elevator. In his heart, he knew he was whistling in the wind.

He had expected it to be a long and anxious journey. He was wrong. There was almost no sense of time passing. Perhaps this was due to his fatigue. He had now long passed the point where he was sleepy. He felt an almost ecstatic feeling of floating, as though all the poisons in his system had somehow transmuted themselves into a fine lubricating oil. Never had his joints moved with such ease. Never had he felt so capable of commanding the slightest movements of his body with absolute precision, aware withal that in the back of his head there lay a small active pool of unease.

His cab ride and the shuttle to Kennedy were of a piece, almost instantaneous. He must have slept on the plane, but it was only a half-sleep. He took the limousine into New York still buoyed up by his hollow bones, his manageable muscles.

The world snapped back into focus only when he found himself in Times Square, looking for Deborah. He didn't see her for a few moments. When he finally spotted her, he could hardly recognize her. They were tearing down a huge building and a painted crane, ablaze with arabesques of glowing lights, was standing, motionless, in a roped-off area. Deborah too was standing, her white face upturned, looking at the crane. Jeff came upon her from the side. Her mouth was open, in a small gape of astonishment and terror. When she turned and saw him he had one awful second in which this girl, with the huge black eyes, taut white face and hooked nose, was a stranger. Then she was in his arms, and she was gasping, "Oh, Jeff, you came, darling, you came!"

He could feel her trembling and he held her tight and murmured comforting sounds into her ear, small noises of reassurance. After a few moments, she stepped back.

"What were you looking at?"

"That." She pointed with loathing at the crane. "I hate it."

"Why?"

"I don't know." She smiled nervously. "So many things have happened to me in the last twelve hours."

"Bad things?" Jeff put his arm around her. She felt thinner.

"I don't know. That's why I called you. I don't know anything anymore."

So there it was, Jeff thought. He, whom Debbie had cosseted and fed and loved and protected, was now the one to cosset, the feeder, the protector. He felt an obscure resentment that was washed away by Debbie's white face and the way she clutched his hand with convulsive fingers.

"All right," Jeff said. "Let's get out of here."

"I'd like a cup of coffee," Debbie said. "I'm cold." She shivered in the heat of the night.

They sat in a cafeteria. Debbie cradled her fingers around her cup. She and Jeff shared a cigarette. Color had finally returned to her face. As Jeff stubbed out the cigarette he said conversationally, "You've got the book?"

"Yes."

"It's got to be returned, you know."

Debbie took a sip of coffee. "I had to take it. You didn't know, but Simon called early yesterday morning, while you were asleep."

"He mentioned it."

"He wanted to know where you were. Something had happened to me, just before, that I can't talk about, something private, and I was off in a world of my own — you know?"

"Yes," Jeff said, though he did not know.

"So when I talked to him, I took it for granted that he knew all about it. Not only Ricardo's report, but the . . . book too. And Jeff, he did. He *did* know. You hadn't told him, no one had told him. But I could tell he knew what was in the briefcase. He knew all about . . . *him* . . . being alive.''

"No one knew but Consuelo and me," Jeff said. "And Franzl.''

"He knew," Debbie said.

"Simon and I had a talk.'' Jeff played with a paper napkin. "He's bucking the whole thing up to the President. It's been declared need to know.''

"Something came over me," Debbie said obliquely. "Something happened to me. Jeff, I've changed. I didn't think it was possible for me to change, to lose and find myself in such a short time. I was happy, did you know? I was quite happy with me, with you, with my life. And all the time, I wasn't happy at all. I was desperate. I wasn't even a human being . . . and I didn't know it. All these years, I haven't been me, I've reneged on everything . . . Jeff, I never used myself completely with you, when we made love. Did you know that?''

"No," Jeff said. "I thought we were good together.''

"We were," Debbie's hand clasped his. "But not good enough. I mean, I never was able to be *me*, to be really *me*, not just in bed, but — everything, everywhere.''

"What has that got to do with the fact that you've stolen a top government secret? You know, Deb, Simon is really quite kind. They could have picked you up. They have ways, they didn't have to let it work out this way, the comfortable way. If it were wartime, you could be shot. Let's go back to Washington right away.''

"But don't you see?'' Debbie said softly. "People have got to know. Everyone's got to know. Not just Simon and the President. It's not Simon and the President that *he* killed by the millions. It's people like me. We're the ones owed. We're owed the truth. I'm going to make sure we get it.''

"You can't buck the whole system," Jeff said. And out of his unconscious, from the deepest part of him, he dragged forth, ''And nobody'll thank you for it. Everyone will be angry. They're angry as hell right now.''

''That's not important.''

''But they're angry at *me*,'' Jeff said.

''That's not important either, darling.''

''Well, it's damn important to me. You've got no right to do this to me.''

''I have the right to do anything I want,'' Debbie said, her voice abruptly factual and firm. ''Nothing, no one, is more important than what I've got to do. What *we've* got to do. You must help me, Jeff. I'll do it alone if I have to, but it would be so much better if you'd help.''

''Help in what?'' Jeff said angrily.

''I called the *Times* this afternoon. They think I'm just a crank. I could tell. If you were to come with me, they might believe both of us. You can show them your identification.''

''And . . .?''

''And then they'll publish the whole story. There'll be headlines all over the world, and Paraguay will have to give him up. They'll have world opinion against them.'' Debbie's eyes glittered. ''There'll be a revolution, a big one, if something isn't done about him.''

Jeff put a tip down on the table. ''But,'' he said, ''no one yet knows if the inscription is real or not.''

''It's real,'' Debbie said. ''It's got to be. They wouldn't have tried to kill you, they wouldn't have murdered that girl if it had been a forgery.''

''Maybe they didn't know it was a forgery.''

''The inscription's addressed to Franzl, remember? He would know it was true, he must have stood there while . . . *he* . . . wrote it.''

''Let's get this straight,'' Jeff said as they both got up from the table. ''You want to get this published, you want everyone to know this story?''

''Yes.''

"Then I don't see you and Simon are at odds over anything," Jeff said. They threaded their way out into the street and turned, Jeff supposed, toward Debbie's hotel. "He just wants to have the whole thing checked out before anything is done. He just wants to move more slowly than you. I think he's right."

"No. The *Times* can find handwriting experts as well as we can. They've got an even bigger morgue. They can check it out. They will check it out. Oh, Jeff, do you think I *want* him alive?"

Debbie had always walked separately from him. She said that women who hung onto men in public places disgusted her. Now she put her arm under his, and they walked the short blocks linked together, in silence.

"I told them at the desk I was expecting my husband," Debbie said. "It's all right. I even wore a ring." They walked past the desk and into the elevator.

The first thing Jeff saw when he entered the room was Debbie's handbag on a chair by the window.

"You left it here, just like that?"

"Don't be silly."

"Where is it?"

"Taped to me," Debbie said. "Under my slip." There was a peculiar look of gratification mixed with loathing on her face. "I want to take it off. I don't like to be so close to it." She went into the bathroom, and five minutes later Jeff heard the shower running.

He could phone Simon now, he thought, while she was showering, but decided against it. The best thing to do would be to sleep on it. She'd go back with him in the morning; she'd be more herself then.

Debbie came out, her hair piled on top of her head, gleaming with water.

"I'm dog-tired," she said.

"Let's let it go till morning," Jeff said. "We'll decide what to do then. My head's buzzing."

There were twin beds in the room. Jeff undressed quickly, showered, and lay down. He was asleep before his head touched the pillow. He looked older, Debbie thought, and then she remembered his voice in the cafeteria: "But they're angry at *me*."

We all, Debbie thought, grow up lopsided. Bits of us years ahead of other bits. Perhaps it's better that way. You get emotional indigestion if a large piece of you grows up too fast. That's what happened to me, she thought. It hurts.

Then she too was asleep. Her dreams were vague shadows against a dun-colored background.

When she awoke, in the early morning, she was awake all at once, altogether, like a child. She was aware of how hungry she was for Jeff. She looked at her watch: five-twenty. She slipped into Jeff's bed and put her arms around him. He was naked. She just held him, passively, and let his warmth flow through her.

After a while, Jeff woke too. He kissed her, and she felt his arousal. But she herself was not as she had always been: active, a willing and inventive partner, intent as much upon her own pleasure as pleasuring Jeff. She kissed him back, and when she felt his mouth begin to descend her body, she stopped him.

"No," she whispered, "I don't want that."

"You always liked it before."

"That was before. Come inside me."

"But . . ."

"Just get inside me," she whispered fiercely. "That's all, that's everything. Inside me."

He went into her and she felt the smooth, sleek longness of him in her. She put her legs around his waist, and her arms were clenched about his back, and she half closed her eyes, and she — relaxed. If that was the word, she thought, as a strange new turmoil began to move inside her.

"Softly," she said. "Slowly. Oh."

There was a bubble in her belly. It swelled slowly until it

pressed against every convolution of her interior. She threw back her head and her lips worked soundlessly, and the pleasure grew and grew, softly, contentedly, quietly, solidly, forever.

For Jeff, this was something strange and wonderful. It was so unlike the sharp, ecstatic lust that he and this girl had successfully made so many times before, that it was almost frightening. He felt as though he were drowning, as though he were in a pool of warm and living water, and it was rising slowly to lap at his shoulders and his neck, to caress his mouth, and finally to engulf him, so that he was working now, in long slow thrusts, in an aqueous world, green and peaceful. Then the turbulence began; he could feel the moving of the deep waters. The storm gathered and gathered. He caught its quiet fury, and he began to mount his own desire, letting it carry him deeper and deeper, and the fright held him for another moment, like the taut string of a violin, a silver thread stretched across the heavens of the world, unbearable. It snapped. He entered a world of slow consummation. He surmounted the fright; it was no more; it had never been; and in him, as he worked upon the quiescent, and then moaning female flesh, there was born a small victory. It grew with his mounting drive, with his increasing attention and concentration, until he suddenly cried Deborah, thinking, This is *Debbie*, I am in *Debbie*. And he came.

He stayed in her, feeling her long, long orgasm, her cheek wet with her tears, his ears ringing with his name, as Debbie said over and over again, Jeff, Jeff, dearest Jeff, and his own name was exciting to him. He held himself proud in her, though he was finished, and he could feel the slow ebb now of her excitement, until it faded away. Deborah gave a loud sob and they separated, yet did not really separate, but lay close together, wondering at this thing they had made, this frightening, primordial perfection upon which they had stumbled, unaware.

They rested together in intimacy for a long time, and neither of them rolled over to smoke or, as had been their custom, to look contentedly into their own, separate souls. But rather, it was as though their fusion had been only a beginning, a precursor to yet another intimacy. Debbie said softly, "It's as though we're still making it," and Jeff said nothing, because he was awed, and proud, and, somehow, sad.

When they finally dressed and went down to breakfast (neither of them was very hungry), all was somehow decided. Debbie again had the book taped to her, next to her naked skin. Jeff paid the room bill, and they turned into the hot sunshine of 51st Street, and Debbie took his arm, and he hailed a cab. They both knew they were going to La Guardia and home. It had been decided, almost against their will.

As the cab pulled up, a familiar voice behind them said conversationally, "That's it, kid." Jeff turned and there they were, Fred and Larry. Only this time there wasn't anything pleasant about Fred at all, and he held his hand in his pocket. "Pointing at you and the lady," he said coldly. "We have instructions to shoot if necessary. You're coming with us." He motioned the cabbie away, and the driver's lips shaped a silent curse as he revved up his cab.

Jeff said, "You've been tailing us."

"Since yesterday," Fred said. "We had to wait to pick you up. The order just came through."

Jeff thought to himself, They're treating us, they're treating *me*, like an enemy. I've got to get them to trust me again. I've got to get myself out of this mess.

Somehow he knew Debbie could take care of herself. She didn't need him; she'd changed. Jeff knew he was afraid. In the back of his mind he knew too that this fright might drive him into dishonorable action. I'm going to cop out on this one, he thought unhappily. I know I'm going to cop out.

Larry said, "It's in the handbag." Fred reached over and picked it off Debbie's shoulder with a delicate motion. He opened it and said softly, "It's not here. Where is it?"

"Where's what?"

"The book. We were told to look for a paperback book."

Jeff took a chance they didn't know. "Sounds pretty odd to me," he said.

"Shut up." That was Larry. "We don't know why we're looking. We're not supposed to know why, we don't want to know. Where is it?"

"Where you'll never find it," Debbie said.

There was a pause.

"We were on our way home," Jeff said. "We were going straight to Mr. Lee's office."

"You've got an appointment with Matheson," Fred said coldly. "He's waiting for you, and he doesn't like to wait."

"Why don't we search the woman?"

"No," Fred said. "We were told to look in the handbag. We were specifically instructed not to touch the damn thing. Just to see it was there. If they say they have it, they have it, as far as I'm concerned. The rest of it's their red wagon. Let's move."

"I could strip the girl," Larry said quickly. "She's got it on her, I know she has."

Jeff said softly, "If he doesn't stop talking to us, I'm going to knock him down, and the hell with your gun."

Fred said, "Shut up, Larry." He turned to Jeff. "Let's go."

"Okay," Jeff said. "This is where I came in. Don't you guys ever learn any new lines?"

"We've got a car," Fred said. "There's a small jet waiting at La Guardia. What the hell did you kids do, anyhow? Kill someone important?"

Presently a battered Volkswagen drove up alongside

them. The traffic hooted mercilessly, and they squeezed their way in. If we wanted to make a break for it, Jeff thought, noticing Fred's corpulence, this would be the time. There's nothing so helpless as a fat man getting into a Volkswagen.

At the airport they walked out to the corner of the landing fields reserved for private planes. A small aircraft waited there. The pilot must have seen them coming, because the door was open. Even as it closed on them, the engine started, the small plane shivered and was in the air.

"That's the way they do it on Air Force One," Fred said. "They don't lose a moment. You're getting the VIP treatment, all right."

Then they sat in silence until the familiar airport came in sight. It had taken twenty-two minutes. A black car waited for them. They rode out toward the Langley complex in silence, neutrally, almost peacefully. It was all so unnecessary, Jeff thought. They would have returned by themselves. His anger at Simon Lee was a slow burn within him.

Debbie said nothing. She huddled against him, and he noticed that she was crying. He didn't even try to comfort her. He didn't know if he could.

After a while, he put his arm around her, and Larry smirked. But you couldn't hit a man for smiling. So Jeff stared fixedly out the window as they rolled along.

7 ❧

THE anteroom of the head of the CIA was kept quite cold by air conditioning. Though Washington sweltered outside, here a fire burned in a small blue faïence fireplace. The feeling of coziness, of vaguely Victorian comfort, was reinforced by the Empire furnishings, the boulle desk at which the general's executive secretary sat. Her phone was in keeping with the rest of the anteroom, all headpiece and speaker, made for those who want such things by the Bell Company. It was, of course, entirely modern inside, transistorized, in fact. Mrs. Flynn, the general's secretary, was much like her phone. She was a gentle-seeming lady of over fifty, with white hair and a pleasant, lined, rather grandmotherly face. She was also a demoniacally swift, entirely efficient, practical woman. She had a low, sweet voice, but on occasion she could swear like a marine. With her help, the general ran one of the largest agencies in the United States.

Here, on two ornamented, uncomfortable chairs, Jeff and Debbie awaited the general's pleasure. Mrs. Flynn spoke few words to them. "Sit down," she had said when they entered. "The general is in conference." She had turned to Fred and Larry. "You may leave," she said. They left.

Debbie's handbag was on Mrs. Flynn's desk. Mrs. Flynn was at her typewriter, rattling off copy at ninety words a minute.

Jeff sat rigidly, remote from everyone. The overcomfortable, overpretty anteroom did not reassure him; it filled him with dread. There were some people he never wanted to see: General Matheson ranked high on that list.

255

His palms sweated. He looked at Debbie almost with hatred. He could feel the disapproval in Mrs. Flynn's stiff shoulders. He could feel it emanate from behind the polished walnut doors that led to the general's office.

Debbie sat with the book taped next to her skin, her legs crossed at the ankles, her hands demure in her lap. She was trying to understand why she was here at all.

By now she had divided her interior life into two parts, Deborah One and Deborah Two. Like a snake shedding its skin, she thought. Deborah Two had always been there, waiting to walk into the sunlight. What am I doing here, then, among these people, who are not my people, and who keep pushing the small ones of the world around? I needn't have come with Jeff, she thought, though I was willing to go back with him and fight it out. I'm not afraid.

But why did Simon have us picked up like that? She answered herself, Because he's afraid, and he doesn't want to make a mistake.

She knew something Jeff did not yet fully realize. She was through with the CIA. She didn't care at all, she discovered. Deborah Two was not as interested in politics as she was in people. Or in power, or in human frailty. Somewhere, Debbie had stopped running a marathon with herself. She was approaching an interior stillness, a quiet worth waiting for. For when it came, it would never leave her.

She thought, At least, last night, I was a woman for the first time in my life. Poor Jeff! I don't think he's going to like Deborah Two as much as he liked Deborah One. I think I scared him last night, and he doesn't yet know it.

She found herself praying fervently that Simon would understand what she had to say, that he would let her say it, that the general (whom she had only seen twice in her life, and then at a distance) would understand. She realized that she had come here, that she had returned, because in her heart she believed Simon would help her.

She looked covertly at Jeff and she was sorry for him all

over again. He hated all this so, and it was none of it his fault. She regretted Consuelo's death for him, painfully. That girl might have been good for Jeff, she thought; I would have been able to get out from under, it would have been easier. But did she really want to let him go? She was still uncomfortable in her new skin. She was not yet fully knowledgeable about what Deborah Two wanted or did not want, how far she would go, or how she would go about getting there. I'm thinking like a madwoman, she thought placidly, aware now that her sanity had never left her, except possibly for those few minutes during that awful dream she could not remember even though she knew it was important, even though she tried and tried until her head hurt.

Besides, she reflected with sudden practicality, you can't buck the system, not on its own terms. She would have been picked up anyway. She had known that her gesture of flight was just that — a gesture — and that whatever road she chose, it would have ended up here, in this office. She had to fight with her own weapons, but part of the trouble was that she did not yet know the power of her new armament.

But one thing she did know. Whoever she was to confront that morning, they were only men like other men. She was no longer frightened of men.

The outer door opened and James Whitson appeared. He was dressed beautifully as always, and his bald head gleamed. He took a few swift steps and stopped uncertainly by Jeff's side.

"Uncle Jim," Jeff said.

"I have to go in there," James Whitson said. "I'm sorry, Jeffrey. It looks like we're all in trouble." His expression was weary. "I told you not to rock the boat," he said. "Looks like you not only rocked it, but you may well have sunk us all."

Debbie giggled. She couldn't help it, he was so dour, and poor Jeff's eyes had widened until he looked like a trapped rabbit waiting for the huntsman's knife. James Whitson cast her a look of dislike, and Mrs. Flynn nodded her head to him. She rose from her desk and opened the general's door. She opened it just enough so that he could pass through. There was a vague murmur from within.

Ten minutes passed in ever thickening silence, and then Mrs. Flynn's intercom buzzed. She picked up the nineteenth-century phone and said, "Yes, sir." She pointed an authoritative finger. "Go in now," she said. "The general is ready for you."

She did not escort them to the door. Jeff opened it for Debbie. She could hear the hissing of his breath as he inhaled deeply. She was tempted to tell him that it couldn't possibly be all that bad, that these were only men. But she understood that this was a woman's secret, that it could not help Jeff.

The room beyond was large, sparsely furnished, brilliantly lit, with the standard desk at one end. Six men were grouped around a large round coffee table, sitting on a semicircular couch.

Simon rose as they entered.

"All right," he said. "I'd better introduce you. This is your boss and mine, General Matheson." The general did not acknowledge the introduction. He was a tall, thin man in a double-breasted gray suit. His eyes were brown. His mouth was thin, the lips severely set. He wore his iron-gray hair World War Two style, close-cropped. His fingernails were buffed, not manicured, and his black shoes gleamed. He was perusing a red file, opened in front of him.

"Mr. Whitson you know." James nodded his head austerely. "Mr. Leland, Secretary of State." John Leland was a white-faced, moon-faced man with the build of an athlete gone to seed. His hair was still carrot-colored, and his hands were enormous, twisted, calloused, and ridged. He had been a famous football star in his college days.

"His excellency, Vladimir Abakumov, Ambassador from the Union of Soviet Socialist Republics." The Russian ambassador was a small man with a round face and spectacles and small, pudgy hands. He smiled, showing a great deal of dental work, and nodded his head. "How do you do?" he murmured in excellent, faintly accented English.

"Cecil Lord Reston, Ambassador from Great Britain," Simon continued. The Englishman had a transparent complexion, with wispy blond hair that was almost white. His eyes were small, blue, and sharp. He nodded distantly.

"Monsieur Poincaré," Simon concluded. The Frenchman was dark and small, with perfect lips and a sharp ferret face. He did not change expression as he was introduced.

The atmosphere in the room was electric. "You may sit," Simon said. There were two straight-backed chairs arranged so that they faced the semicircle of sitting men. Jeff held Debbie's chair while she sat down stiffly, and he himself sat down as though he were ready to spring to attention at a second's notice.

"Now," the general said, still not looking up, "you have caused us considerable concern. You are the cause of this meeting, which is expensive, in time and money." He glanced up. "This nonsense has gone on long enough. Where's this book?"

For a moment neither of them said anything. Then Debbie said softly, "I have it."

"Where?"

"Next to my skin, taped to my stomach," Debbie said. "Don't you think you owe us an explanation?" She was talking directly to Simon, appealing to him.

"We *owe* you nothing," Matheson said. "We will, however, *give* you an explanation. We have decided it would be better to let you know the whole picture rather than only a small part of it. Mr. Lee believes half-knowledge is dangerous to everyone."

There was a pause. Simon rose and began to pace the carpet in front of them.

"In 1945," he said, "Adolf Hitler left his bunker, and

259

through a carefully planned escape network, made his way with some of his staff to Paraguay and Asuncion. This you already know from Ricardo's report.

"What you do not know is that the governments of Great Britain, France, and the Soviet Union have been aware of that fact since July of nineteen forty-five."

Debbie went rigid with disbelief; Jeff sat stunned.

"Hitler was traced to Asuncion," Simon continued. "The governments of the Free World demanded him of Paraguay. Paraguay informed them categorically that they would not comply."

The door opened. The obese man who entered, apologizing in American English for his lateness, was familiar to Jeff, but it took him a moment to place him.

"You know General Díaz, I believe," Simon said imperturbably. "Your Excellency, this is Miss Deborah Bernstein."

The general bowed, smiled, and waddled to one end of the huge couch. The men made room for him. He sat down and lit a long black cheroot.

"We could have forced the issue," Simon resumed. "Paraguay was in no position to back up its negative attitude. There were conferences at the presidential level. It was decided to do nothing. Neither the President, nor the Prime Minister, nor the then head of the Soviet Union, felt that Hitler's life or death in the body was of any prime importance. He was dead politically, Germany was dead as a world power. The information was labeled top secret, and the reports were filed away. We have inherited this decision, and its implementation.

"Over the years, we have kept track, with the help of General Díaz and men like him, of the Sons of Liberty. We have some thousands of feet of film showing Hitler in his room at various stages of his existence. At all times, we have had operatives high in the ranks of this neo-Nazi organization.

"The situation has been kept under control. At no time have there been more than twenty-five people in the world who knew what you know now. We now, regrettably, have twenty-seven.

"What Ricardo learned," Simon continued, "he was not supposed to learn. But Bormann and Franzl have grown too secure with the years, soft and careless."

"Yes," Díaz said in his idiomatic English, "that is true. We had to force Ricardo's death. It was regrettable. On the other hand, we saved this young man's life."

"You could have saved him?" Jeff said. "You could have saved Consuelo?"

"Not Consuelo, no," Díaz said, "nor would we have wished to, since she too knew. We could have saved your friend. But we found it better not to. We took good care of you, however. You could have been killed on the road to the airport had it not been for us."

"Your own death was thoroughly discussed," Simon said. "General Díaz consulted with General Matheson and me. In a sense, none of this was your fault. You were incompetent, true. But I had expected that. Besides, we do not eliminate our operatives for mere incompetence. We simply retire them."

"You knew what Jeff was sent to bring back?" Debbie said, her voice low. "You knew all the time?"

"Oh, yes," Díaz said. "We have known about Hitler since he came. Your Ricardo was not the first operative to discover the secret." He smiled again. "The Sons of Liberty are businessmen as well. They bring much money to our country, and we are poor. We appreciate it. Ricardo went too far. He was assigned to a surveillance job, that was all. We told him just to infiltrate and to keep quiet. We emphasized that."

"Whose side are you on?" Jeff asked quietly from his chair.

"Ours," the fat man said. "Mostly ours. If Ricardo had

been content with a verbal report, when he discovered Hitler's room, we might have saved him." He puckered his lips together and made an odd, disgusted half whistle, half hoot. "But he proceeded to write down what he'd learned. We had to get that report out of Paraguay. We could not destroy it" — here he inclined his head courteously toward General Matheson — "since our Washington friends asked to see it. And there was only one copy. An embarrassing copy. The book, the signed copy of *Mein Kampf*, that was different. We had not suspected its existence. Franzl had kept that as his own secret.

"Unfortunately," Díaz said after a short pause, "it was obvious that Ricardo could no longer live. It was his life against a matter that had been kept confidential for a quarter of a century. We allowed his death. But, as I said, we watched over you as though you were made of gold." The general smiled again, sweetly, and leaned back on the couch, smoking his cigar in peaceful puffs.

Matheson spoke up. "What better operative could we have found than this young man? No one would suspect him. He was too obvious."

"Now, look . . . ," Jeff said loudly and clearly.

"Keep quiet, Jeffrey." His uncle rose, and spread his hands. "I tried to keep you out of it. It was Deborah who first gave Simon the idea. You wanted so badly to be an operative."

"Had it not been for your callow insubordination," Matheson said, "it would have worked as it should, and we would all have been spared this juvenalia."

"Agents are not permitted to mix socially," Simon said coldly. "Now you know one of the reasons for that rule."

"I don't like being used," Jeff said. "I don't like it at all."

"You have no choice. We use you as we see fit. It all goes with the job. That's what you take a loyalty oath for. You're talking like a civilian." Matheson was obviously angry. "Go on," he said curtly to Simon, "finish it up."

"It is not in the interests of this country's security that proof of Hitler's continued existence be broadcast. The President agrees. Please give me the book. We do not wish to take it from you by force, but we will if we have to."

Debbie got slowly to her feet and faced them all. Her hands were splayed on her stomach. Her eyes were cold.

"May I speak?" she asked. "Or am I a prisoner?"

"Please." Abakumov looked disgusted. "No histrionics before lunch, I beg of you."

"I dislike you all," Debbie said. "What gives you this right to keep alive this man who murdered six million of my people, who was the cause of millions of American and British and French deaths? Because that's what you're doing, you know you're deliberately helping to keep him alive. It's the most profoundly evil thing I have ever heard. You aid and abet him cynically, for your own reasons. I despise the lot of you."

She sat down, breathless with anger.

"You'll moderate your tone, young lady," Matheson said. "Try at least to be as polite to us as we are being to you."

"You know," Abakumov said softly, "we too suffered from Hitler's SS. We lost whole cities. How many hundreds of thousands of us died in the concentration camps? We too were burned, gassed, shot, tortured, our women raped, our children's brains spilled upon forest floors. You do not have a monopoly on the righteous anger of the world. It is shared equally."

Simon stepped forward and took Debbie's hands in his. "My dear, can't you see?" he said quietly, "If we were to do as you ask, if we were to let all this be known, then we would be truly raising the dead. What does it matter if a blind, paralytic, diseased hulk who sits all day in his own ordure, who has to be fed pap, who neither thinks nor speaks but lives out his days as a rotting vegetable, continues to exist a little longer? Do you want to rescue him from his hell, resuscitate his name, profoundly disturb the peoples of the world, all for no reason? How good do you want to be to this man? Hasn't he caused enough suffering? Why should we disturb him? He no longer exists, either as a power or as a thinking being. His punishment has been long and terrible. We could not have done as well. And you want to take him out of his misery!''

There was a pause. The Debbie said softly, ''You're eloquent, Simon. More eloquent than I'd dreamed. And you are profoundly immoral. All of you'' — she looked at the ring of men — ''you have good reasons for what you're doing. Excellent reasons. But if what you're doing is despicable, and you know, you alone know how despicable it is, then of what importance are your good reasons?'' She paused again. ''Are you cleverer, wiser, better than other people? What makes you think you have this right, this God-given authority, to decide what we will and will not know?'' She choked a little in her anger. ''You're insulting the stuff of which this country is made — and it is made up not of you, but of everyone. You are only a small part. Why, in the long run, you don't count at all. Not at all,'' she repeated, and the tears were running down her cheeks.

Matheson cleared his throat.

''And *I'm* surprised at *your* eloquence,'' Simon said. ''However, the point is, perhaps, that the morality of government and the personal morality of the individual are different. It is my belief they have to be.''

''In any case,'' Matheson said impatiently, ''we cannot alter this decision, even if we wanted to — which we don't. And, young lady, let me remind you that you took a loyalty oath when you became a member of our organization. You are a woman, and upset. I'll take that into consideration. What I have just heard, I have already forgotten. But we must have that book.''

Debbie heard herself cry out. She turned. "Jeff!" she said softly. "Please. Help me."

Jeff, his face white, sat there. His lips trembled, but he said nothing. There was another long pause.

"The truth is, I'm alone," Debbie said at last. "I cannot do anything alone."

She laughed, and it was not a pleasant sound. It was a hard and whinnying cackle. It did not seem possible that Debbie could laugh like that.

"I'll have to undress," she said. And almost to herself, "When rape is inevitable" — she raised her voice — "I *do not* enjoy it."

"We'll turn our backs," Simon said. "I'm afraid you can't leave this room." The men rose and stood, their backs to Debbie. Only Jeff sat, his burning eyes upon her.

"Please, Jeff," Debbie said. He looked at her for a moment and then rose and joined the other men.

Debbie unzippered her skirt, grimaced as she ripped off the tapes. The book fell to the carpet with a small thud.

"All right," Debbie said. The men sat again. Simon picked up the book and handed it to Matheson. The general opened it, read the inscription, and passed it to his left. All of the men read in turn, silently, except for the Englishman, who murmured, "Extraordinary," as he passed it along.

Matheson went to his desk and returned with a pair of scissors. Quickly, delicately, he cut the page bearing the inscription from the book's spine, hauled a standing ashtray toward him, took out a gold lighter, and applied flame to the paper. The page flared brightly, giving off a pungent, unpleasant odor. Then it crumpled into charred ash. Matheson pressed a button and the ash itself disappeared into the ashtray's well.

"All done," he murmured. The Secretary of Defense rose, and everyone rose with him. He went to Debbie, and framed her head in his hands for a moment.

He said: "I have a daughter older than you. I love her.

265

You have said some harsh things to us. We have sat here and listened to them. That should mean something to you.''

''Not enough,'' Debbie said.

''I would not like to think that anyone like you hates me,'' Mr. Leland said tiredly. He looked absurdly powerful, his huge body almost blocking Debbie from Jeff's view. ''But if you must hate, then hate me. And the President. And twenty-five years of supporting this decision. Because we must decide these things. We watch over the people. That is our sworn responsibility.''

Matheson ushered his visitors out. He said briefly to Simon, ''Finish up. I'm going to lunch with Leland.''

The door to his office closed behind him, and the three were left alone. Simon looked at them, and at the copy of *Mein Kampf* still on the coffee table.

''If you want to talk about all this,'' he said, ''we can't stop you. In fact, we wouldn't want to. You have no proof, and I can assure you that none of us would back up your story. If you do talk,'' and he turned to Jeff, ''you'll be considered cranks, if not insane. Remember that.'' He paused. ''I have no objection to your continuing to work here,'' he said to them both, ''if you wish to. Your days as an operative are over, Jeffrey, but you knew that.'' He faced Debbie. ''I could find you another job in the organization.''

Debbie just looked at him.

''Can I think it over?'' Jeff asked.

''If you're here tomorrow,'' Simon said, ''your office will still be here for you. In all fairness, I must tell you that I don't foresee much future for you with us. But you will have a permanent job. It's the least we can do.'' He turned to Debbie. ''Would you like *Mein Kampf* as a memento?'' he said. ''You can have it if you want it.''

''Yes,'' Debbie said fiercely. ''Oh, yes, I want it!'' Simon handed her the book and she tucked it under her arm.

At the door she turned.

''It's all wrong,'' she said to Simon. Jeff felt she was

somehow still speaking to the assemblage of power that had lately stood there. "It's wrong because it can't be cut off at will. First one decision, and then another, and another, and all the time, ordinary people, what happens to them? How many decisions will you make for them? Until there are no decisions left to be made? You say it is your job to watch out for us. But who will watch the watchers?"

"We can be replaced," Simon said.

"You can't hide behind that," Debbie said. "You're murdering America. I don't know what we'll have in the future. Whatever it will be, if this continues — and it's getting worse, you know it's getting worse — you won't have an America. Not the America I want for my children. Or for myself. Or, for that matter, for you. I'm sorry for all of us."

Jeff opened the door for Debbie, and she walked out. She was crying again, he noticed, but her back was straight.

Mrs. Flynn, still typing with astonishing ease and celerity, did not even look up as they passed her.

Simon remained alone in the room. Jeff caught a last glimpse of him, looking out the window.

He took Debbie's hand and they walked out of the building together. Jack, the old policeman who shepherded VIP cars outside, got them a cab.

"I want to go home," Debbie said. "I'm very tired." She put her head on Jeff's shoulder and closed her eyes. The book lay in her lap, and she put one hand on it.

"They used me," Jeff said aloud. "I'm sorry, Deb."

"They think they have to use everyone."

"What are we going to do?"

Debbie did not answer. Then she put her hand on Jeff's arm. "We never discussed it," she said, "but think back. Why did you take this job?"

"I told you. Uncle Jim wanted me with him."

"But why? Jeff, he was trying to expiate his own guilt. You were used even then. He didn't think of you as good

CIA material. He thought perhaps he could make himself more comfortable about you if he gave you a job. You had a bad start, Jeff.''

''He liked me,'' Jeff said defensively. Debbie made a sound halfway between a laugh and a sob.

''Jeff, it isn't that important to be liked. You've got to go beyond that. You have to live with your own actions and not worry so much about other people's opinions.''

For some reason, Jeff found himself angry. ''It's all right for you,'' he said loudly. ''You're a girl. Someone'll take care of you. I've got to look out for myself.''

''Exactly,'' Debbie said. ''But you go about it wrong.'' She sighed deeply. ''You know,'' she said again, ''I've changed.''

''How?''

''I'm not sure yet. I'm different from the girl you knew. I don't know why, or in what exact ways, but I do know I'm going to be different. Do you think you can get used to that?''

''Of course,'' Jeff said. He tried to make his voice casual and convincing, but it sounded hollow.

''If you can't,'' Debbie said, ''I'll understand.''

''But why?'' Jeff's tone was passionate. ''Why does all this have to happen? Can't we just forget the whole thing? It's over, done with, there's nothing we can do about it. Why must we continue to live with it? Why must it make us miserable forever? Let's drop it, Deb, please. You always want me to be mature. Isn't this the mature thing to do?''

Debbie looked at him but she said nothing. They rode the rest of the way home in silence.

At her apartment house door, Debbie turned and looked at Jeff searchingly.

''Kiss me,'' she said.

They kissed. Her lips were tender. She passed her hand through Jeff's hair and held him tightly. Then she broke away. She was crying again.

"What's the matter?" Jeff asked.

"I don't know."

"Will I see you tomorrow?"

"I've got to get someone to clear out my stuff at the office," Debbie said. "I can't go back there."

"I'll do it."

"All right." She knew he had made up his own mind. He was staying on.

"Can I come up?" Jeff asked abruptly. "I want to."

"No. I'm tired."

But still they stood, unwilling to leave each other. Jeff thought, She doesn't want to be with me, she isn't going to marry me at all.

"You were terrific," he said, knowing now it was too late to say anything.

Debbie looked down at the book in her hand. A strange expression crossed her face. Suddenly she thrust the book at Jeff.

"Get rid of it," she said. "I don't want it at all, really."

Jeff took the book. "Are you angry with me?"

"No," Debbie said, "of course not. Call me tomorrow, I'll wait for your call." And she thought, I'm not the girl he wants to marry at all, I'm not even the girl he wants to sleep with anymore. She's dead. I don't want to hold him to a promise he made to someone else.

"I must go," she said swiftly. She pushed at his chest with both her hands, and smiled up at him. Then she was gone, and he was alone in the afternoon sunlight. The book was in his hands.

In her room, Debbie kicked her shoes off and sank down on her bed. He'll have to work it out himself, she thought hazily. It's his decision. I hope, whatever it is, it's the right one for him. She sank into a deep and dreamless sleep.

Outside, Jeff walked down the block to a garbage can. It was at the mouth of a dark alleyway, and some children had knocked off the battered lid. An afternoon shower had turned it into an evil half-liquid in which swam orange rinds, apple cores, and swill scrapings. Jeff wrinkled his nose, and he dropped the book into the steaming mess.

Then he turned and walked away.

Behind him the book settled in its filth, and the sun caught the title in a sudden blaze of light. It sank slowly into the garbage and was gone.